Praise for Anthony O'Neill's

Dr Jekyll & Mr Seek

'Clever, gripping and reverent. Recommended.'

IAN RANKIN, author of the Inspector Rebus series

'O'Neill infuses the narrative with suspense and meticulously researched detail. A gripping novel.'

KAITE WELSH, author of *The Wages of Sin*

'A strange and wondrous tale beautifully told.'

LIN ANDERSON, author of the Rhona MacLeod series

'Fiendishly ingenious.'

RONALD FRAME, author of *The Lantern Bearers*

'A clever and entertaining sequel that will leave Stevenson fans delighted.'

KEVIN MACNEIL, author of *The Brilliant & Forever*

'Dazzling in its own right.'

LESLEY MCDOWELL, author of *The Picnic*

'Written with verve and humour, this is an entertaining tale which weaves an ingenious web of mystery and suspense.'

The Independent, 9 Best Scottish Fiction Books 2017

THE
Devil
Upstairs

ANTHONY O'NEILL

BLACK & WHITE PUBLISHING

First published 2019
by Black & White Publishing Ltd
Nautical House, 104 Commercial Street
Edinburgh, EH6 6NF

1 3 5 7 9 10 8 6 4 2   19 20 21 22

ISBN: 978 1 78530 261 9

A CIP catalogue record for this book is available from the British Library.

Typeset by Iolaire Typesetting, Newtonmore
Set in 12.4/16.4 pt Dante MT
Printed and bound by CPI Group (UK) Ltd, Croydon, CR0 4YY

'If you injure your neighbour, better not do it by halves.'

George Bernard Shaw

'Those who make peaceful revolution impossible will make violent revolution inevitable.'

John F. Kennedy, 1962

PART

ONE

CHAPTER

ONE

I F YOU ASKED CAT THOMAS on ten separate occasions why she moved to Edinburgh she would have been able to give you a different answer each time. A yearning for a different climate, after spending most of her life in Florida. A cooling of UK house prices, owing partly to Britain's decision to leave the EU. The strength of the US dollar against the pound sterling. A sudden influx of inheritance money, on top of the savings she had been accruing for nearly twenty years. Family tensions and a legacy of failed relationships. A certain dismay at the intellectual and political climate in her home country. And, on a very practical level, her ability to gain UK residency thanks to her late mother's birth in Inverness.

But three reasons stood out. The first related to her job at a Miami bank and a routine fraud investigation that had evolved into something much larger and more sinister. When her life was repeatedly threatened by an organised crime syndicate – dead animals on her doorstep, spray-painted warnings on her car – Cat had defied the advice of senior management and resolved to remain in Florida until court proceedings were complete. But then, once the guilty parties were sentenced (some with serious jail time), she opted to relocate for her own safety to another country.

The second reason related to her overheated brain and the need to retreat and reassemble in a fresh environment. The chaos of the previous three years – coordinating the investigation, her subsequent legal obligations and the care of her ailing father – cried out for new scenery, new horizons, new minutiae, and the overwhelming distraction of setting herself up a new home.

The third reason – and the one Cat was most willing to share, particularly with Scots themselves – sprang from her long-time fascination with all things Scottish and her particular passion for its capital city. She'd first been taken to Edinburgh, where her mother's uncle was a prestigious civil engineer, at the impressionable age of eight. Already advanced for her tender years, with a field of vision that was unusually discriminating, she instantly fell in love with the sooty sandstone, the crowstepped gables, the cobblestones (actually setts, her uncle explained grandly), the elegant crescents and sloping streets of the New Town, the maze of lanes and bridges in the Old Town, and the general air of perpetual twilight that pervaded at the time of her visit (early December). She boldly declared, to the amusement of all present, that she was going to purchase a home there one day – preferably a Georgian terrace-house like that of her uncle, in some fashionable street like Inverleith Row (where her uncle lived), with a conservatory out back where she could read the morning paper over freshly brewed tea (as her uncle did), before taking a dog (a Border Terrier, like her uncle's) on a bracing walk down one of the tree-flanked bicycle paths that crisscrossed the north of the city (just as her uncle liked to do on his morning constitutionals).

Management in Miami made noises about wanting to retain her in the US, in any city of her choice, but having reached the age of thirty-five Cat was determined to fulfil her dreams while she had a chance. So the bank, 'sad to lose such a fine operator', had duly arranged her transfer-in-principle to its sister institution, the venerable Alba Banking Company, or ABC, headquartered in Edinburgh.

For three months Cat studied the real estate websites, collated a list of properties that suited her dreams and her means (as it happened, terrace houses in Inverleith Row were at least one zero outside her budget), and commissioned a relocation agent in Edinburgh to check out these places in person and compile a list of her own recommendations. Then she flew into Scotland, in glorious blossom-infused April, to make her all-important decision.

Everything went remarkably smoothly. As soon as she stepped out of the airport Cat was greeted by the relocation agent, a bubbly mother of three called Janine, who over the next two days whisked her around Edinburgh in a battered silver Vauxhall. They visited ten properties altogether, including a spacious duplex apartment in a converted schoolhouse in Danderhall (superb and under budget, though Cat feared it might be prohibitively expensive to heat); three top-floor flats in the New Town (each with its own charms and deficiencies); a tiny pied-à-terre in the Old Town (there wasn't enough room to swing a kitten, let alone a cat); a well-appointed second-floor place, owned by a widowed surveyor, in the charming riverside suburb of Colinton (the relocation agent warned that it was a little far from the nearest supermarket); a sliver-thin terrace house in the eclectic area of Leith (Cat was alarmed by the sight of beer bottles spilling over the top of a neighbour's wheelie-bin); and an eccentric old residence, formerly a potter's studio, that had everything going for it except for openable windows and a functioning bathroom (it was also disturbingly close to a traffic-clogged arterial road).

In the end it came down to two choices. Cat's favourite was a two-bedroom flat in an incredible keep-like building in so-called Dean Village, a sleepy enclave set in a picturesque gorge half a mile from the city centre. Built in the late 1700s as a sort of office block for the various millers, skinners and tanners that once operated in the area, the building's sandstone walls were three feet thick. The ivy-covered façade was abutted by a spiral stairway, fully enclosed, that was like something out of a Robin Hood movie. Both bedrooms – large and small – faced onto a leafy quadrangle where traffic was minimal. There was a burbling little river, the Water of Leith, just eighty metres away. A private garden across the road. Even a designated parking space directly outside the front door.

The second property was a basement flat, under a dental surgery, in an elegant Georgian tenement in Dundas Street. Cat enjoyed the idea of living huddled away and out of sight. She especially liked the idea that the dental surgery would (presumably) be unoccupied overnight. And since the owner's asking price was considered 'a real steal' by the relocation agent, Cat was getting ready to pounce when the owner of the flat in Dean Village suddenly announced that she was willing to lower her own price to something not dissimilar – an incredible bargain by any measure.

Scarcely believing her luck, Cat instructed her Scottish solicitor, an easy-going fellow called Stuart, to accept the fresh price immediately.

The sale, however, proved unbearably suspenseful. Stuart put in an offer that was ten thousand pounds lower than the already reduced price. Cat's misgivings – she was a virgin to Scottish real estate protocols but thought it never wise to look a gift horse in the mouth – were only exacerbated when there came news that an eagle-eyed 'other party' had sprung out of the woodwork with a last-minute competing offer. Cat reminded Stuart that she was perfectly willing to pay the full price but the solicitor was adamant: 'Don't worry, this place has been on the market for a year. It's just a ploy, trust me – the "other party" doesn't exist.'

Cat wasn't so sure. She had no patience for financial games. And she hated the prospect of missing out. But, as a stranger in a strange land, she figured it was best to shut up. So she spent three torturous days pacing restlessly around the city, trying to 'keep calm and carry on'. A score of times, just to assure herself it wasn't some sort of Brigadoon-like mirage, she negotiated the steep inclines down into Dean Village, dreading the prospect of finding the FOR SALE – UNIT 5 sign removed from the railings outside 'her' building.

But then, on the afternoon of her fifth day in Edinburgh, while standing pensively atop the Salisbury Crags, she received a call from Stuart: 'Congratulations! You now own a tiny piece of Scotland.'

Cat was incredulous. 'They accepted the offer?'

'I got another three thousand off in the end.'

'Really? It was as easy as that?'

'I told you the other buyer didn't exist. Go get yourself a whisky.'

'I don't drink.'

'An Appletiser, then.'

Poised on the clifftop, with her coat flapping about her, Cat pocketed her phone and stared over the rooftops of the sunlit city, trying to exult, like Friedrich's *Wanderer Above the Sea of Fog*, from the precipice of a momentous and thrilling future. But at just that moment a cloud curtained the sun, Edinburgh fell into deep shadow, and she was lanced by a brief but disorientating feeling of portent.

It was Friday, 28 April.

CHAPTER
TWO

FOR A WHILE, EVERYTHING SEEMED to be going splendidly. Cat had allotted two weeks in Edinburgh to formalise the sale of the flat but in the end the whole deal was settled within eight days. She signed a good deal of paperwork, transferred a deposit amount from her bank account, and on a whim purchased a hamper for the owner as a gesture of goodwill or even guilt (she still couldn't believe she'd nabbed a place in Dean Village, so close to the city centre, for such a price). But the owner's solicitor claimed that her client was 'unavailable' and Cat ended up passing the basket to Stuart, who, embarrassed by the largesse, promised to share it with his family.

She spent the rest of her stay roaming around the city, methodically noting the prices of items she'd need to purchase, making reconnoitres of the local stores and supermarkets, and walking repeatedly past her future home with a giddying sense of dominion. Then, in early May, she flew back to Florida to pack up her belongings, dispose of everything not precious enough to ship, and say farewells, sometimes stilted, to family and friends.

In fact, Cat was the last – and by far the youngest – of five children and had always felt like something of a fifth wheel, alienated both by

her age and the nagging suspicion that she was an unwanted financial burden. She had learned not to rely on love – to be constantly
suspicious of it, in fact – and to mine her sense of self-worth from
within. Anticipating a day when she might shift overseas, she had
also maintained a studied distance from family, friends and work-
mates. Her greatest fear, indeed, was that she might make herself
vulnerable to the same overwrought emotions she had observed
in them. So there were no tears shed at her farewell dinners and
get-togethers, just a lot of laughs, good wishes, and the occasional
expression of disbelief: 'I can't believe you're leaving Miami for that
cold, cold place at the ends of the earth.'

To which Cat was quick to point out that Edinburgh, despite its
latitude, never got as cold as Philadelphia, where her family had
lived prior to an unmentionable scandal, and never as uncomfortably hot as Miami, either – so who was the foolish one?

* * *

She expected a transition period of around three months but the
owner was quite happy to move out at once – she already had
another property, apparently – and Cat, with a new life beckoning,
was equally happy not to delay things. She donated most of her
clutter to Miami thrift stores, left boxes of her more substantial
items with a shipping company and, armed with two large suit-
cases and a jam-packed carry-on, took a direct flight from Orlando
Sanford at the start of June, just before the official moving-in date.

In Edinburgh she booked into a budget hotel near Dean Village
and, by some miracle, was allocated a room from which she could
see her own building – the windows of her own flat! – amid the
cluster of steeply gabled residences in the gorge below. Two morn-
ings later she collected the keys from Stuart – one standard door

key and two impressive Chubb keys, of the sort you'd expect to see opening safes – and, with some difficulty, wheeled her luggage from the hotel down into the village, across the wrought-iron foot-bridge where tourists were snapping photos of the palatial Wells Court, and up through the cobbled (correction, *setted*) streets to her building. Here she unlocked the black stair door and hefted her luggage up the granite steps to her own flat on the fifth floor. She half-expected to meet the former owner there – Stuart had indicated that the woman would probably greet her in person – but as it happened there was only a Manila envelope taped to the door containing six pages of dog-eared instructions: the location of the stop-cock and gas meter, the proper way to open the casement windows, and extensive details on the stove, the fuse-box, the radiators and the combi-boiler.

The place had been stripped of furniture but for an oversized wardrobe that Cat guessed had been too cumbersome to wangle down the stairs. The splintery floorboards were bare. There was a curious ambience of abandonment. But the views were intoxicating. The tranquillity was profound. The invitation to occupy was palpable.

That evening Cat sobbed herself dry – an occasional purging process whenever she thought of her ill-fated parents and her own failure to fully connect with the world – and afterwards slept on the bedroom floor under a single blanket she'd purchased at a Princes Street department store. The next morning she welcomed the delivery of a double bed (which she had to assemble from the ground up). Then came a mattress. Later a sofa and an armchair. She went out and ordered a flat screen TV. A computer. A kitchen table that had caught her eye in a Heart Foundation store. A funky chest from a Leith Walk auction house. A few bookcases from a closing-down sale at a homeware outlet. A couple of faux-vintage lamps. Floor rugs, throw rugs, towels, bath and bed linen. Pots and pans and cutlery and crockery for the kitchen; sculptures, trinkets and clocks for the walls and ledges; flowers for the window boxes; and bird feeders to attract the robins, tits, chaffinches and dunnocks that she had seen flitting about the surrounding trees.

She spent a glorious two days shopping for new outfits, head-wear and shoes. She bought a SIM, opened a phone account, got herself connected to the Internet, purchased a TV licence, joined the nearby Drumsheugh Baths Club for the swimming pool, and acquired a key to the neighbouring Belgrave Crescent Gardens (an immense private garden across two dramatic levels, featuring river, bridge, weir, church and crescent views). She registered at the Stockbridge Medical Centre, had a basic check-up, and received in the mail a letter informing her that she was now registered with the National Health Service. More of a surprise – since she had done nothing to apply – was the news that she was listed on the Scottish electoral roll (this minor technicality seeming to announce officially that she had been embraced as a Scot).

Early in July her belongings arrived from the US and an overly solicitous delivery guy helped her lug the boxes up the stairs (before lingering disagreeably, like a man who'd watched too many porno movies). When he left, with a surly glance at his £10 tip, Cat was finally able to hang up her most cherished artworks, stock her shelves with her favourite books, crowd her closets with the remainder of her best clothes, and generally unpack and squirrel away a lot of things which she would have done better to leave in America.

In all these actions she found an invigorating sense of recon-struction.

Four weeks into her residence – just as she was beginning to have too much time to reflect on things – she started work in ABC's headquarters in Lauriston Place. She was guided around the building (a block of green-tinted glass known locally as 'the Aquarium'), met her new colleagues in the Internal Fraud Department (Ross, Fergus, Jenny, Skye, Isla and Agnes), was shown to her closet-sized office, and handed the keys to her company car, a VW Golf, in which she would soon be visiting branches across Scotland.

'You and I are gonna get along fine,' declared Agnes, a fearsome Goth who'd taken up the task of showing her the ropes.

This now, for Cat, was the time for routine: awake at six-thirty, twenty laps at the pool, a hot shower, granola and black coffee, a quick drive to work, home at six, dinner, chores, some down-time, a five-mile run, bed just before eleven, rinse and repeat, every movement from the flick of the kettle switch to the return of her trainers to the shoe rack an integral component in a reassuring daily ritual. This also was the time for Edinburgh to assume its new role of a comforting backdrop, for her flat to become a cosily familiar sanctuary, and for Cat to consider how idyllic it was, to be living in such an enchanting building in such a remarkable city.

And Cat did that – all that – for another two blissful weeks.

And then, on Friday, 28 July, she became aware of the problem.

CHAPTER
THREE

'WHEN I BOUGHT THE PLACE,' Cat admitted, 'I didn't even realise there was an apartment upstairs. You can't really see it from the street – the roof slopes in dramatically – and I just assumed it was a storage space or an empty loft or something.'

Agnes grunted. 'Lots of buildings in Scotland have old nooks and crannies that've been converted into living spaces. You should've been more careful.'

'Uh-huh. And then, for my first five or six weeks in Edinburgh, the flat was empty. The guy who lives there was away somewhere. I think he was away when I inspected the place, too, or just super quiet. But now he's back. And suddenly I get why the previous owner was so eager to sell.'

'He's some sort of maniac?'

'He's a musician.'

'Same thing.'

'And he makes noise. Lots of noise.'

'All musicians do.'

'But it's not just the music – though that's bad enough. It's all sorts of things. Dropping stuff. Stamping around. Banging doors.'

'All through the night?'

'Day and night. Every night. He never seems to sleep.'

'Just kill the cunt.'

'I wish I could,' Cat said, grimacing. 'I wish I could.'

It was an unusually humid early August evening and, with Agnes at the wheel, the two women were hurtling down the A91 towards Edinburgh after interviewing staff at the ABC branch in Montrose. It had only been Cat's third such expedition since reviving her career in Scotland, so she had let Agnes take charge while familiarising herself with the local idioms and procedures. In fact, Agnes, though wildly different in most ways – as plump as Cat was slim, as loud and impulsive as Cat was prudent and methodical – had become her closest colleague in the department, and the nearest thing to a friend outside office hours, for all her fondness for booze, deep-fried food and the c-word.

'Is the cunt renting?'

Cat grimaced again. 'I don't know ... I don't know.'

'Complain to the landlord, if he is. Tenants need to maintain good records, you know – especially in a compact city like Edinburgh.'

'The previous owner surely would have done that, if it was going to do any good.'

'Complain to the factor, then.'

'I don't know what a factor is,' Cat admitted.

'The building superintendent.'

'I don't think there is one.'

'How many flats in the building?'

'Six, one atop the other.'

'Maybe the place is too small.'

Honking the horn at a motorist who swung into her lane, Agnes mouthed the c-word again.

Cat shook her head. 'In Florida I lived for a while in a condo, and there were strict rules in place. Anyone with floorboards had to cover at least seventy per cent of them to reduce noise.'

'Got bare floorboards, has he?'

'They creak like ship timbers. And – I swear to God – I think he deliberately leans on them, at their weakest points, just to make a racket.'

'It's an existential thing,' Agnes said. 'Some people are like toddlers – they only feel alive if they're making noise.' She honked the horn again.

'Maybe that's why he's a musician.'

'Does he shag?'

'Sorry?'

'I used to live beside a couple that shagged like rabbits. Round the clock like newlyweds. I had to thump on the walls to get some peace. That's what you should do, you know. Bang on the ceiling and shout at the top of your lungs: "Oi! What are you playing at?"'

'I didn't come here to make enemies.'

'You didn't come here to tolerate cunts, either.'

'Do you have to say that word?'

'Which word?' Agnes thought about it and sniggered. 'Hey, you're in the wrong country if you blush at a bit of swearing.'

'Isn't there anything else—'

'Prick?'

'Not that, either.'

'Fud?'

'Like Elmer Fudd? That'll do.'

Agnes chuckled. 'OK, then.'

'And, in answer to your question,' Cat said, 'I haven't heard him shag. Not yet, anyway. I have heard him on the toilet, though.'

'Ha! Seriously?'

'I set up an inflatable mattress in my second bedroom – I use it as a study mainly – and tried to sleep there. But it must be directly below his bathroom. I swear, he pees directly into the water, this great thunderous stream, just for the hell of it. Then he slams the lid down.'

'He puts the lid down? You sure he doesn't have a girl?'

'I've never seen one, if he has.'

'What's he look like?'

'No idea,' said Cat. 'The building has a common mailbox, though, so I've seen his name on envelopes. Mr Dylan Moyle.'

'Dylan Moyle . . .' said Agnes, nodding. 'Sounds tasty.' She roared past two lorries carrying freshly sawed logs. 'Maybe he's hung.'

'I can't imagine why you'd say that.'

'Said he pissed "thunderously", didn't you?'

'I don't think that signifies anything.'

'You never know,' said Agnes. 'Go up and introduce yourself. You might be sharing his bed before long.'

'I assure you I won't be doing that.'

'Why not? It's one way to solve your noise problem.'

'It's one way to *make* problems, if you ask me.'

'Not frigid, are you?'

Cat, who in general could shrug off insults and even enjoy them, made a disapproving noise. 'Abrasiveness can be another "existential thing", you know.'

Agnes laughed. 'Well, we've all been wondering about you. Coming all this way, all by yourself, living alone. Either a prude or burned out, we figure.'

'The truth, as usual, is in the middle.'

'That makes not a jot of sense.'

'Whatever,' said Cat. It was too difficult to explain how much she enjoyed being alone. How she had learned the hard way not to trust people. How she had not even contacted her surviving relatives in Scotland, including the sons of her mother's uncle, for fear of needing to socialise with them. 'No,' she said, 'I wouldn't care if he looked like George Clooney. He's inconsiderate, I know that for a fact, and that's a deal-breaker for me.'

'If you have a quiet word with him, maybe he'll change his ways.'

'If he doesn't already know he's making too much noise, then he's dumb as well as inconsiderate. I mean, as soon as I moved in, I bought rugs and carpets for the floors. And every night I creep around to make sure I don't disturb anyone downstairs. And I've never even *met* the people downstairs.'

Agnes shook her head. 'You'll go mad judging people by your own standards. Time to play by his rules, I say. Play loud music, bang on the walls, see how *he* likes it.'

'No . . .' Cat stared out at the heather-dotted pastures of Fife.

'You *really* don't want to confront him, do you?'

'I doubt it will do any good. It might even make him worse.'

'So, what are you gonna do?'

'I dunno . . . Pray.'

Agnes glanced at her. 'Not religious, are you?'

'Don't think so.'

'You don't *think* so?'

'Well, my parents were. And I'm American. So it'd be silly to suggest I hadn't taken on some influences.'

Agnes, who had a pentagram swinging from her rear-view mirror, nodded approvingly. 'Wise answer,' she said. 'Wise answer.'

Shortly afterwards they whisked across the Firth of Forth via the Queensferry Crossing – one of three majestic bridges linking Fife to Edinburgh – and Agnes made a sceptical sound. 'George Clooney's a bit long in the tooth for you now, isn't he?'

But Cat was too distracted to answer. The heat, the waves, the sun-seared evening sky: she had been impaled, briefly but disturbingly, by a totally unexpected feeling of homesickness.

CHAPTER

FOUR

A T NINE P.M. THAT NIGHT Cat heard Moyle leave his flat and trudge down the stairs. She knew enough about his habits by now to suspect that he'd be out for a few hours, possibly at a pub or club, and would return well past midnight. But once or twice he hadn't come back at all. And that meant there was the *possibility* of a full night's sleep.

She'd started going to bed much earlier than was her preference. In Miami she had routinely hit the sack at eleven and risen no later than six-thirty for an early morning run. In Edinburgh she had been forced to move her run to the early evening and go to bed as early as nine-thirty, so she could snatch at least five hours of sleep in bits and pieces across the night. The only alternative was to retire only when exhausted, when it was impossible to keep her eyes open, hoping that the sheer intensity of fatigue would allow her to ride out the loudest of disturbances. But – in her case, anyway – that rarely seemed to work.

She lay there for a while, hearing the booms and whistles of Edinburgh Festival fireworks. The rattle of someone's wheeled suitcase on the setts. The distant whoop of a disturbed bird, probably in the riverside trees. And somewhere along the way she must have drifted off to sleep.

She was chasing a red balloon through a forest of fire-blackened trees. She couldn't understand why the balloon was so important but she knew she had to catch it. The balloon, which was pulsing like a heart, bobbed and curled through the air towards a huge twisted oak tree. There was a hollow in the tree, of the type that animals nest in, and the balloon was disappearing into it. Cat made one last frantic effort to catch it but it was too late. She edged closer to the trunk, and was reaching, very tentatively, into the hollow (her hand so tiny it could only belong to a child), when suddenly—

BANG!

Cat jolted to her senses.

She thought for a moment it was a firework.

But then:

Clap clap clap.

A footfall so loud that it had to be Moyle, stomping up the stairs.

Clap clap clap. His customary jackbooted staccato. *Clap clap clap.* Every step like a gunshot. Around and around, past Cat's door, stopping at the flat above.

Jingle jingle jingle, went his keys.

Kee-waaah, went the door with its pneumatic hinge.

Ka-lunk! He'd let the door fall shut.

Cat knew that the residents downstairs would have heard this much as well. Hell, it was likely that people all over Dean Village had heard it.

But what came next was a symphony played exclusively for her.

Klonk klonk, went something dropped on floorboards. *Whump,* went some inner door that he had thrown closed. *Ga-wonk,* went something else. *Creak creak creak,* went the floorboards as he crossed his living area.

For a minute or so there was nothing. Cat shot a glance at her alarm clock: 2.07 a.m.

Kawissssshhhhhhhhhhhhhhhhhhhh, went the sound of the toilet flushing. Then the noise of the water pipes hissing and clanging – for some reason these pipes, which ran down behind Cat's own bathroom, were loud enough to be heard even from her bed.

Silence for a minute or two, then Moyle moved into the room directly above her. Cat prayed he was about to flop onto his bed and go to sleep.

Klunk klunk – probably boots being thrown on the floor. *Ka-woot* – possibly a belt. *Skaweeeeeeee*, went something like a closet door. Then the squeak of bedsprings. It sounded as though he'd dropped onto his mattress.

Cat held her breath. Could it be? Could she really be in luck?

The silence lasted possibly fifteen minutes – Cat was drifting into dreamland again – when there was another jagged noise.

BA-KLONK!

She spasmed awake as if electrocuted. For a moment she didn't even know what had happened – her heart had registered the noise before her ears.

Then:

Creak creak creak. Moyle was shuffling again across the floorboards. *Skaweeeeeee.* He was opening the closet. *Creak creak creak.* He was leaving the room.

PLONK. He'd dropped something in his living area.

'Fuck!' he cursed to himself.

Nnnnnnnnnhhhhhhhhhrrrrrrrrr. He was dragging a chair across the floor.

Bahlunk lunk lunk. He was plugging something into a socket.

Silence for thirty seconds.

TWAAAANG. He'd struck a chord on his electric guitar.

Cat gasped. If precedent was anything to go by, Moyle would be awake for the next couple of hours. Experimenting with his music.

Repeating riffs. Shifting around. Watching television. Drinking. Turning taps on and off. Dropping things.

She glanced again at her alarm clock. 2:52. She figured she'd get just fragments of sleep before 7:45, the latest she could rise and still make it to work on time. But she'd have to make do with the briefest of showers, don her clothes in a mad rush, and gobble down her breakfast or sacrifice it entirely.

Wrapping the pillow around her head, Cat remembered fondly her early days in Dean Village, not two months earlier, when her biggest problem had been trying to decide between an early morning run around the neighbourhood or a vigorous swim in the heated pool of the Drumsheugh Baths.

Somehow she had to regain control.

CHAPTER

FIVE

TWO NIGHTS LATER CAT ARRIVED home just as the couple in Number Four – she'd seen them a couple of times from the window by now – were getting out of their Prius. They introduced themselves at the stair door and continued chatting as they mounted the steps. Maxine was an artist who'd spent some years on the Continent and was now working as a tour guide; her partner Michael was some sort of legal expert, originally from Wales, who'd also spent a lot of time abroad. Cat accepted their invitation to dinner the following evening.

'We're vegans, if that's a problem,' Maxine added before parting.

'Not a problem,' said Cat, smiling. 'So am I.'

Though the meal wasn't great – a middling goulash and a soggy strudel; Maxine apologised constantly for missing ingredients – Cat warmed to the two of them immediately. They were a bohemian couple, interested in arts and travel and fitness and good wine; they didn't own a TV because, in Michael's words, 'It's nothing but shit.' They were also devoted nudists – they'd met during a Spencer Tunick photo shoot on a Swiss glacier, apparently – and often walked around the apartment au naturel. 'That's why we keep the blinds down,' said Maxine.

'And the heating up,' chipped in Michael.

'I don't mind,' said Cat, chuckling. 'It'll help keep my own power bills down.'

Maxine showed off her sculptures, which were suggestively erotic, and over glasses of some sort of mulled Bavarian liqueur – of which Cat sipped only to be sociable – they discussed the charms of Edinburgh and the hikes that Cat just 'had to do'.

'You can go all the way from Dean Village to South Queensferry without hitting more than two sets of traffic lights,' Maxine enthused.

'You take the bike paths first,' Michael explained, 'then follow Queensferry Road for a mile or so, then wander down through the Dalmeny Estate. We do it all the time.'

'How far is it?' Cat asked.

'About 18,000 steps,' said Maxine.

Cat, who wore a fitness tracker while running, struggled to calculate. 'Which is—?'

'About nine miles. Then we have lunch by the Firth and walk back.'

'And I thought *I* was a health nut.'

'You should join us sometime,' Maxine said, grinning. 'At the gym too. There's a new place in Murrayfield. We do all sorts of classes there: high intensity, boxing, jazzercise. It's great fun.'

'Yeah?' said Cat, shifting uncomfortably. 'I'll keep it in mind.'

She quickly steered the conversation on to some of the difficulties she'd encountered in the building, wanting in truth to talk about Moyle but hoping that they'd raise the subject first. She mentioned the stairwell light outside her door, which flashed like a strobe lamp ('A maintenance fellow used to visit but he passed on,' noted Michael). She spoke of the flies that frequently invaded her flat because there were no window screens ('That's only a problem in summer,' Maxine assured her). She drew a laugh by imitating, with a creditable Scottish accent, the wayward delivery men who sometimes phoned up for directions: 'Ah cannae foond the plais, ken ya gaid may un?'

'And what about TurMoyle?' Maxine asked.

Cat was momentarily flummoxed. 'Turmoil?'

'Moyle, Mr Moyle – "TurMoyle", as we call him. The guy in Number Six.'

'Oh' – Cat was surprised – 'you mean you know all about him?'

'Oh yeah,' said Maxine. 'Oh yeah.'

It turned out that Moyle – he was a bass player in a heavy metal band ('a friend saw them in a Gorgie pub and said they were rank') – had for years been the black sheep of the building, rarely doing his bit with clean-ups, or contributing to the maintenance fund, or being sociable in general. Sometimes he threw raucous parties and left stacks of empty beer cans at the bottom of the stairs; once Michael had tripped over them in the dark and dislocated a finger. Confronting him had made little difference, though; his usual response was to walk past as though he hadn't heard.

'Well, he hasn't thrown any parties since I moved in,' Cat said. 'At least there's that. But I can hear him clearly. *Everything.*'

Maxine nodded. 'The top flat wasn't even an apartment until ten years ago.'

'They were still converting it when we moved in,' added Michael.

'And apparently there's *nothing* between your floor and his. It's like a drum.'

'It might not even be legal, you know,' Michael noted. 'There are regulations about separating floors, even in old buildings like this. I'll look into it, if you like.'

'I'd appreciate that,' said Cat, adding, 'My hairdresser suggested applying for something called an ASPO.'

'ASBO,' Michael corrected. 'Anti-Social Behaviour Order. But you can't apply for one of those yourself.'

'No?'

'You have to lodge a complaint with the police, who in turn lobby the council. And unfortunately the council is so flooded with applications – particularly with all the new holiday lets around – that ASBOs take ages to process, when they're processed at all.'

'What about the former owner? Do you know if she tried?'

'Connie?' said Maxine. 'She certainly *mentioned* it, but as for whether she ever did anything official—'

Michael interrupted: 'Wasn't there that time when—'

'Oh yeah, I forgot about that,' said Maxine. 'But that had nothing to do with noise. TurMoyle flooded his bathroom once and the water dripped through Connie's ceiling onto some priceless maps she was storing in her box room. She asked TurMoyle about his insurance policy and he just laughed at her. So she demanded compensation from the landlord but things dragged on and on. I'm not sure what happened in the end.'

'I think she gave up,' said Michael, 'and just repainted the ceiling.'

'Yeah,' said Maxine, 'there was a big brown stain for a while. Mind you, this was years ago now.'

Cat tried to see a precedent she could strive for. 'So she ended up *adjusting* to the problem? Just *living* with it?'

'Oh no,' Maxine said with a mirthless chuckle. 'Oh no. Connie left the building a long time ago. Moved to Glasgow, I think. Then she rented your place out a dozen times, but no one lasted longer than a few months.'

'The noise?'

'I think so,' said Maxine, frowning sympathetically. 'I know this isn't exactly what you want to hear . . .'

It wasn't, but Cat tried to be positive. 'Oh well, Moyle himself might move out soon – I can always hope for that.'

But now Maxine's frown deepened. 'I hate to disappoint you, but from what I understand his landlord is his aunt. He pays hardly any rent – a peppercorn. Maybe nothing at all. For him it's a deal that's just too good to be true. And he's not likely to ever become famous, from what I hear, so the odds of him shifting anytime soon, I'm afraid to say, are pretty remote.'

Cat felt her spirits drain. 'You know, I've never met him,' she said, still clutching at straws. 'Never even *seen* him, not even from my window. He doesn't look like George Clooney, does he?'

'George Clooney?' Maxine laughed. 'More like Charles Manson.'

'Eyes that are pure evil,' Michael added, also chuckling.

And Cat laughed too, though in truth she was finding it increasingly hard to see anything remotely amusing.

She sipped some more liqueur.

★ ★ ★

Cat had been trained to deal with difficult people – to charm them, establish a rapport with them, manipulate them. She was proud of her record in doing so. And she backed herself to get results now.

The following evening she raced home from work and changed into her running gear. She felt slightly out of shape – moving in, setting herself up, then adjusting to Moyle's routines had all taken their toll – but she knew she still looked OK in Lycra pants. She tied her hair back in a swishy ponytail. Even considered stuffing her bra.

Then she sat in her armchair, trying to read a book about Julius Caesar, and waited for Moyle to come home.

Frustratingly, it wasn't until ten p.m. But when she heard the *kah-lunk* of the building's stair door and *clap clap clap* of his boots on the granite steps, she was ready. She took a deep breath and started down the stairs past the malfunctioning light.

She met him for the first time outside the door to Number Three.

'Hi,' she said as brightly as possible, thrusting out a hand. 'You must be Dylan.'

He had unruly shoulder-length hair, a lank beard, a bloodless complexion and ruthless dark-brown eyes. He was wearing an inflexible scowl, a dog-collar tattoo and a leather jacket over a ragged T-shirt bearing the words HOUNDS OF HADES. He couldn't have looked more like a hard rocker if he'd stepped off the cover of a death metal magazine.

He accepted her hand with a desultory shake but was still giving her a million-mile stare.

'I'm Cat, Cat Thomas,' she went on, still smiling. 'I'm living in Flat Five, right beneath you.'

He continued looking at her blankly.

'I'm sorry I didn't introduce myself earlier,' she said. 'But I think you were away for the first few weeks I was here. This is really some sort of place, huh? So atmospheric – I love it.'

He finally seemed to have realised she was talking to him. 'Cat,' he said. 'Thomas Cat. Tom Cat.'

'Yeah!' She laughed, as though nobody had ever made that joke before. 'Catriona actually, in the Scottish style, but where I grew up no one knew how to pronounce it, so I shortened it to Cat. Tom Cat, yeah.' Another pointless chuckle.

Moyle continued staring at her. His eyes roamed her body, but he didn't look impressed.

'Oh, well,' said Cat, 'better be on my way. It was great to meet you.'

She turned away and started down the steps. But almost

immediately turned back. Because now came the 'afterthought'.

'Oh – Dylan?' And when he slowly rotated back in her direction: 'I don't know if you're aware, but apparently there's nothing insulating the space between our two apartments – just empty air. So I can hear everything. *Everything.* And, you know, I'd really appreciate it if you could be mindful of that. At night, I mean. The boards in your place creak. The pipes clang. The doors bang. And sometimes I find it a little hard to sleep. Which is a problem because I'm settling into a new job and . . . well, you understand.'

She'd said it all with upraised eyebrows and the sweetest of smiles – completely unthreatening and non-aggressive, just a new friend asking for a favour.

But in response Moyle's forehead furrowed, as if he was struggling to work out why she was bothering him with such trivia. And finally:

'*American.*'

He said it as though he'd belatedly recognised her accent. As though it explained everything. As if her nationality were some sort of *disease.*

Cat could only laugh politely, treating the reaction as a joke, then turn around, head down the stairs again, and go out for her run.

But as she scaled the hills of Ravelston – half-heartedly, and absurdly late at night – she had a terrible feeling in her gut. A sense that her charm, her wiles, all her strategic manipulations, had come to naught.

And so it turned out to be.

That night she lay awake in bed, hearing the *klunks,* the *creaks,* the *kee-wahs,* and the *shhhhhhhhhhhh* of the hissing pipes. If anything, the noises were more insistent than ever. She slept in fits and starts, drifting in and out of psychedelic dreams, her solutions becoming ever more biblical.

CHAPTER
SIX

THE FOLLOWING WEEK CAT AND AGNES were in the pretty town of Callander, 'gateway to the Highlands' – the sort of place where the ageing demographic doesn't understand the intricacies of online banking and has no desire to learn them. Consequently there were more tellers at the local branch than ABC usually considered necessary; there was even talk of shutting the place altogether and forcing the locals to make do with a basic-services outlet at the post office.

When two elderly customers – so set in their ways that they insisted on filling out withdrawal forms – complained that their printed statements registered debit amounts well in excess of what they'd received, the internal fraud team – Cat and Agnes, in this case – were called in to investigate. And it immediately became obvious they had their work cut out for them. The internal CCTV cameras at the branch had been switched off. The branch manager stored the key to the cameras in an easily accessible office drawer. And all three tellers – and some of the senior staff – sometimes shared the cash desk without officially logging on.

Nevertheless one staff member in particular – a locum teller called Connor Bailey – ticked all the boxes. He was male. He was twenty-four to thirty-two. His body language was defensive. His responses during initial interviews were self-contradictory. Most significantly, he had been at other branches in the Stirling region when similar activity had occurred.

But he was proving a tough nut to crack. He denied everything. He claimed to be wounded by their suspicions. He insisted repeatedly that he was 'a good man'.

Cat and Agnes were wearily familiar with such tactics but that didn't mean they were on firm ground. The department had earlier conducted a misconduct test – they sent in two 'customers' who drew out hundreds of pounds while feigning general forgetfulness and distraction – and Connor had passed with flying colours. There was no indication he'd altered any withdrawal forms or stolen cash for himself. His own accounts, including those he held with other banks, showed no signs of unusual activity. Nor did he appear to be living above his means.

But Agnes – with just a couple of hours to wrap up the investigation – thought she had him.

'Listen here, young fellow' – an amusing way to address him, Cat thought, since Agnes herself was scarcely older – 'we *know* you did it. We *know* you're lying. And we know all the nuances, trust me. This isn't just instinct, it's *everything*. You're giving off so much radiation you'd make a Geiger counter click. You're swinging this way and that in that chair. Your voice is low and tight. Your eye contact is irregular. Hell, even the tip of your nose is red – what we call "the Pinocchio effect". You're *embarrassing* yourself, fella.'

Connor, whose eyes had flickered at the mention of eye contact, shook his head. 'I'm sorry. I know nothing about that. If I'm nervous it's because I don't like being here. Because I don't like being suspected of anything. But I'm a good man.'

'Aye right,' said Agnes, with a jaded glance at Cat. 'Well, we've asked around, you see. We know your mother has gambling problems. We know she spends most of her day at the betting shops. And we know you've been supplementing her pension most of your adult life. So how about admitting the truth, Connor? She was in a spot of bother – maybe about to lose her home, eh? – and you needed to cover her debts. But you didn't have the cash so you had to make do with someone else's. You fiddled with the cameras and put the sting on some wealthy old geezers – no real harm done, right? You gave old Mrs MacAskill a few hundred less than it said on the withdrawal form. You altered the withdrawal form of old Mr Mitchell so it looked like he took out £1,500, not five hundred. A wee bit here, a wee bit there, but it all adds up. You knew the old fossils wouldn't notice immediately – in fact, you were hoping they wouldn't notice at all. Not only do they rarely check their statements, most of them can't even *read* their fuckin' statements. So as far as you were concerned it was worth the risk. No one would ever find out. Yet here we are.'

Connor responded with another head shake. 'I'm sorry,' he said, 'but that's not true. My mother has nothing to do with this. My mother raised me good and proper. She'd be *horrified* if she thought I'd done anything like what you're saying.'

'But you did it anyway, didn't you!' Agnes barked, slapping the table so hard that Connor – and Cat – flinched. 'You did it because you love the old dear, right? Who cares! You talk about good and proper, for Christ's sake. What about the other staff here we've put through the griller? You ever think about them? You *do* know that if we don't get this sorted HR is gonna have to assign you all to different branches, right? Just to break you up? So why not own the hell up to your misdeeds like a proud Scot?'

They were in the bank's tiny lunchroom and Agnes, in full bad cop mode, was speaking louder than strictly necessary – itself a form of humiliation. But Connor, though clearly discomfited, wasn't buckling.

'I *am* a proud Scot,' he protested. A vein in his temple was pulsing and there was a sheen of perspiration on his forehead. 'And I'd own up if that was the right thing to do. I've always been honest. I'm proud of my record. If I'd really done those things you're talking about, I'd never be able to look anyone in the face.'

But at just that moment he *wasn't* looking anyone in the face. And he must have realised it, belatedly, because he tore his eyes off the table and stared at Agnes again.

'Oh, for fuck's sake, Connor!' she said. 'Have you not heard a word I've said? This case is what we in the trade call a walk-up start. It should be done and dusted already. Now, you can choose to make it easy for us or you can choose to prolong the suffering. But we'll get you in the end because we always do. And the longer it takes the more annoyed we'll get. So own up now or kick the can down the road and face the consequences. Do you understand what I'm saying?'

Connor tried appealing to Cat instead. 'I'm a good man,' he said hoarsely.

'Oh, Jesus!' Agnes said to Cat. 'Did you see that? The Balkan Shake? Shaking his head while claiming he's a good man! This guy might as well be wearing a guilty sign around his neck!'

It was at this point that Cat chose to intervene. While technically there chiefly to observe – and to disconcert suspects with her cool demeanour and the occasional injection of a legal technicality – she had also, by pre-arrangement with Agnes, assumed the role of the good cop, the sympathetic voice that nevertheless lures the victim to the same destination. But what she did now, sighing, was very much off script.

'Yeah, yeah,' she said, 'you're a good person, Connor. You can say that a thousand times and maybe you even believe it. But it's a defence mechanism. It's something the guilty say to reassure them-selves. Because *no one* is a good person all the time. And you need to face the truth – you need to immerse yourself in reality for a change.'

She registered Agnes's surprise – not to mention Connor's – and felt a brief stab of shame. This was not her way. But it was getting late and they needed to get back to Edinburgh. She was fatigued from lack of sleep. She was fatigued in general. So she ploughed on.

'*Everyone*, if the circumstances are right, is capable of bad things. Everyone certainly contemplates bad things. And everyone, when backed into a corner, is liable to criminal actions. Look at me, for instance. Three months ago I moved from Florida into this idyllic flat in Edinburgh. It's everything I ever dreamed of. And yet there's this guy upstairs, this heavy-metal musician, who seems hellbent on turning my life into a nightmare. He makes noise constantly – day and night, every night. He doesn't respond to polite requests or threats. He doesn't respond to anything at all. He just goes on being the way he is. And you know what? I sometimes lie awake thinking of ways to kill him. Actually kill him. I wonder if I can drill a hole in my ceiling, feed a rubber hose through his floor and fill his place with carbon monoxide. I wonder if I can set fire to the building at night and burn him to a crisp. I wonder if I can loosen a step, or set up a tripwire, so that he goes tumbling down the stairs and cracks his skull open. I wonder if I can attach something to his car so that it blows up when he turns on the ignition – that sounds ridiculous but I know how it's done. And it goes without saying that if you could kill someone by pressing a button – just pressing a button and leaving no forensic evidence whatsoever – I would've finished him off a hundred times, a *thousand* times, by now.'

Cat could hear her own voice in her ears – with a sort of disem-bodied horror – but she couldn't stop.

'And even when I'm not thinking of ways to kill him, I'm

dreaming of ways he might be killed. Maybe that light plane I hear buzzing overhead will drop out of the sky and crash into the top floor – just the top floor. Maybe the landing gear will fall off that jetliner. Maybe that storm will send a branch spearing through his window. Maybe that shooting star is a meteor heading straight for his head. You can't imagine how many ways I've fantasised about this guy getting crushed, sliced open, ripped apart. And yeah, that's shocking, and yeah, I wake up in the morning thinking, "My God, what's the matter with me?" But that's what happens when you're at your wits' end. When you're tired. When you're not thinking straight. When your peace of mind is suffering, when your *health* is suffering, when the only answer seems to be doing something that was previously unthinkable. You don't need me to tell you that people under pressure can crack. The very best people can crack. I've been close to cracking – *ridiculously* close to cracking – this very week.'

She glanced at Agnes, who was staring at her with awe, and back at Connor, whose mouth was as wide as a sideshow clown's. But still she hadn't finished.

'So I understand you, Connor. You're not a bad man, of course you're not. Trust me, I've investigated hundreds of people and some of them are genuinely bad. People who ignore the consequences of their actions, people who feel no remorse, people who seem to enjoy the thrill of crime. Next to them, Connor, you're pocket lint – and I'm not saying that to belittle you. You stole minor amounts of money to protect your mother. In similar circumstances I might have done the same thing. Bottom line is, your case is nothing. It's kids' stuff. And we can arrange to have the whole thing settled with a minimum of fuss. This region you're in – Stirling? – is charming but it's small. I can tell that everyone knows everyone and word gets around fast. Well, we don't want to embarrass you any more than necessary. So what we can do is this. If you agree to resign from the bank and pay back the money you stole, we'll guarantee two things. One, not to inform the police. And two, to fudge the reasons for your resignation. You can even tell people that you were insulted by the suspicions and decided you'd had enough. Whatever. You get to move on with your life with dignity. You get to apply for another job without fear that your record will come back to haunt you. Did you ever believe you'd hear such a thing? Well, I'm putting myself out on a limb for you, Connor. But I need you to tell us the truth. That's non-negotiable. Just admit what we already know and then we can get back to hunting down the *real* bad guys.

'So how about it, Connor?' she said, leaning back. 'Did you deactivate the cameras? And take some money to help your mother? A simple nod of the head will suffice . . .'

Connor Bailey stared at her, then stared at Agnes, then stared at Cat again . . . and looked as though he didn't know what to say.

CHAPTER
SEVEN

'WELL,' SAID AGNES, 'that was quite a show.'

Cat, at the wheel of her own VW this time, shook her head. 'I didn't mean to take over like that. I really don't know what got into me. Displaced aggression, probably – anger with the guy upstairs. And I *hate* displaced aggression. It's a cardinal sin for me.'

'What are you talking about? You manipulated him perfectly. And gave him the kid-glove treatment in the end. That offer you made, I mean – shit, he couldn't do anything *but* confess after that.'

'Yeah, yeah, I overstepped my boundaries, right?'

'Let's just say I don't think the Wing Commander is going to approve.' Nick 'Wing Commander' Bellamy was the officious department chief.

'Bellamy doesn't like me anyway. He's never been happy about the way I was foisted onto him – I can tell.'

'Bellamy is a fud. Everyone – even his wife, even his dog – thinks it. He's a fud.'

'Well' – Cat sighed – 'I'll deal with his objections later. We got a quick result, didn't we? Connor Bailey will pay back what he stole.

And it's always better to get the money back in dribs and drabs, from some guy in gainful employment, rather than writing it off as a loss because he can't get another job.'

'Sounds a wee bit logical for the Wing Commander. He likes his pound of flesh.'

'Then he's in the wrong industry. He should be a butcher.'

'Or an op-ed writer.'

'Bottom line is, Bailey isn't an evil person. There are plenty out there, and he's not one of them. It was a release for him to acknowledge his dark side.'

'And you sure showed him how to do that.'

'You have to,' Cat insisted. 'For your mental health. For your sanity. It's why the Catholics have confession. You up for a snack, by the way?'

Agnes giggled at the change of tone. 'Say again?'

'You hungry? I think we deserve a good meal – on me.'

'Thinking about the dark side gives you an appetite, does it?'

'Not eating all day gives me an appetite. Just keep your eyes peeled for a decent bar.'

'Pub.'

'Sorry, pub.'

Ten minutes later, changing gears, Cat steered into the car park of the Snarling Wolf.

★　★　★

Agnes ordered pork and haggis sausages with hand-cut chips, garlic bread and three beers. Cat had aubergine stew and a mineral water with a slice of lime.

'Don't know how you can eat that shit,' Agnes said, finishing the last of her chips.

'I've been vegan for so long now,' Cat said, 'that I gag as soon as meat hits my tongue.'

'Best not mention that on a first date.'

Cat ignored her. 'This is richer than I prefer, really, but I always cave in when I'm under stress.'

'The guy upstairs?'

'Yeah,' said Cat, 'I'm not getting time for any of the things I usually like to do. Running, reading, cooking. It's affecting my work too.'

Agnes wiped her mouth with a napkin. 'You really thought of all those ways of killing him, by the way – that stuff you mentioned to Connor?'

'Oh yeah.'

'And that bit about murdering him in his car – that for real?'

'The only reason I know how to do that is because someone tried it on me once.'

'Ha! You're serious?'

'Dead serious,' said Cat, putting down her fork. 'A crime syndicate in Florida. The fallout from that investigation is the real reason I'm here in Scotland.'

'Oh aye? You never did tell me the full story.'

In fact, Cat had resolved to be circumspect about the full details: people in her field were almost superstitious about discussing the ins and outs of major cases openly. But the cosy nature of the pub – oaken ceiling beams, crackling fire, quaint illustrations of cravat-wearing wolves – served to lower her guard. So she took a sip of water and went for broke.

'There was a bank manager in Miami, sixty years old, a pillar of the industry, and someone from head office happened to see him in New York in a five-star grill dining with the kingpin of a crime syndicate. Or thought he did – the details were a bit sketchy.

Anyway, I got lumped with making a routine check on his financial history. Now there wasn't much to see at first, and in normal
circumstances I would've given up after a week. But I thought I
smelled something fishy. So I went into his branch, because I
wanted to see him personally. Not officially: I only wanted to look
at him. And when he breezed past wearing a thousand-dollar suit,
not a hair out of place, whitened teeth, botoxed forehead – well,
my radar told me this guy was shifty. So I kept digging. I looked
into all the loans he'd approved and the accounts he'd opened.
And finally I found something. Largo Hospitality. Supposedly an
employment agency in Florida and the Carolinas, but with no
website, no mention in the yellow pages, nothing. I dug deeper.
The company turned out to be a subsidiary of Scicluna Holdings,
a company I knew had links to organised crime. I looked at its
account transactions. And a lot of them turned out to be amounts
paid into the accounts of hotel staff across the south-east. Always
hotel staff – maids and janitors and what have you. But that's still
nothing to ring any alarm bells, right? Maybe Largo Hospitality is
a temping agency. Maybe their clients get a few days of employment here and there at hotels or guest houses or whatever. Maybe
that's why the payments are irregular. But I kept digging anyway.
I put myself in the shoes of these people – subsistence workers
on crappy wages and shift patterns who change filthy sheets, mop
the pee off bathroom floors – and in the end I had a hunch. So I
booked into one of the hotels where these people worked – after
hours, mind you, and on my own budget – and set up a hidden
camera. Now this—'

'I thought entrapment was illegal in the US.'

'This wasn't entrapment,' Cat said. 'I wasn't interested in the
hotel staff or using the footage as evidence. And at first it showed
nothing unusual anyway. So I tried again. Still on my own money,

you understand. And eventually I got exactly what I suspected. The cleaners were breaking into the luggage of the guests. They were taking address details. Passport details. Credit card numbers. Wax impressions of house keys.'

'Jesus.'

'And, to cut a long story short, the impressions were immediately forwarded to an intermediary so that duplicate keys could be cut. And then the duplicate keys were dispatched to accomplices in the guests' home state. This is before the guests, whoever they were, even got back from their vacation. So for the thieves it was like stealing candy from a baby. The houses were empty and they literally walked in the front door. They ransacked the place and took anything that was valuable, including cash if they were lucky, and later the guests would come home, discover they'd been burgled, and never link it to the hotel they'd stayed in. Someone must've been watching our house, eh? Those light timers didn't fool anyone. The crime syndicate got cash and jewels and contraband to sell on the black market. The maids and janitors, the ones who'd waxed the keys, got a small kickback for every robbery they'd made possible. These payments were distributed through Largo Hospitality in the form of temp payments. Our guy, the bank manager who helped launder the money, was also getting kickbacks. But it wasn't just him. Turned out this was a nationwide scheme with bank managers in twelve states implicated. A huge story. And all because my nostrils flared.'

'Bloody hell,' said Agnes. 'You should be famous.'

'No,' Cat said. 'Fame was the last thing I wanted. In fact, my name was supposed to be suppressed for safety reasons, but it got out anyway. And I started to get these threats from the crime syndicate. The usual stuff. Rocks thrown through my windows. A dead cat on my doorstep. They tampered with my car. I was lucky I wasn't blown up.'

'No wonder you're here.'

'Hmm,' said Cat, with a philosophical air. 'But you know what bothered me the most? It was the people they chose as victims – the dupes, the hotel guests. They were never rich because the wealthy can afford round-the-clock surveillance and sophisticated security systems. It was always the battlers – penny-pinching couples in three-star hotels on their first big vacation in years, heading out to take in the sights and leaving their cases back in the room with the locks off, never knowing any better. Then they get home and find they've been ransacked and everything – even the memory of the vacation – is ruined. And they live in fear for the rest of their lives. Ordinary, everyday, lower middle-class schmucks. Just like my parents. Just like me, for that matter. I spent years scrimping and saving, right from my first job as a teenager, just so I'd have enough capital to buy a place of my own. And now it's a nightmare. A goddamn nightmare.'

Cat drained the rest of her mineral water and slammed the glass down on the table.

'Anyway,' she said. 'Let's get out of here. I need to get home to bed.'

'Why? Sounds like you won't sleep anyway.'

'True,' Cat said, rising. 'True.'

★   ★   ★

They were hurtling down the M9, having just passed the Kelpies – the colossal water horse sculptures at Falkirk – when Agnes, unusually self-conscious, made a suggestion.

'You should come with me, you know. I might be able to solve your problem.'

Cat blinked. 'What problem?'

'You know. With the guy upstairs.'

'How, exactly?'

'Come with me and find out.'

'Come with you where?'

'To a meeting. With some friends of mine.'

'What sort of friends?'

'Friends friends.'

'Hitmen?'

'Not hitmen, exactly.'

'Then who?'

'Come along and find out. I don't do this for everyone, believe me.'

Cat, shifting lanes to avoid the choking black exhaust of a campervan, shook her head. 'Well, this is all very *mysterious*.'

'Only if you want it to be. In reality, this is very logical. Supremely logical. You have all the right qualities, you know.'

'What qualities?'

'Certain attitudes. Inclinations. And intelligence.'

'Intelligence.'

'Aye.'

'And why is intelligence important?'

'Because we don't tolerate stupid people nowadays. Fanatics. Exhibitionists. Perverts. Times have changed.'

'You still haven't told me who "we" are.'

'Come along and find out,' said Agnes. 'Put in your request. See what happens.'

Part of Cat felt the need for clarification; another part told her it was best not to ask.

'I must be dreaming already,' she said. 'Because for a second I was taking you seriously.'

'You should take me seriously.'

'I'm a realist,' said Cat.

'So's *he*. The ultimate realist, in fact.'

'Who?'

But Agnes didn't answer. Didn't say a word. And Cat decided that she'd heard enough.

'Let me concentrate on the road, will you? This is the first time I've driven this far in Scotland. And on the wrong side of the freeway, too.'

'Motorway.'

'Sorry, motorway.'

They drove in silence until they neared Edinburgh Airport. Overhead, a huge jetliner, like an oversize Christmas tree, was lumbering through the darkness.

'Hope the landing gear doesn't fall off,' mused Agnes.

'Huh?' It took Cat a few moments to realise Agnes was referring to her confession. 'Oh – you're not still thinking about that, are you?'

'I'm still thinking about how to solve your problem.'

Cat was silent, negotiating some complex lane-changes, but something continued to niggle at her. 'You know,' she said, 'I've been meaning to ask you something...'

'I'm all ears.'

'It's about that tattoo on your arm.'

'The Saltire?' Agnes sniggered. 'It's the Scottish flag, dummy.'

'I mean the other one. The one higher up.'

Agnes peeled back her sleeve. 'This thing?'

Cat looked back at the road, nodding. 'Yeah – what is it?'

'It's an autograph.'

'Whose autograph?'

'Who do you think?'

'I've got no idea.'

'Let's just say he goes by many names . . .'

Cat thought about it and snorted. 'Uses a tattoo needle, does he?'

'A pen. I *later* had it tattooed.'

'I'm surprised he didn't use a talon.'

'Now you're being silly,' Agnes said, and both women laughed.

'But seriously . . .'

'But seriously,' Agnes admitted. 'I got this on my eighteenth birthday – that's why it's so faded. It was copied from a book about the Loudun witches. The pact that Urbain Grandier made with Lucifer.'

'The Loudun witches,' said Cat, vaguely remembering something. 'Now that was a famous case of fraud, wasn't it?'

'That's the consensus. Though only an expert would be able to say if it was a genuine fraud.'

'Pity we weren't around back then, I guess.'

'Pity for a lot of people,' said Agnes, and the two women laughed again.

They plunged into outer Edinburgh and Cat was pleased to end the bizarre conversation. This was a moment to be alert, not distracted. She certainly didn't need to be dealing with the sense that her life was about to take another monumental detour.

It was Friday, 24 August.

CHAPTER
EIGHT

O VER THE NEXT THREE WEEKS, as festive August surrendered to stately September, Cat ignored Agnes's suggestion about the mysterious 'meeting' and deflected any questions about the ongoing problem with the guy upstairs. As predicted, her supervisor Nick Bellamy was less than impressed with the deal she'd cut with Connor Bailey in Callander and even sought interdepartmental advice about overturning it. When the legal team suggested that might create more problems than it was worth – the stolen amounts being so minor – Cat was removed from field investigations for two weeks and ordered to put together an intra-office lecture on a new study, written up in *Psychology Today*, measuring the traits inherent in a fraudster's mind.

Trying to reduce this into the form of a soundbite-friendly speech drove Cat to the brink of exasperation:

Insensitivity ($ß = .16$), Self-Interest ($ß = .27$) and Moral Disengagement ($ß = .12$) increased in measures consistent with the HEXACO model (see Chin, Monagle and Rodway, 2008) but well beneath the threshold of expected Psychopathy ($ß = .38$) as predicted by Contoyannis, Arrigo and Ahern (2012), keeping in mind the free parameters, manifest variables, and the possibilities of misspecifications in the log-likelihood ratio (LLR).

In better times Cat might have made sure she understood it, at least in essence; now, she resorted to quoting large chunks of it verbatim, feigning full comprehension of its principles, and trusting that no one would seek a coherent explanation. And mercifully no one did.

In truth, she lacked the energy to concentrate. She had taken to drinking at least five cups of coffee a day. She had sacrificed nearly all of her exercise regimen. Her muscles had loosened. There were loose hairs on her pillow each morning. Dark circles under her eyes. And a subcutaneous pimple on her chin. Though she disliked the idea that she was vain, Cat had always been proud of her clear skin, her lustrous hair, her general fitness. Now she felt like a frump.

She had tried fitting gel plugs into her ears every night. She had experimented with earmuffs and headphones. All-night music on her clock radio. 'White noise' to harmonise with Moyle's racket. Prescription sleeping tablets from the NHS. She had even tried spending the night in every room in her flat barring the bathroom. She'd slept on the living room sofa. On the floor beside her desk. Even, on one especially torrid night, on the kitchen table. But there were no easy answers.

Clap clap clap, went Moyle's boots on the sixty-six steps.

Kee-waaah! went the pneumatic hinge.

Ka-LUNK! went his front door.

Creak creak creak, went the floorboards.

Kawisssssshhhhhhhhhhhhhhhhhhhhh, went his toilet.

Whump! went something dropped on the floor.

Nnnnnnnhhhhhhhhhhrrrrrrrrrr! went a chair he'd dragged into position.

Twang, went his electric guitar.

'*Aaaaarrggggggghhhhh*,' growled the man himself

And all this at 11.30 p.m., at 12.12 a.m., at 1.22 a.m., at 2.06 a.m., at 3.35 a.m., at 4.01 a.m., at 5.26 a.m.

There was simply no getting used to it. Cat decided that, paradoxically, it was not the sounds themselves that were so disruptive. It was Moyle's blatant disregard for her welfare. The seething rage that accompanied every one of his louder noises precluded the possibility of just shrugging it off and sliding back into sleep. She couldn't treat him like a noisy songbird or a barking dog or something else that could not be controlled. Nor could she convince herself, as much as she tried, that it was just part of the local culture – something she needed to acclimatise to, and quickly, if she wanted to fit in. Even her willingness to entertain the idea that she was punishing herself with some form of neurosis – because in her heart she didn't believe she deserved full happiness – failed to help. And the sporadic nature of the noises meant that there was no point *trying* to sleep until Moyle himself was at rest – and typically that was not until four or five o'clock in the morning.

Again and again homicidal fantasies ranged through her delirium. She saw herself painting his door handle with a deadly toxin. Climbing from her window to the top of the building, in the middle of the night, and somehow weakening the roof so that it collapsed on him while he slept. 'Accidentally' dislodging her window box, from forty feet above, just as he arrived at the stair door. She even saw herself buying a Magnum – this wasn't America but she figured she could get one if she really tried – and blowing him away as he came up the steps.

Each of these imaginings offered nothing but a fleeting catharsis, and again and again she awoke recoiling with shame. But the problem never faded.

Frantically warding off fond memories of Miami – the palm trees, the art deco architecture, the melting pot intensity – she started studying the Edinburgh real estate websites again. Alas, there seemed no apartments remotely in the same league, and certainly not the same price, as the one she already owned. And any change of premises would mean a substantial hit to her finances – stamp duty, agency commissions, moving costs, and so on. Besides, she simply couldn't tolerate the idea of palming the problem off to someone else. Some innocent buyer like herself, full of hopes and dreams, eagerly moving into the flat only to discover the horror of the guy upstairs. It would be like selling a house you knew was riddled with termites or destined to be demolished in a freeway extension. No amount of rationalisation – trying to convince herself that Europeans are more tolerant of neighbourly intrusions – could satisfy Cat's conscience on the matter. Nor could she imagine leasing the place out, quite apart from the fact any self-respecting tenant would quickly pull out, or complain constantly of the conditions, or cancel the lease entirely (she was unfamiliar with the relevant Scottish regulations).

In desperation she wrote to the department of Building Standards and Public Safety, seeking proof that the separating floor had been soundproofed to existing standards. But in response she received only a muted letter stating that the department's power was limited 'where there is no risk to public safety'. They had, however, written to the registered owner of the property 'outlining their obligations as per Building (Scotland) Regulations 2004'. Cat was further dismayed by the coda: 'Should we fail to receive a reply, you may find that the most satisfactory conclusion involves legal action.'

Cat baulked at the prospect of summoning lawyers. She could live with toxic atmospheres – had done so during the crime syndicate investigation – but was reluctant to play the role, in her very first year in Scotland, of the litigious American.

She devised an alternative strategy whereby all the building's tenants would sign a letter to the owner of the flat – Moyle's aunt – matter-of-factly noting her nephew's unsociable habits and imploring her to have a stern word with the lad. The spectre of an ASBO would be insinuated. But though Maxine and Michael agreed to be co-signatories – somewhat sceptically, as they seemed to think the aunt would take little notice – the gay guys in Number Three were in Majorca for a couple of months, the woman in Number Two didn't want to get involved, and the Romanian couple renting Number One were standoffish, claiming they hadn't heard any disruptive noises.

'Oh, come on,' Cat said to them. 'Your place is right beside the stair door here. You must have heard him come home at all hours?'

But the couple, clearly averse to hostilities for whatever reason, looked away and would not reply.

Starved of the numbers necessary to constitute a rear guard, Cat elected not to send the letter after all.

She sought out a quotation from a soundproofing firm.

The avuncular tradesman who showed up to measure her ceilings asked her – in a wonderful brogue, full of 'naes' and 'oots' and delightfully rolling 'r's – exactly what sort of noise was coming through: 'Airborne or impact?'

'Both,' said Cat.

He scratched his stubble for a while and told her the only real answer was suspended ceilings for the whole flat, 'Tho' that'll take a guid four or sux unches off yer cillin, and yer cillins are low enough noo.'

Cat thought she understood. 'You're saying that you'd need to hang a new soundproofed ceiling under the existing ceiling, and fill the cavity with soundproof insulation or whatever?' She'd done her homework.

'Aye,' said the tradesman, impressed.

'And how much would that cost, exactly?'

'For the hull place?'

'For the whole place.'

He stroked his chin again, and narrowed his eyes, and looked almost apologetic when he said, 'Ah couldnae do it for less than ten thoosand, lass, and that's jest for the cillins.'

Cat grimaced. 'Why do you say "just for the ceilings"?'

'There's the wulls as well.'

'The wulls?'

'Aye, the wulls. Sound leaks doon the wulls as often as it comes through the cillins.'

'I see,' Cat said, nodding. 'So you think I'd need to soundproof the walls as well?'

'It's the only way to be sho-ar.'

Cat nodded. 'And that would add another ten thousand to the bill, I assume?'

'Ah could do the wulls for five.'

Fifteen thousand, thought Cat. It would carve a sizeable chunk out of her diminishing savings. Then again, the purchase price of the place had been a steal. Maybe she could combine the two amounts and try to convince herself she had paid the proper price after all.

But she hated the idea of lowering her ceilings – as the tradesman himself had noted, they were already conspicuously low – and she couldn't really be sure that the added strain on the joists wouldn't make the floor above even more prone to creaks (one of the potential drawbacks of suspended ceilings, if what the Internet forums said was true). Moreover, she dreaded the possibility of discovering – after defacing her own property and parting with a gruesome amount of money – that Moyle was preparing to move out anyway. That'd be just her luck.

'I just need to be sure of one thing,' she said. 'If I go ahead with all this stuff – suspended ceilings and what have you – you can guarantee that the noise will be reduced, right? Enough for me to get a decent sleep?'

Now at just that moment – before the tradesman could even answer – Moyle erupted from hibernation in the bedroom upstairs. It was as if he'd been eavesdropping on their conversation, awaiting the right cue, and was intent on proving that any measures against him would be futile.

Creak creak creak, went the floorboards.

PLONK, went something dropped on the floor.

Nnnnnnnhhhhhhhhhhrrrrrrrrrr! went a dragged chair.

Kah-lunk, went a door.

Looking to the tradesman, Cat discovered that he had gone as white as his overalls. He was *shaking*. Because he was *mortified*.

'Lassie,' the man said hoarsely, swallowing and licking his lips, 'you've got yerself a prrrrrrrrrrroblem.'

CHAPTER

NINE

C AT'S BREAKING POINT CAME in October, just as the autumn air was whispering of winter. Her quest for an adequate sleep had become so desperate that she was now spending at least a couple of nights a week in a local hotel – the same hotel, ironically, that she had used prior to moving in (she couldn't imagine what the desk staff thought about it). Sometimes she was assigned the very same room she had occupied on her first visit, the one where her flat was visible from the windows (she wistfully remembered a lost age, not four months earlier, when the building had seemed like a castle awaiting its princess).

Then, a miracle. Driving up to the building on the evening of Tuesday, 3 October, Cat noticed that Moyle's black Peugeot hatchback was missing from its designated space. But she was fatalistic: this usually only meant that Moyle would be coming home later. She went inside and did her chores – cooking, washing, ironing – with her ears tuned to his inevitable return. It was shocking, when she thought about it, how much time she spent monitoring his movements – being *tyrannised* by his very existence. But Moyle did not return that night. She lay in bed, wide awake until after midnight, waiting in dread for the growl of his car's mistuned engine, the insistent slam of the driver's door, the cacophony of his entry into the building, the stomp of his boots on the sixty-six stairs. But when she woke up, to the trill of her alarm clock, she was amazed to find that she'd been blessed with a full seven hours of uninterrupted slumber – the first such stretch, not counting her nights in the hotel, that she'd enjoyed since first becoming aware of his existence.

He was absent the following two nights as well. And Friday.

She expected him back for the weekend, along with a drinking buddy, perhaps, but Saturday night was clear also. And Sunday.

The change in her well-being was immense – a tantalising glimpse at life as it should have been. Walking home at night she took the long route, down to Stockbridge and up through the Water of Leith gorge, glorying in the beauty of autumnal canopies, burbling water, lichen-coated walls and steel-blue twilight flecked with gold and amber leaves. Oh God, it was so beautiful. She dared imagine a full week, or even a month, during which she could revel in such a life again. She even entertained the possibility that Moyle might be away frequently, for sustained periods – on tour, perhaps – giving her ample time to regain her energy and wallow in the charms of her chosen city.

But on Monday evening, just as she was settling in for a bowl of peanut noodles, Moyle returned to his lair. *Bang, clap clap clap, kee-wah, creak creak creak, twang tawang tawang.* Cat's heart sank. Then again the following night. *Bang, clap clap clap, kee-wah, creak creak creak, twang tawang tawang.* And Wednesday night as well. *Bang, clap clap clap, kee-wah, creak creak creak, twang tawang tawang.* The new 'normal' was back.

Cat was contemplating another night in the hotel – she had a daunting examination the following day on Scottish legal procedures – when, on the evening of Thursday, 12 October, she finally snapped.

The first sign that some new horror was imminent was the sound of a vacuum cleaner humming and scraping across his floors. She'd never known Moyle to use one. Then she heard him dragging furniture around. Opening windows. She wondered if, by some miracle, he was preparing the place for inspection.

But then came the muffled buzzing of his intercom. The voice of Moyle himself – 'Yeah, come right up!' The *kah-lunk* of the stair door being released. A symphony of *clap clap claps* as three people, at least, whirled up the spiral stairway. The jingle of bottles. The *kee-waaah* of Moyle opening his door. The booming laughs and welcomes as he ushered the newcomers inside. The infernal clatter of four or more people walking backwards and forwards, in boots and dress shoes, on wooden floors.

To Cat it seemed incredible that Mr Moyle had *any* friends, let alone two or three. What on earth did they see in him? Charm? Generosity? Compassion?

There followed such incessant movement – she could barely hear the TV news – that she assumed the group was getting ready to go out for the evening, perhaps to a pub or party before returning for more drinks.

A prospect that was itself deeply unappetising. But the reality proved even worse.

BZZZZZZZZZ, went his intercom.

Kah-lunk, went the door release downstairs.

'Just leave it open!' came Moyle's voice – he was shouting down the stairwell.

Clapclapclapclapclapclapclapclapclapclap, went footsteps on the stairs.

Hey ha hey ha hey ha, went people being welcomed inside.

Then:

BZZZZZZZZZZZZZZZZ again.

And: 'Come right up!'

And the *CLUNK CREAK CLUNK PLONK* of a growing crowd shifting around the small apartment.

Hey ha hey ha hey ha. And some guy with a particularly obnoxious laugh, like a braying donkey: *HAW HAW HAW HAW HAW.* And some girl with a hyena's giggle: *HEE HEE HEE HEE HEE HEE.*

And then the party really started.

BOOM BOOM BOOM BOOM BOOM BOOM.

Moyle was playing music. At the sonic limits of his sound system. Cat's whole flat was shaking – the crockery in her kitchen was rattling.

BOOM BOOM BOOM BOOM BOOM BOOM.

Hard rock. Way out, hell-for-leather stuff. Cat couldn't identify any of it – the *Very Best of Hounds of Hades*, probably – but it sounded *horrific.*

BOOM BOOM BOOM BOOM BOOM BOOM. And *THUNK THUNK THUNK THUNK.* And *FARK YOU FARK YOU FARK YOU FARK YOU TOO!*

Music so aggressive that it almost drowned out the *klunks* and *clinks* and *plonks* and *creaks* and *blams* and *hahahahas* and *hawhawhaws* and *heeheehees.*

Cat sat rooted in place for half an hour before changing into her Lycra and heading out for a run – her first in weeks – hoping that the party might have moved on by the time she got back. But halfway up a hill in Ravelston, just a couple of miles from home, she came to a stop, bent over, hands on hips, her leg muscles refusing to drive her further. Vitamin deficiency, she figured, exacerbated by lack of sleep. She trudged home, shivering from chilled sweat, just in time to see a Hyundai pull up behind her VW.

'Hey,' she said, when the driver got out, 'you can't park there.'

Tall and straggly-bearded, wearing a Hounds of Hades T-shirt, the driver looked down at her with squinted eyes. 'Who are you, hen – the traffic warden?'

'I *live* here,' Cat said.

'Aye?' he said. 'And you got a problem with our car being here for a few hours?'

'It's blocking my space. The other spaces, too.'

'Not planning to head out, are you?'

'How would I know? There might be an emergency.'

'What sort of emergency?'

'You *can't park here*,' she barked.

He stared at her for a few moments, as though perfectly willing to continue the argument, but finally turned back to his friends as they spilled out of the car.

'Back inside, lads – Shania Twain here has spoken.'

With a few colourful expletives the crew piled back into the car and reversed recklessly down the street, looking for another place to park. Cat, still livid, had only been back in her apartment a few minutes, peeling off her running pants, when she heard them trundle up the stairs. Yet more *clap clap claps* and *hey heys* and *ha haas* and *come in, come ins* and BOOM BOOM BOOM BOOM BOOM BOOM.

Clearly the party was going to go on for a very long time.

She packed her overnight bag with clothes and toiletries, stuffed her work notes into a folder and marched around the corner to the hotel. But the place – for the very first time in her experience – had no vacancies. Cat nodded resignedly and said she'd try somewhere else. Melanie, the friendly desk clerk, shook her head: 'I doubt you'll find a room nearby tonight, Ms Thomas – there's an evangelical convention in town, you know.'

Cat thanked her and tramped back to her flat. Upstairs, they were playing 'Black Betty' and people were jumping up and down in time to the music.

BAM-DA-LAM. BAM-DA-LAM. BAM-DA-LAM.

Cat could see her ceiling rising and dipping. She feared the joists might break. She wondered if the whole party might crash down on top of her in a hail of plaster and splinters. She decided to shift out of the way, move into her kitchen, just to be sure of her safety.

Her mobile phone chimed with a message from Maxine.

Wow!!! What are you going to do about it?

Indeed, what *was* she going to do about it? To this point Cat had refrained from confronting Moyle in person, keenly remembering the sting of his pejorative '*American*'. But when the party rumbled on well beyond eleven-thirty and, if anything, seemed more boisterous than ever, her inhibitions crumbled.

She gritted her teeth, stomped upstairs and rapped on the door.

No answer.

She knocked again.

Still nothing.

It seemed incredible, but the music was so overwhelming that the people inside couldn't hear her. She pounded down the vortex of the spiral stairway, all sixty-six steps, and buzzed on Moyle's intercom. She held the button for perhaps thirty seconds. And eventually heard Moyle's slurred voice: 'Who is it?'

She inhaled. 'It's Cat Thomas from downstairs. I really must ask you to turn down the music. It's nearly midnight and—'

'*What?*' said Moyle. 'I can't hear you!'

'You can't hear me because the music is so damn loud! Can you turn it down, please?'

A disdainful pause, then Moyle hung up.

Cat re-entered the building, fuming. She went right to the top of the stairs and banged on his door again. She banged and banged. She wasn't going to take this any more.

Finally, the door opened. *Kee-wah!*

Moyle stood there in black vest and jeans, droopy eyed, holding a beer bottle in one hand and a hand-rolled cigarette in the other. He stared at Cat with his serial killer eyes.

'I'm sorry,' said Cat, using her most authoritative voice, 'but you're gonna have to dial that music down. *Please*. I have an exam tomorrow and I really need my rest. Everyone in the building needs their rest. So please turn it down – turn it off – or I'll have to make a formal complaint. And I really don't want to do that.'

Moyle looked stunned – speechless – that she would dare speak to him like that. Then one of his friends in the room behind, the straggly-bearded driver of the Hyundai, noticed her.

'Hey, hey, it's Shania Twain! You're still the one, baby! Still the one!'

And Moyle smirked and sneered. 'Whatsa matter, darling? Music not *American* enough for you?'

'Just turn it down,' she growled, then wheeled around and returned to her flat downstairs.

A minute later, to her surprise, the volume went down. Right down. A few more minutes, then it went off entirely. And Cat registered a small moment of triumph. She'd done it. By standing up for herself, fearlessly, she'd achieved something.

But at the same time she sensed it couldn't be that easy. Moyle wouldn't just give in like that. She listened to the footsteps, the clinking bottles, the laughing, the shifting furniture, waiting for something. The stinger. And then it came – the sound of people singing.

'I'm Gonna Getcha Good . . .'

'That Don't Impress Me Much . . .'

'Man! I Feel Like a Woman . . .'

They were singing Shania Twain songs. At the top of their lungs. To mock her. And just to make more noise.

'*Uh uh oh oh!*'

Over and over and over.

'*Uh uh oh oh!*'

Shania Twain is *Canadian*, you dimwits, she thought bitterly.

The dimwits went on and on until they rang out of Twain hits and got back to 'Black Betty' and started jumping up and down again.

BAM-DA-LAM. BAM-DA-LAM. BAM-DA-LAM.

BOOM BOOM BOOM BOOM BOOM BOOM.

Cat waited until it twelve-thirty and then called 101. She got through quickly – because it was mid-week, she guessed – and lodged her complaint. Thirty minutes later, staring out the window, she saw a police car draw up in the street outside. Two uniformed cops, barely out of their teens, got out and glanced up at the top floor. They shook their heads. She heard them come around to the building's stair door and buzz through to Number Six. She heard the people upstairs shifting, frantically flushing the toilet. Voices. The stair door springing open. The cops ascending slowly: *clap . . . clap . . . clap* – the measured gait of the law. She heard them arriving at Moyle's place and knocking commandingly. The door opening. Stern words issued. Grudging acknowledgments. The sound of the cops, with radio transmitters squawking, heading back down the steps. Reluctant movements above. Grumbling. Bottles being thrown together. The toilet flushing again. Muffled farewells. People clopping down the stairs. Laughing as they spilled out of the building. Car doors slamming. Engines rumbling. The party was over.

Cat brushed her teeth and got into bed. She shoved the gel plugs into her ears, wrapped the pillow around her head and waited for the inevitable statement from above. A protest. A howl of rage. A signal from Moyle that he would never gracefully surrender.

In the event, it took much longer than expected – Cat's mind was a swirl of hallucinatory images – before she heard the deeply ominous announcement.

TWAAAAAAAANGGGGG.

★ ★ ★

The battle was on. Over the ensuing nights Moyle stepped up both the volume and frequency of his aural attacks. If he had not previously been waging a war of attrition then he was now. Objects were not so much dropped as hurled down. Doors were not just closed but slammed. Jagged bursts of hellish music rent the night air. Varieties of DIY work – ten seconds of hammering or drilling – were performed at the most unlikely of times. He even began using his washing machine in the middle of the night, so that every fifteen minutes or so there was raucous whirring and stammering as it reached the peak of a spin cycle.

Trapped in a spin cycle of her own – weary, nodding off at her desk, constipated, suffering piercing headaches, gaunt inside her clothes – Cat one morning marched into Agnes's little office.

'You still have those meetings?' she demanded. 'To make requests?'

Agnes looked up, surprised. 'Aye,' she said, nodding.

'Book me in,' Cat told her with a sigh. 'Book me in.'

CHAPTER
TEN

THE MEETING TOOK A FEW WEEKS to organise; so long, in fact, Cat started to wonder if it was going to take place at all. But it turned out that Agnes had been busy submitting details.

'All sort of things,' she explained, driving past the pebble-dash bungalows of southern Edinburgh. 'Everything I know about you. Your work history. Your attitudes and ethics. Your religious beliefs.'

'My religious beliefs?' Cat raised her eyebrows. 'Sounds like you know more about me than I know about myself.'

'Well, certainly more than anyone in Scotland. You've been very open with me.'

'I have?'

'More than you've probably realised.'

Now that she thought about it, Cat couldn't deny that she'd been more revealing than usual with Agnes – probably a means of establishing rapport in a foreign land. She doubted she would have been so candid back in Florida.

'I had to endorse you, in effect. I even had to send pictures of you.'

'Pictures?' Cat frowned. 'Where on earth did you get those?'

'I snapped a couple when you weren't looking. The office in general, actually, but I cropped them down to just show you.'

'Very . . . creepy, of you.'

'Hey, I'm a trained investigator, remember. I swiped a photo off the Net, too.'

'There are photos of me on the Net?'

'From that case you mentioned – the organised crime thing in America.'

'But I was told those photos had been taken down. I was assured *all* photos of me had been taken down.'

'They're still out there, if you know where to look.'

'This isn't exactly what I want to hear.'

'Relax,' said Agnes, with a suggestive glance. 'They're good photos. You look good. You *always* look good. Anyone with a pulse would kill to do you.'

Cat, nodding noncommittally, was still unable to get a handle on Agnes's sexuality. She spoke as lustily of women as she did of men, and often registered her desire to 'do' someone. But she didn't seem to be 'doing' anybody – despite boasting constantly of her sexual prowess and the 'magnetic attraction' of her enormous 'assets'. For tonight, for the meeting, she'd glammed up in a preposterously low-cut frock, dramatically swinging earrings, siren-red lipstick, and lashings of mascara and rouge. Cat refrained from saying it, but she looked like a music hall prostitute. Marinated in some sort of lilac perfume, she even smelled like one. Cat herself, ignoring Agnes's exhortation to 'dress to impress', had merely thrown on a respectable outfit – tailored wide-leg pants, a striped top, dark-blue denim jacket – and feathered some concealer under her eyes to hide the shadows.

'Any reason,' she asked, 'why I need to look good, by the way?'

'Well' – Agnes laughed – 'everyone responds better to a pretty face.'

Cat couldn't argue with that. 'And why were all the other details necessary?'

'Security. They needed to be sure that you're not some sort of spy or undercover journalist. There've been a lot of stories in the press lately.'

'What stories?'

'Drugs, orgies, cavorting in the moonlight, that sort of thing.'

'Stories about your group specifically?'

'Not mine in particular.'

Cat looked out at the open fields, where skeletal electrical towers were marching off into the darkness. 'This group,' she ventured, 'is some sort of cult, right?'

'Cults are for gobshites. We don't like that word.'

'Something Satanic?'

Agnes made an ambivalent noise. 'Not in the traditional sense.'

'*Traditional* sense?'

'Well, you can't believe everything you read. You can't believe *anything* you read, really.'

'A Satanic cult,' Cat said, tasting the words. 'You know, I can't imagine why I'm surprised.'

'That's because you're *not* really surprised. You know what you're getting into and don't pretend otherwise.'

In truth, Cat had already experienced numerous misgivings about the whole charade. But then Moyle would bang a fist against his bedroom wall at one a.m. Hammer a nail at two a.m. Fire up his washing machine at three a.m. Cat even suspected that he was stealing her mail from the communal mailbox: she'd gotten an email from Stella, the one sibling who'd been halfway sisterly to her, asking why she hadn't acknowledged a birthday gift. Meanwhile, her enquiries to Building Standards and Public Safety – her last hope for some alterations to the ceiling – had proved as fruitless as she feared: 'We apologise for not responding, but to this point we have received no correspondence from the landlord of the property in question. The matter has been referred to the Acting Surveyor, Mr McIver, though we are unable to confirm when he will be free to visit you.'

So ultimately Cat figured that Agnes's 'meeting' – or whatever it was – would be cathartic. She understood the power of symbolic actions. Saluting the flag, planting a tree, flipping a coin to a war veteran, voting in an election. Or tearing an ex-boyfriend's photo into pieces, plunging pins into a voodoo doll, slamming a door in frustration. It was like hypnosis. The mere act of seeking a solution might expel the negative energy. It might paradoxically exorcise a few demons. It might even make her less sensitive to Moyle's astonishing disrespect.

'And the others – the ones in your coven or whatever – they're devil worshippers too, I suppose?'

Agnes shook her head. 'You're using old words. Old words with old associations. Everything's different now. The world's upside down – you know that.'

'Then I won't have to drink anyone's blood? Or kiss anyone's behind?'

'Would you really be here if you thought that?' Agnes said. 'It's more of a game.'

'I don't like games.'

'Well, not *really* a game. But you'll see. You'll see.'

Cat stared pensively out the window again. Having crossed the city bypass, they were into a region of rolling hills, ranks of hedgerows and acres of dark pastureland.

'Where's it being held, exactly?' she asked. 'You never did tell me.'

'A castle,' said Agnes. 'Aileanach Castle.'

'A genuine castle? With towers and turrets?'

'The living quarters are at ground level and the castle is underneath – fourteenth century, I think.'

'The castle itself is underground?'

'No, the house is at the top two levels. The rest of the castle sort of clings to a slope overlooking the River Esk. When you see it, you'll know what I'm talking about.'

'Uh-huh. And who lives there?'

'The Laird of Howgate. It's been in his family for centuries.'

'This Laird of Howgate being a Satanist?'

'Well, he doesn't advertise it – and neither should you.' Agnes chuckled to soften what might have sounded like a threat.

All evening, Cat noticed, Agnes had been tightly wound. Her hands were gripped tight to the steering wheel. Her voice was high-pitched. She was giggling excessively. She might even have been sweating more than usual.

'He'll be in attendance tonight? The Laird?'

'He might be.'

'And the others?'

'People from all over. Slovakia. Japan. Austria. Ireland. Sri Lanka.'

'The United Nations of Witches.'

Agnes giggled again. 'Some of them were in Montenegro for the autumn equinox celebrations in September. Then they were in Norway last week for Hallowe'en. That was one of the reasons it took a few weeks to organise.'

'They're not all coming for me, I hope?'

'No, not really. Not really.'

'Then who?'

But Agnes didn't titter this time. Didn't answer at all.

In awkward silence she steered down a serpentine side road flanked by bristling conifers. They passed what looked like a ruined granary and a deserted cottage. The forest thickened and darkened, and Cat had the disorientating sense of having visited the place in a dream. Finally Agnes flicked the indicator and they turned into a driveway, pausing before ornate wrought-iron gates flanked by sentry boxes. Two slab-faced guards in padded jackets lumbered up to the windows. One of them lanced Cat's face with a flashlight beam. Agnes nodded at them and muttered a strange word: '*Shenhamforash.*' Still expressionless, the guards drew back, the gates swung open, and the VW eased into the thickly wooded estate. Mounted cameras rotated to follow them.

Cat looked around. 'What's going on here, exactly?'

'I told you,' said Agnes. 'There's been a lot of trouble lately.'

'But do they really need all this security?'

'Sad, isn't it?' Another evasive laugh.

The driveway seemed endless. Cat thought she saw more guards moving like wraiths among the trees. She could've sworn that some of them were carrying assault rifles.

Eventually the VW entered a clearing. The headlights swept across several parked vehicles – a Rolls, an Aston Martin, a Porsche 911 – and Agnes pulled up in a spot that seemed reserved for her.

'Now I see why you advised me to dress up,' said Cat.

'Aye,' said Agnes, 'some of these folk have done pretty well for themselves.'

They got out of the car to the sound of owls hooting in the forest. They passed a surreal oak tree with a trunk that resembled fifty serpents entwined around one another. Cat was again ruffled by déjà vu. The Laird of Howgate's residence – the top of the castle – looked like a well-tended hunting lodge, but as they approached she discerned a huge gulf behind it. She made out a precipitous slope. She thought she heard flowing water.

She spared a moment to appreciate the absurdity of the situation. Five months earlier she was shielding her face from the Florida sun. Now she was approaching a remote and well-guarded Scottish castle to participate in some mysterious Satanic ritual. Or game. Or something.

'I'm not going to regret this, am I?' she whispered.

'If things go to plan,' Agnes assured her, 'you'll more likely look back on this as the greatest moment of your life.'

It was Saturday, 4 November.

CHAPTER
ELEVEN

RRIVING AT A HEAVILY BEAMED DOOR, Agnes rapped seven times with a jackal-headed knocker and the door swung open almost instantaneously.

'Och, look at the two of you! Let's get you inside and oot of this cold!'

The first 'witch', if that was what she was, was a personable old biddy in a knitted cardigan, tartan skirt and pussy-bow blouse – everyone's vision of a perfect Scottish grandmother.

'I'm Maggie Balfour,' the woman chirped. 'It's so good to see you noo!'

'I'm Cat Thomas.'

'Of course you are, dear – Catriona Thomas, our wee visitor from America. Come right through noo, come right through.'

After scraping her shoes on a doormat, Cat stepped into a stuffy, dimly lit chamber with oaken panels and ceiling beams. Above was a mediaeval-style chandelier fixed with electric candles. On the walls were sconce-lights, swords, hunting trophies and smoky paintings of Highland scenes. Stretched across the floorboards was a threadbare Persian carpet that looked as old as the *1001 Nights*. The whole effect was baronial but insistently cosy.

'You want to take off yer jacket?' asked Maggie.

'I'm OK,' said Cat.

'It can get a wee bit warm in here, I warn ye noo.'

'I'm fine for now, thanks.'

Cat's nostrils had already curled at an unpleasant odour. She noticed a black cat in the corner, licking its privates.

'This way, dears, they're waiting for you.'

They were ushered into a sizable salon – ancient tapestries on the walls now – where a group of eminent-looking personages, like something out of a wax museum, were partaking of drinks and canapés. Not one of them looked younger than fifty. Much tweed, velour, brooches, tiepins and plaid. Upon Cat's entry all of them turned simultaneously, like clockwork automatons, as though her arrival had been announced with a trumpet.

'Hi there,' said Cat, hoping an all-purpose greeting would suffice.

But Maggie, guiding her by the arm, insisted on introducing everyone individually. 'This is Akinari Ito, our good friend from Japan . . . and Tamsin Blight from Cornwall . . . and Petra Varga from Bratislava . . . and George Pickingill from Dorset . . . and Éliphas Lévi from Provence . . . and Johannes Junius from Innsbruck . . . and Priya Benedicto from Madras . . .'

And and and and . . .

Cat was fielding all the names in a blur, confident that, with her wearied and malfunctioning memory, she would later remember not one of them. She was distracted by the increasingly unpleasant odour. And, as knotty hand after knotty hand slid into her own, disconcerted by the suspicion, bordering on conviction, that none of this was as innocent as Agnes had led her to believe.

' . . . Alice Kyteler from County Westmeath in Ireland . . . and Absalón Salazar from Cuernavaca in Mexico . . . and Zara Mashasha from Harare ... and Elspeth Ross from Derbyshire ... and Melvin Rose, the famous magician from America ...'

'The Great Sheldrake', corrected the magician, who had an Easter Island head, eyebrows like aggravated porcupines, and a multitude of rings cluttering his gnarled fingers. 'You may not recognise me,' he suggested grandly, 'out of black hat and tails.'

'No,' said Cat, not recognising him anyway.

'I hear you're one of ours,' he went on, 'from America. From the Sunshine State, no less.'

'From Miami, that's right.'

'I played in Miami just last year. At Stage 305. Were you there?'

'Um, no.'

'In August I performed at the Edinburgh Festival. Perhaps you caught my show?'

'Nope.'

'But you must have seen the posters around town?'

'I've been a bit ... preoccupied lately.'

'I understand, Catriona.' Rising to his full height, the Great Sheldrake enclosed her hands between his own spidery pair. 'I understand.' His eyes vibrated as though trying to mesmerise her. 'And you've made a very brave decision indeed. Let no one tell you otherwise. And let no one—'

'Some tea, dear?' It was Maggie, insinuating herself between them.

'Tea?' Cat felt herself being tugged away from Sheldrake. 'No, I'm good.'

'You must be thirsty though?'

'Now that I think of it, do you have anything cold?'

'Irn-Bru?'

'That's some sort of orangeade drink, right?'

Agnes answered from the side. 'More like cream soda.'

'Cream soda? Yeah, sure – that'd be great.'

'And treat yerself to a wee biscuit or two, dear, while you wait,' Maggie added. 'You're thin as a reed.'

'I think I've lost weight,' Cat admitted.

'It's all that stress you've been under, dear. All that stress.'

At the sideboard Agnes held out a silver platter covered with soft cubes of tablet and slices of black bun. 'This'll fatten you up,' she said. 'Couldn't be more Scottish if they were deep-fried Mars Bars.'

Cat took a cube of tablet but was surprised by the flavour. 'I thought this stuff was supposed to be sweet?'

'Depends on your taste.'

'I think it's got whisky in it.'

'I told you it was Scottish.'

Maggie returned with a goblet filled with Irn-Bru. 'Drink up, dear, it'll cool you doon.'

Cat took a sip and grimaced again. 'Whoa,' she said to Agnes, when Maggie retreated. 'I swear this has got whisky in it too.'

'It's the Laird of Howgate. He owns some distilleries up north. One in Edinburgh, too. Ever smelled that malty stench in the air?'

'Sometimes – I think.'

'I rather like it myself,' said Agnes. 'Anyway, his distillery is one of the places it comes from.'

'Is he brewing something right now?'

'Huh?'

'There's a terrible odour in the air,' Cat said, wrinkling her nose. 'Don't tell me you can't smell it?'

'That's just the cats. The Laird loves cats.'

'*I* love cats. But not if they stink.'

'You'll get used to it.'

'Hmm,' said Cat, looking around. 'Is he here now?'

'The Laird? Who knows? But that's a picture of his great-grandfather on the wall.'

Above the fireplace was a majestic gilt-framed painting of a hawk-faced man in a green felt jacket and dark kilt, his right arm bracing a rifle, his left hand resting on the head of a hunting dog. Black cats were curling around his ankles; stags were fleeing in the background.

'Looks about two hundred years old.'

'The painting or the Laird?'

'Both,' said Cat, and it was true – the man's face suggested the wisdom of the ages. 'I think he's looking at me.'

'The Laird of Howgate is always looking at you.'

Discomfited, Cat turned to see the others in the room – Sheldrake and Lévi and Salazar and Mashasha and so on – also staring at her.

'Why do I get the feeling I'm the centre of attention here?'

'Relax,' said Agnes. 'You *are* the centre of attention. It's not often we get a gorgeous young cheese toastie at one of our conclaves.'

'Conclaves?'

'That's what we call our get-togethers.'

'Why?' asked Cat. 'Are we electing a pope? Or antipope?'

'Listen to yourself.'

'I'm not gonna be offered up as a human sacrifice, am I?'

'I told you that was stuff and nonsense. Just remember why you're here.'

'I've forgotten why I'm here, to be honest.'

'You know that's not true. Anyway, this isn't remotely what you think it is.'

'Is that supposed to reassure me?'

'Just relax,' said Agnes, looking terribly uneasy. 'You'll be home in bed before you know it.'

'Very well then!' Maggie, who seemed to be the emcee, was clapping her hands together. 'Time noo to get proceedings under way, don't you think? Anyone who feels like another nip just wave and I'll fill yer cup for you. Anyone who needs a tinkle, there's a bathroom just around the corner. I ask only that you turn off yer phones and other devices, to make as few distractions as possible. Are we all happy with that noo?'

General nodding and grumblings of approval.

'Very well – let's make our way doonstairs to the banquet room.'

Maggie proceeded to lead them through a panelled corridor to another oak-beamed door. Then down a spiral stairway, not unlike the one in Cat's own building. They went round and round, deep into the castle proper, the warmth and the sulphurous stench all the time intensifying. Finally they came to a huge chamber that looked like it had survived a terrible inferno. The walls were blackened with soot. The ceiling beams were charred. The ash-grey furniture looked as though it might crumble at a touch. The back half of the room, despite a raging fire in the hearth, was eerily, supernaturally dark, as though separated from the rest of the chamber by a series of black mosquito nets. Another clutch of cats was evident.

Oh well, Cat thought, it could be worse. There was no Satanic statuary, no upside-down crucifixes, no black candles, no arcane inscriptions. There was only a large round table under a tasselled lamp. And, painted around the rim of the table, Roman numerals from one to twelve in the manner of an oversized clockface.

'Take yer seats, all. Take yer seats,' ordered a fussy Maggie, guiding Cat by the elbow. 'And young Catriona, you come here to the midnight seat, and I'll put yer wee friend Agnes next to you at one o'clock, just to make sure you don't feel oot of place. Noo, would you like another Irn-Bru?'

CHAPTER
TWELVE

C AT WOULD LATER REMEMBER the increasing heat (she had her back to the fireplace), her mounting thirst (she gladly accepted more and more of the orange soda pop) and the troubling stench (which she was convinced didn't emanate exclusively from the cats). The ritual itself, as Agnes had predicted, proved more subdued – at least initially – than she expected.

A flat white box was placed in the middle of the table and the Great Sheldrake, sitting at nine o'clock, deftly extracted a large deck, thatched on the back like playing cards. For a moment Cat wondered if he was going to deal a hand.

'Are we ready to begin?' he asked, in a most theatrical tone.

When everyone nodded he gave a lupine smile and peeled off the first card, holding it in front of his eyes for a few pointed seconds before proceeding.

'You are walking through the woods with your dog,' he intoned. 'The dog stops to dig behind a tree. You try hauling the hound away, but in so doing notice that it has unearthed an old suitcase. Intrigued, you open the case and discover gold pieces, cut diamonds and thick wads of cash.'

The Great Sheldrake now looked around the table, not even

reading from the card – he seemed to have committed the remainder to memory.

'Do you (a) put the suitcase back in the ground and kick dirt over it; (b) take the suitcase to the police and hope for a reward; or (c) spirit the suitcase home and keep the riches for yourself?'

Cat almost laughed at the banality: it sounded like the old board game Scruples.

'Alice?' the Great Sheldrake asked the old crone to his right.

'I'd take the money for myself, of course,' said the Irish-accented Alice. 'If it's buried in the woods there's some criminal act involved, surely, and you can't steal from a thief.'

The Great Sheldrake smiled indulgently and turned to the lady at seven o'clock. 'Petra?'

'I concur,' the grey-haired Slovakian replied.

'George?'

The Cornishman at six o'clock chuckled. 'No need for debate. The system is as crooked as the Mafia in most parts of the world, so handing the case over to the authorities would only see the treasure disappear into the vortex of corruption. Under the circumstances, you'd be daft not to take the money for yourself.'

The Great Sheldrake's smile looked painted on.

'Johannes?'

'The guilt reflex is an artificial construct for remotely control-ling the masses,' said the well-spoken Austrian. 'And a central tenet of Satanism is to liberate us from such mind-shackles. Only a fool would hand over a windfall or put it back in the ground for someone else to discover.'

And on it went, anti-clockwise around the table, everyone agreeing that the only proper response was to take the money and make the most of it. Some of the answers were as clipped as Petra's; others seemed too eloquent not to have been rehearsed.

But Cat herself was rarely one to compromise her opinions for social harmony. Her conviction, borne from experience, that the world is a whole lot more complex than people generally care to admit, was a cornerstone of her personal philosophy. So by the time the question had reached Agnes at one o'clock – 'If you'd seen my bank balance, you'd know this was a no-brainer for me' – she had resolved to unleash her full argumentative self.

'Look, I don't want to come across as difficult,' she said, when her turn came, 'but I really have to take issue with the imprecise nature of the question. Because in circumstances like this there are always lots of possibilities to take into consideration. Maybe, for instance, the woods where the suitcase is buried is a known hiding spot for criminal gangs. Maybe that'd make you less inclined to get involved, or maybe it'd make it easier for you to take the money. Maybe there've been a series of home burglaries in the area, making you suspect that the riches are not stolen at all, just hidden by someone who doesn't want to keep them under the floorboards. Maybe the police are in league with criminal gangs, as someone else suggested, but maybe you know at least one policeman you can trust completely. And in all cases you have to think about your own financial state at the time. Because – if you have enough to live comfortably, with no pressing debts, no family obligations, no desperate need for cash – then the satisfaction you'd get from turning the suitcase over would surely outweigh the risks you'd take in smuggling the thing home. Remembering, too, that riches don't always buy happiness. A cliché, sure, but no less true for all that.'

Cat heard her own voice echoing around the chamber.

'So, I really don't think there's any easy answer,' she went on. 'Nothing that wouldn't be glib, anyway. The truth is, I don't know if I'd take that money, or hand it over, or put it back in the ground.

It'd depend on my bank balance, my sense of well-being, and my familiarity with the neighbourhood. But I'm not trying to be difficult or evasive either. So, considering I'm new to Scotland, I'd have to say I'd rub my fingerprints from the case, kick dirt back over it, then inform the cops that my dog had dug up something unusual in the woods. In that way I could keep myself out of trouble while still leaving open the possibility that I'd get a reward if the police proved as honest as I hope they are in this country.'

The comprehensive nature of the response surprised even Cat herself. But such things, as a fraud investigator steeped in the study of ethics, came so naturally to her that she could not resist.

She raised her eyebrows. 'Hope that doesn't make me sound like a jerk?'

No one laughed. No one sneered. No one coughed. But everyone was still smiling. Looking at her serenely, with an air of rapt approval.

It was the Great Sheldrake who ruptured the silence. 'Not at all, Catriona. That was most enlightening.'

'*Well done*,' whispered Agnes, nudging her under the table.

There were further, ambiguous responses – Cat wasn't really concentrating – and then the Great Sheldrake laid the first card down and plucked another one from the deck. Cat meanwhile looked around, seeing four or five figures – Maggie Balfour, Absalón Salazar and some of the other witches – watching her from the side of the room. All of them seemed to be grinning approvingly as well.

'Second dilemma,' Sheldrake announced, milking the suspense again. 'The person you most desire ends up marrying someone else, a person for whom you have a very little regard. One weekend, while staying with the couple at their summer retreat, the two of them have a spiteful argument and the partner – the one you dislike

– storms off. Shortly afterwards, over intimate drinks, the one you most desire invites you to bed for the evening. Do you (a) refuse outright; (b) suggest that you might be interested at a later date; or (c) fulfil your life's desires?'

Sheldrake rotated to eight o'clock. 'Alice?'

The old crone cackled. 'Well, I hope I don't sound glib,' she said, with a good-natured glance at Cat, 'but I reckon I'd be up for some slap and tickle. Can't see any reason to be holding back at my age, assuming anyone'd want me.'

In normal circumstances this might have occasioned some mirth, but again no one laughed. Not even a polite chuckle. It was almost as though everyone was too nervous – or too well-rehearsed – to respond with any sort of spontaneity.

'I concur,' agreed Petra (who Cat was beginning to suspect was less than fluent in English).

George the Cornishman: 'In a heartbeat. Life is too short – far too short – to be hamstrung by bourgeois morality. I can't see any reason why a person shouldn't enjoy the pleasures of the flesh in those circumstances. This is supposed to be the twenty-first century.'

Johannes the eloquent Austrian: 'This is one of the central tenets of Satanism. *The Satanic Bible* is very clear on the matter. One *must* be free to satisfy one's sexual needs with whomever one chooses, as long, of course, as there's mutual consent. In this instance two grown adults have a desire to engage in sexual intercourse. The circumstances are irrelevant. Neither of these people is motivated by anything they should be ashamed of. And there's genuine affection, not just sexual attraction, involved. In fact, what would be unnatural, what would be *cruel*, would be if the two people *restrained* themselves – surrendered to outdated inhibitions – and denied each other an innocent evening of physical pleasure.'

Around the clockface it went for the second time, with mutual agreement all the way to Agnes at one o'clock. 'Is this a serious question?' she asked with a guffaw. 'You know me – I'm the Seven Deadly Sins in one package. So I'd be in, hammer and tongs, of course I would. Even if the one who walked out was my best friend. *Especially* if it was my best friend.'

But at midnight Cat was ready to pounce again

'I'm sorry,' she said with another apologetic chuckle, 'but again I have an issue with the original question. Because this isn't something you can predict without knowing all the facts. You say the partner I'm not supposed to like – the wife, in my case – storms off, and it's implied that she's being unreasonable . . . but can that really be assumed? What if the husband has been intolerably rude? What if he's a terrible womaniser? What if the wife has good reason to be angry? Not to mention all the other considerations. What if the couple has kids, for instance? What if the husband has a habit of bragging about his sexual conquests? Do we know, for that matter, that the wife, having stormed out in a huff, wouldn't return just as impulsively? I mean, would it really be without consequence to go to bed with the husband under those circumstances? An hour or two of fun might lead to a lifetime of complications. But – let me be clear – that's not to say I'd rule it out. Not at all. Because what if, hypothetically, I happen to know that the wife, on top of being an unpleasant woman, has been having affairs behind her husband's back? What if the heated argument is about just that – her infidelity? What if the marriage has long been a farce, it's been crumbling for years, and for me this is a chance to convince the husband that he made a terrible mistake in not marrying me in the first place? The bottom line is, this isn't an open and shut case of free love versus sexual guilt. Not at all. Impulse control is essential to emotional maturity, but we're all prone to lapses under pressure, and the sexual urge is one that generates an unusually large number of regrets. So in all honesty it's impossible to predict how anyone would respond within the confines of this dilemma. I sure can't say how I would. I'd need to be there, and juggle all the variables, in order to make a calculated decision before jumping right in. Or not, as the case may be. I'm sorry I can't give you a straight answer, but that's the way I see it.'

Cat looked around the table and found everyone beaming at her again. They appeared positively *enthralled*. Even one of the cats miaowed. And the Great Sheldrake made a flourishing gesture with his hand, like a courtier before the Queen.

'Another splendid answer, Catriona. You really are something to behold.'

Cat again gathered that she was meant to be pleased with herself. But she *wasn't* pleased with herself. She was only *impatient*.

Then came the third, considerably darker dilemma.

'You're working for a secret government agency,' read the Great Sheldrake, 'when you uncover evidence of a terrorist plot to assassinate a leading political figure whom you despise. Do you (a) inform your supervisors in order to prevent the politician's murder; (b) let others find the information for themselves; or (c) actively bury the evidence?'

Of those sitting between eight and one o'clock Johannes the Austrian was again the most well-spoken: 'This illustrates a central tenet of Satanism – that the power of God, the right to kill, should be delegated to the common man. Now, if everyone had a right to kill then there would be barbarism, that's true, but that right is currently exercised freely by those on the highest rungs of power, and very often such people only reach those positions through psychotic levels of deceit and narcissism. So if a Satanist is given the opportunity to participate in the assassination of a man he or she judges to be a menace to society – simply by burying the evidence – then it's one's duty to do so, without guilt or second thoughts. *Not* burying the evidence, in most cases, would be an act of irresponsibility.'

At twelve o'clock Cat was wondering if this was all an oblique reference to her own desire, privately shared with Agnes, to eliminate the guy upstairs – the very reason she was here. So she forced herself into another challenging response.

'This sounds like the Hitler dilemma,' she said. 'Would you assassinate Hitler in the 1930s and prevent the Second World War? The answer is yes, of course you would. And if you had nothing to do with the actual assassination, well, so much the better. But is it really as simple as that? I mean, who are the people – these so-called terrorists – arranging the assassination? Members of some ethnic minority? Wouldn't then the assassination only empower the tyrant's cause? Turn a maniac into a martyr? Make things even worse than they are? Because there's now proof that a minority is acting against the nation's will? Besides,' she said, 'is there any real evidence that Hitler's replacement – Himmler, say – is any less of a psychopath? Or that a war would be prevented? Who can say? I mean, you can't really judge these things unless you're immersed daily in the detail and fully aware of all the variables. In light of that, I can understand how someone might pass the information on to her superiors or pretend not to see it at all. Suffice to say the devil is always in the details.'

It wasn't intended as a joke and Cat, when she realised what she'd said, blinked self-consciously. She wouldn't have blamed the Satanists if they were offended; if they decided to give up on the game entirely. Part of her wished that they would. But the people around the table – and those off to the side – didn't look remotely upset. They were still wearing their wax-museum smiles. Their adoring eyes. Their tense postures.

'Can I take my jacket off?' she asked. 'It's hotter than … than Florida in here.'

'Of course, dear.' Maggie sprang to attention. 'I'll pour you another Irn-Bru!'

'Thanks,' said Cat, wriggling her arms out of the sleeves just as the Great Sheldrake reached for another card.

'So there's to be more of these questions?' she asked, annoyed.

'Oh yes,' said Sheldrake. 'The devil, as you say, is always in the details.'

And then things started to turn really dark.

CHAPTER

THIRTEEN

IRST OF ALL, THE CHAMBER HAD literally become darker. The
tiny overhead globes had dimmed and the only illumination
came from the hearth. The figures around the table,
splashed with wavering light, now looked like genuine old-time
witches around a bonfire.

Second (and this would later cause Cat much consternation),
there seemed to be someone in the velvety darkness behind the
mosquito nets at the other side of the room. Observing her. A
man who'd never been introduced to her, a man who was making
everyone else edgy. He was sitting in what looked like a high-backed
chair, or a throne, and when he leaned forward, resting his chin
on steepled hands, Cat thought she saw his eyes – bestial eyes, like
those picked out by a flashlight in the woods.

Third (and most disturbing of all), the dilemmas were now deeply
discomfiting and personal, as though someone had plundered her
mind of its darkest and most closely guarded secrets.

'You're busy with an important work project, integral to your
professional career, when you receive word that your elderly parent
is close to death. As chief carer, you know very well that your
parent has been deteriorating for years and suspect that the nurse

has made a premature evaluation. Do you (a) drop everything and rush to your parent's side anyway; (b) wait for further evidence before you commit yourself; or (c) continue guiltlessly with your work and wait for an opportunity to present itself?'

In fact, the parent had been her father, stricken with leukaemia. Cat had been deeply immersed in the crime syndicate court case in Tallahassee. The call had come from one of her brothers, Mark, who'd had little contact with his father in years and seemed ill-qualified to judge his condition. And Cat's decision – to remain with the court case at a critical stage – had never stopped haunting her. Because she had not been there – no one had – when her father had slipped into eternity.

So she listened blankly to the other responses and when her turn came she was unusually reserved.

'No details are provided about the "important work",' she pointed out. 'No details on the location of that work in relation to the parent. No idea if there are other relatives, sons and daughter and so on, in the mix. No real idea if the parent would even *want* anyone to come rushing to his or her side. There's so much we don't know that no answer can be categorical. So I'm really not sure what I'd do in similar circumstances,' she said, struggling not to wince.

There followed an extended silence, as though everyone was waiting for her to continue. But she'd said enough this time. She refused even to look around, to check for a reaction. She only stared at the Great Sheldrake, imploring him to get on with it.

Which, eventually, he did. In wavering flamelight he picked up the next card. He held it in front of his face. He read it in silence for a few moments. Then he returned his knowing eyes to Cat.

'A young girl who has been sexually abused by an older relative contrives to take violent revenge. She confesses this to you after the fact and throws herself at your mercy. Do you (a) inform the police or the girl's parents; (b) counsel the girl to confess to the authorities; or (c) advise the girl to stay silent on the matter and assure her you would have done the same thing in the circumstances?'

Cat squirmed. She herself had been such a victim. And the way she had responded – heroic, understandable or shameful? – continued to plague her nearly three decades later.

'I wish I could say,' she responded self-consciously – was it just her imagination or were the witches surveying her with particular cunning? 'Violence often begets violence but that doesn't make revenge forgivable. And there's no indication what sort of "violent revenge" we're talking about anyway. Like so many other arguments, it might boil down to semantics. And, of course, how close you are to everyone involved.'

She shot a glance across the chamber and thought she saw the glimmering eyes of the man on the throne. She sensed that he – *everyone* – wanted her to elaborate. But she only lowered her gaze to the table, like Connor Bailey in Callander, and waited for them to move on.

By now her vision, fixed on the number XII in the table, was becoming blurred. Her head was starting to swim. And she must have blacked out for a second, or simply lost sense of time, because when she looked up she found the Great Sheldrake already reading the sixth dilemma.

'A dying relative sends you a letter revealing that your late brother, lauded in his lifetime as a pillar of the community, was in reality a sexual predator responsible for a string of assaults. Do you (a) inform the authorities; (b) inform the authorities only after those close to your brother have passed away; or (c) destroy the letter and tell no one, in order to preserve the family name?'

This too seemed a distorted reflection of the truth. The predator had been her cousin. And the decision not to speak out about him, while complicated for many reasons, had years later caused her intense, life-changing guilt.

'The brother is "late" – meaning dead?' she asked, struggling for a coherent response. 'Does that mean he was old? Does that mean his victims have died also? Again, there are a lot of things here that need to be . . .'

And she waffled on without even hearing what she was saying. In truth, she had lost control of her own thoughts. She might have started slurring. All she knew for certain was that she was tired. The soda pop was making her tipsy – she was convinced now that it had been spiked with something less innocent than whisky. The warmth, even with her jacket off, was furnace-like. And the sulphurous odour was impairing her ability to think straight – did the Satanists not realise that the use of unbearable smells could influence ethical judgements? Or was that the point? Were they toying with her? *Experimenting* with her?

'Are you OK?' Agnes was asking.

'I'm OK,' said Cat. But she most certainly was not OK. She was dizzy and scared.

'Final dilemma,' the Great Sheldrake announced from three o'clock. He was reaching for the last card. He was studying it. He was smiling. He was turning his eyes directly to Cat.

'You purchase a perfect apartment in a picturesque city and every-thing seems to be going splendidly. But then the tenant upstairs, a worthless loafer, returns to his own apartment and, disregarding all your pleas, begins a campaign of malicious disruption with the specific intention of driving you mad.'

Cat squinted – was she really hearing this?

'Do you: (a) move to a different residence at considerable finan-cial cost; (b) try to live with the nuisance or hope that the problem resolves itself; or (c), make moves to eliminate the troublemaker at the source?'

My God, Cat thought, *this is my very own dilemma*. Starkly and indisputably. But surely it hadn't been written on one of the cards?

Alice: 'The fellow sounds like a right royal prick. I'd kill him without a second thought – with my bare hands.'

Petra. 'I concur.'

George the Cornishman. 'People with that level of sociopathy don't deserve to live. They're like a virus. It's a duty to wipe them out, for the good of society in general.'

Johannes the Austrian. 'Sounds like what LaVey calls a "psychic vampire". A man who only feels relevant if he's creating pain and displeasure. Such men are often crying out to be terminated. I see no reason to disoblige them.'

And around the table it went, though Cat for the first time couldn't work out what to say. She wanted to advocate her fervently held belief that nobody has the right to appoint himself judge and executioner. She wanted to point out that the people most willing to kill others are invariably the least suitable to kill anything. She wanted to declare that she had always opposed the death penalty, even for mass murderers and terrorists. She wanted to insist she couldn't kill an animal, let alone a human being – it was the principal reason she was a vegan. She wanted, in short, to indulge in yet another high-minded analysis. But how could she do such a thing, considering the very reason she was here? Under the circumstances, would it not be supremely disingenuous? Could she really do anything but admit to her own raw impulses – to *own* them by echoing the replies of those preceding her? And by so doing acknowledge that such dilemmas are in fact a good deal simpler than she cared to admit?

Not that it mattered, in the end, because somewhere between

three o'clock and midnight Cat's mounting fatigue overwhelmed her. She had a last glimpse of the Great Sheldrake smiling at her, and over his shoulder, in the satanic darkness, the ghostly face of the man with the gleaming eyes.

And then her head dropped onto the table and she plunged into delirium.

'Rege Satanas!' she thought she heard in the darkness.

'Ave, Satanas!'

'Der Mensch ist Gott!'

'Gott ist der Mensch!'

'Hail Satan!'

'Shenhamforash!'

Through half-lidded eyes Cat saw, or thought she saw, the black mosquito nets rising like velvet stage curtains. She saw the others gathering around the distinguished man in the darkness. She saw him gesturing to her regally. She slipped again into unconsciousness but awoke now and then, for fleeting seconds, enough for her later to remember being moved across the chamber, and being fussed over, and being lowered into a chair, and having her head propped up by leathery fingers, and feeling other hands encasing her head, and seeing the two bestial eyes hovering over her face, and feeling hot breath on her cheeks, and hearing a litany of chants and blessings as the sulphurous stench, stronger now than ever, assailed her nostrils.

'Rege Satanas!'

'Ave, Satanas!'

'Shenhamforash!'

'Everything is going to be all right.'

Whoever uttered the last words had a voice so deep and resonant that it shook the chambers of her heart.

'Are you OK?'

It was Agnes now, with streetlights flaring behind her. She was at the wheel of her VW. She was stroking Cat's hair with a tender hand. They were speeding home through the dark and deserted streets of outer Edinburgh.

'I'm not a victim,' Cat protested.

And then she fell into a deep sleep, with no idea what she'd just said.

CHAPTER
FOURTEEN

C AT WAS IN HER COUSINS' UNKEMPT back yard in Philadelphia. She was alone. Her siblings had all left home. Her father was working round-the-clock. Her mother was laid up in bed with a mysterious 'bug' that would eventually claim her. So here was Cat, bursting with displaced aggression, setting out into the jungle to exterminate every insect she saw. She roamed the garden with an old fly-spray pump. She overturned rocks and bricks, shifted metal sheets, separated clumps of witch-hair grass. No hiding place was safe from her deadly pump; no insect was swift enough to escape her fatal poison. She was vaguely aware of her brooding twenty-one-year-old cousin watching her from the window of his upstairs bedroom. But it wasn't until she had moved to the back shed – a hive of creepy-crawlies – that she noticed him now standing in the doorway, viewing her from close range, with a curious expression on his face.

'All God's creatures have—'

Cat jolted awake. She was at home in her bed. With the lights on and the blinds down. And that didn't make sense. She liked to sleep with the windows uncovered, so she could watch the moon climb over the tenement rooftops of Rothesay Place. She glanced at the alarm clock. 3.11 a.m. She sat up. She was still wearing her clothes of the previous evening. Only her shoes had been removed. The duvet was covering her. But how had that happened?

She heard snoring. Loud, hog-like snoring. She thought for a moment it must be Moyle upstairs. But then she realised it was coming from inside her own flat. Someone was in her living room.

Her pulse accelerating, Cat flung off the duvet and went to investigate.

She smelled the lilac before seeing her – Agnes, sprawled across the sofa with a half-eaten cracker sitting forlorn on her chest. There were other crackers, piled high with cottage cheese, on the coffee table beside a glass of orange juice. The lights were on and the television was tuned to some documentary about the Vietnam War.

Cat nudged Agnes until she shook herself awake, blinked a few times and focused.

'Well, well, look who's risen from the grave,' she said, grinning.

Cat, feeling not remotely amused, folded herself into the neighbouring armchair. 'I see you've made yourself comfortable.'

'Not angry, are you? I was hungry. But all I could find in your kitchen was rabbit food – damn, girl, haven't you got anything edible? This stuff tastes like wet rice.'

'Never mind that,' Cat said. 'What happened?'

'Huh?' Agnes was brushing crumbs of her chest.

'How did I get here?'

'How did you get here? You fell asleep – don't you remember? And I drove you home.'

'You carried me all the way in here?'

'I almost had a heart attack getting up the stairs.'

'Then how did you get me through the door?'

'You were awake enough to hand over your keys.'

'And you put me in bed?'

'What else was I supposed to do?'

Cat released a pent-up breath. 'I suppose I should be grateful you didn't undress me.'

'Hey, I'm not that creepy.' Agnes laughed and then frowned. 'What's wrong, girl? You're not angry, are you?'

'I *am* angry, of course I am. What do you expect?'

'Why?'

'Because I . . .' *Because I lost control*, Cat wanted to say. 'Because I remember hardly a thing about the end of the ritual.'

'Really?'

'It's a blur, it's fragmented, it's . . .' Cat became aware of her scratchy and sweaty clothes, the dull ache in her head, the queasy feeling in her stomach. 'Was I drugged?'

'No, you weren't *drugged*. You were *drunk*. You had too much of the Laird's whisky, that's all.'

'The whisky that laced the soda pop?'

'That's right. I warned you what might happen.'

'When did you warn me?'

'Many times, but you just kept on drinking. Don't you remember?'

'As a matter of fact, I don't.'

'You were settling your nerves, obviously.'

'I wasn't nervous.'

'The sweat on your brow said otherwise.'

'That was just the heat.'

'It was your *nerves*, lassie – it's perfectly normal.'

Cat, sighing, acknowledged it was possible. 'Then what happened after I passed out?'

'What do you mean, what happened? You passed out. So we wrapped the thing up and I drove you home.'

'I heard chanting . . . satanic chanting.'

'Of course you did – we had to conclude the ritual.'

'Even though I was delirious?'

'Semi-delirious, by the sounds of it. What's the matter?' Agnes reached for the fruit juice. 'Everything went extremely well. You were awesome. And he liked you. He really liked you.'

'Who liked me?'

'Who do you think?'

'The Laird of Howgate?'

'Aye, the Laird of Howgate.' Agnes gave a sort of half-wink.

Cat's head started throbbing again. 'I saw a face in the darkness . . .'

'A reflection of the Great Sheldrake in the mirror. I noticed that too.'

'No, it wasn't the Great Sheldrake. I saw flashing eyes.'

'Just one of the cats. There are so many in that place nobody even notices them any more.'

'No,' Cat insisted, 'it was the face of a man . . . a very distinguished-looking man. He was sitting on a throne.'

Agnes guffawed. 'You saw this fellow when you were passed out?'

'Before I passed out. He had a voice . . . an incredibly deep voice . . .'

'Aye? And what'd he say?'

'He said to me, "Everything is going to be all right."'

'"Everything is going to be all right"? *Everything is going to be all right*?' Agnes burst out laughing. 'That's the sign above the Modern Art Gallery, silly girl! Just around the corner from here!'

Cat, embarrassed, realised that Agnes was right. The message was emblazoned in blue neon across the entablature of one of the gallery buildings: EVERYTHING IS GOING TO BE ALRIGHT. She'd seen it numerous times while out running. So what had happened? Had she imagined the voice? The whole end to the ritual?

Agnes meanwhile launched, victoriously but unsteadily, to her feet. 'Anyway, can I get you something? You must be hungry? Thirsty?'

'No,' said Cat. 'I've got one hell of a headache, though.'

'Then I'll fetch a tablet. Where's your medical stuff?'

'In the bathroom cabinet.'

'That's original.'

When Agnes left the room she seemed, most uncharacteristically, to be blushing. Cat heard her rummaging around in the bathroom and humming 'Only for the Weak' with such awkward enthusiasm that she had to ask to her to pipe down – she had neighbours to think of.

'Oh, that's right, the neighbours.' Agnes returned with a tablet fizzing in a bathroom tumbler. 'Must say I've heard not a squeak out of your musician friend upstairs, by the way. Maybe he's been taken care of already.'

'I'm not sure what you're suggesting,' Cat said, 'but Moyle's been away for a couple of days.'

'Maybe he'll have a car accident on the way home, then. Here.' Agnes handed over the glass.

Cat contemplated the bubbling tablet. 'You know, I still have no idea what happened tonight.'

'What do you mean? You got what you wanted, didn't you?'

'Did I? All I remember was a slew of ethical dilemmas.'

'That was all part of it – to make sure you were worthy.'

'Like an aptitude test?'

'I guess you could call it that, yeah, an aptitude test. And you knocked it out of the park, as you Yanks say.'

Cat remembered the dreadful feeling of having her mind plundered. 'Are you absolutely sure something wasn't done to me?'

'I told you, you weren't—'

'I mean something else.'

'Like what?'

Cat narrowed her eyes. 'Are you sure I wasn't *violated*?'

'*Violated*?' Agnes exclaimed. 'Jesus, Mary and the Cuckold – is that really what you think happened?'

'Like I said, I wish I *knew*.'

'Well, you certainly weren't violated, I can promise you that. You've been suckered by too many horror movies, girl. Satanism doesn't condone non-consensual sex any more – doesn't condone *anything* sexual without specific invitation. It's very strict about that. So relax. Nobody undressed you and nobody got naked. And if you thought anything like that happened then you really *were* delirious. Get that headache tablet into you.'

Cat had been referring to her mind, not her body, but she let it pass. As she sipped the soothing water – the tablet had fully dissolved – Agnes adjusted her breasts, looking remarkably self-conscious. 'Anyway, I'd better get home. I'm not feeling all that well myself. Maybe I got some of that whisky in me too. You gonna be OK by yourself?'

'I'll be OK,' said Cat, feeling ashamed. 'And I thank you for bringing me up here – sorry if I seem a little edgy.'

'You've got a right to be edgy. You *are* on an edge. The edge of a wonderful precipice, that's what. But you'll see. You'll see.' Agnes tugged her frock at its tight points, shaking her head affectionately. '*Violated*, for fuck's sake. Let me tell you, girl, if you'd been had by him, you'd know, girl. You'd *know*.'

'Had by who? The Laird of Howgate?'

'Aye.' Agnes chortled mysteriously. 'The Laird of Howgate.'

★ ★ ★

When Agnes departed, Cat, belatedly troubled by her friend's misinterpretation, removed her clothes in front of her bedroom mirror and checked herself all over. But she could find no signs of interference. Physically, at least, there was no evidence that she'd been violated. But the odd sense of losing control continued to gnaw away at her. She couldn't imagine how the Satanists had divined so many of her secrets.

Returning to bed, she found her headache had eased but she was still sore and swollen with fatigue. She plunged almost immediately into a deep and a disturbingly vivid dream.

As if from a God's eye perspective, she saw a leathery-winged creature rising from the demonic darkness of the River Esk. She saw him soaring over the chimneystacks of Edinburgh. She saw him descend like a hawk into a moonlit Dean Village. She saw him swoop upon her building and effortlessly spring open the stair door.

Clop clop clop. He was ascending the steps.

Clop clop clop. She heard his cloven hooves.

Clop clop clop. She saw him heading for a door.

Kee-wah! She saw the door opening. She saw him stepping inside. She saw his glowing yellow eyes.

And – with a violent shudder – she awoke.

She adjusted herself in the bed.

And lay there, listening.

Creak creak creak.

It was the floorboards upstairs.

Creak creak creak.

PLONK!

Oh, there was a demon in the building, all right.

Creak creak creak.

But it was *Moyle.*

Nnnnnnnnnnhhhhhhhrrrrrrrrrrrrrrrr.

TWANG!

The Hound of Hades was back. Alive and well. And ready to raise some hell.

Kah-lunk!

'*Shit!*'

Glancing at her bedside clock – it was past four a.m. – Cat didn't know whether to be relieved or infuriated. The whole night's chicanery had been a complete waste of time. But at least she'd been spared the ordeal of battling with her sanity, not to mention her conscience, had the ritual actually *worked*.

She rolled over, wrapped the pillow around her head, and when she fell asleep again it was to the image of the ghostly man's face – wicked and yet loving – behind the black mosquito nets at Aileanach Castle.

CHAPTER

FIFTEEN

C AT ENJOYED A RELATIVELY UNINTERRUPTED sleep on Sunday night, waking only at a loud *thump*, which she guessed was Moyle dropping something, and an unearthly shriek, which she figured was a nocturnal bird or a fox in the private gardens. But at the office on Monday Agnes was absent, having phoned in sick, and Cat couldn't help being disappointed that she wouldn't have a chance to discuss in further detail the ritual at Aileanach Castle.

As it happened, she didn't get a chance to discuss anything. As soon as Nick 'Wing Commander' Bellamy arrived – at ten thirty, after Monday morning's customary inter-departmental meeting – he summoned her to his 'cockpit', the first time she'd been allowed inside.

'Can you guess why you're here?' he asked, indicating that Cat should sit down.

'I must admit I've got no idea,' said Cat, obediently taking a seat.

On Bellamy's desk was a model of a Hawker Hurricane. Mounted on the wall was huge print of a Lancaster bomber. Bellamy himself, close-cropped of hair and clipped of moustache, had tried to join the RAF as a youth but had been knocked back for unspecified reasons. A permanently bitter man, he had moved under sufferance to Edinburgh from sunny Torquay, on the English Riviera, in order to help cure the homesickness of his Scottish-born wife. But the marriage had proved by all accounts an unhappy one, sustained only by fear of change, and Bellamy had taken to venting his frustrations on his long-suffering staff.

'They provided a file on you before they sent you here, you know.' Bellamy indicated a folder on his desk. 'And it spoke glowingly of your work ethic, your ambition, your total commitment to the job. But now, I must admit, I'm a little confused. Because when I examine your work record since you arrived here' – he looked at the folder and up again, as if shovelling bad news at her – 'I see lapses. I see a pattern of overstepping your boundaries. I see a performance that, to be perfectly honest, isn't up to the standard I was led to expect.'

Cat knew there was no point challenging him so she nodded guiltily. 'I admit I've disappointed myself.'

'Ahhhh.' Clearly he hadn't expected that.

'I came here with all my ambitions intact, I assure you. But I guess it's taken me longer to adjust than I'd hoped. And there are certain complications which unfortunately I haven't—'

'Now, I must stop you there. I must stop you there.' Bellamy's eyes gleamed maliciously. 'Because I'm sure you can appreciate why I can't allow personal circumstances to be an excuse for poor performance. What happens at home or anywhere else is irrelevant to what happens at work. You shouldn't discuss it with anyone here. I never do.'

Not quite, Cat thought: Bellamy's constant whining about his sickly and passive-aggressive wife, shared with senior colleagues, was legendary. 'You're right,' she agreed. 'It is irrelevant.'

'Besides, I already know about your problems with the fellow upstairs.'

'Ahhhh.' Now it was Cat's turn to be surprised. 'Can I ask . . .?'

'Your good friend Agnes has spoken about them.'

'Ahhhh.' Goddamned Agnes, Cat thought.

'But you really need to adapt. The most effective operators always adapt. It doesn't matter how they do it – they just adapt. They certainly don't let petty distractions get in the way of their work. Because their work is the most important thing in their lives.'

'Absolutely,' said Cat. 'And I'm doing my best to adapt right now. But – you'll have to forgive me – there's no question that my problems at home have had some impact on me. My health has suffered. I'm not as sharp as usual.'

'Your health has suffered, has it?'

'I like to think I don't always look this bad.' Said with a vaporous smile, as if to invite some reflexively positive comment.

Bellamy, however, merely shifted in his chair. 'Did you know I have Type-1 diabetes, Ms Thomas? That I've had it since my youth? And yet my attendance record here is perfect. It's been without blemish for eight years.'

'I – I didn't know about that,' said Cat, trying to sound sympathetic. 'I'm sure it's very difficult for you. But my attendance record too is—'

'Yes, I know all about your attendance record. It's exemplary. It's the best that can be said about you. I dearly wish the same could be said about your chum Agnes.'

Cat felt obliged to protest. 'Agnes has some serious health problems too, but she's a dedicated operator too – I can vouch for that.'

'A dedicated operator, eh?' Bellamy seemed to find that amusing. 'Yes, you and Ms Sampson have quite the double act going on, don't you? Practically inseparable, from what I understand.'

Cat wondered with alarm if Bellamy knew about the ritual. 'I wouldn't say inseparable. Agnes reached out to me when I arrived and I appreciated that.'

'Swanning around the country, making your own rules, dining out at expensive pubs.'

'We dined out after work, and both times I paid for it,' Cat insisted, taken aback by his venom.

'Oh really? Both times Ms Sampson claimed it as a business expense – did you know that?'

Goddamned Agnes, Cat thought again. 'Well, now that I think of it, there were a couple of other meals that were on company time as well.'

'If they were on company time, then why didn't *you* claim them?'

'I'm still finding my feet here. I'm still not sure what's business and what's not.'

It was a ridiculously flimsy defence and Bellamy, his moustache twitching, clearly didn't buy it. He leaned back in his seat, his palm pressed flat on the desk. 'I'll be grounding Ms Sampson for a while, whenever she sees fit to return to the office. She needs to realise that a company car is a privilege, not a right, and field investigations are not an opportunity for "some fun", as she's been known to call them. And I'll be grounding you, too, Ms Thomas, so you've more time to learn about our procedures. We may not have seen the best of you yet – I can't believe that everything I was told about you was an exaggeration – but my goodwill only extends so far. There are budget cuts at ABC, you know. Very likely there's to be significant consolidation of services and staff layoffs. And I'm in the firing line as much as anyone else. So I need everyone operating to their optimum efficiency. Your priority now is to do whatever it takes to get yourself up to your well-advertised standards. In the meantime, you can take Jenny's desk.'

Cat's heart sank. Jenny McLeish, a sweet-natured blonde who'd recently gone on maternity leave, was one of the department's analysts, responsible for preparing stats, liaising with different business units and responding to incoming mail. It was a humiliating demotion, confining her to the Aquarium, but again Cat knew better than to protest. 'No problem,' she said, with a rueful nod. 'Will this mean a pay decrease, by any chance?'

Bellamy was shifting papers now. 'That won't be necessary.'

'Will I have to hand in the keys to the company car?'

'You can keep them in the key drawer. But the vehicle itself' – he glanced up – 'I'd prefer that you keep it downstairs, in case someone else needs to use it.'

'Of course.' She tried to sound hopeful. 'So, just to clarify, there's always the chance, if I improve my performance, that I can resume my proper role?'

Bellamy arched an eyebrow. 'Your "proper role" is what I decide it is, Ms Thomas – though such things might soon be out taken out of my hands anyway. But, in answer to your question, I'm always willing to reward improved performance.'

Cat managed a humble smile. 'Thank you,' she said, rising. 'I promise I'll do my best.'

She left Bellamy's office, wondering if she should click her heels and salute.

★ ★ ★

Cat moved into Jenny McLeish's cubicle, with its happy snaps of a beaming Jenny, her goofy husband and a multitude of evangelical life-lesson stick-ons: GOD HAS A PLAN. TRUST IT, LIVE IT, ENJOY IT. And: GOD WILL ALWAYS MAKE A WAY. And: LET TODAY BE THE DAY WHEN YOU GIVE UP WHAT YOU'VE BEEN FOR WHO YOU CAN BECOME.

Well, Cat thought, that last one is nothing if not appropriate. In order to keep her job – in order to remain in Edinburgh, period – she was going to have to take positive action to get her groove back. Real action. Something more material than taking part in some ungodly ritual with a cabal of weirdos and seeking the help of 'Satan'. She was going to have to soundproof her flat at devastating cost and then sell it off at a crippling loss. And find somewhere to achieve a decent night's sleep, even if it was just a campervan parked on the outskirts of town (her hairdresser had recommended exactly that).

She was halfway through the mail when she came to a mildly interesting letter from a certain Mr Dennis Napier of Dundee.

Dear Sir/Madam,

I have been a loyal customer of ABC Bank for 25 years. Three years ago I opened a targeted savings account at your branch in Glenrothes, Fife. Against my stated wishes, the clerk who served me insisted that I take a credit card as an adjunct to the account. When this card arrived in the mail I purposely destroyed it and failed to activate the account. Two years later I moved to Dundee. It was at this point that a new card was forwarded to my old address (the previous card, it seems, had expired). Somehow the credit card account was then activated without my knowledge and someone (the bank will not tell me who) went on a spending spree. I first learned of this fraudulent activity when I received a stern email demanding full repayment or . . .

And so on.

Cat was intrigued. It looked as though service staff in Scotland, like their counterparts in the US, had been incentivised to foist credit cards on unwilling customers. But the activation process, at least in America, usually required the submission of personal information to which only the customer and the bank were privy. Cat was making a note of the details – there was something that made her radar crackle – when her mobile phone vibrated. She refrained from checking it immediately, because Jenny's desk was in clear view of Bellamy's office, but as soon as she went out for lunch she called up the text.

It was from Maxine in Number Four.

Hear that man screaming last night?

Holy fk! What a noise! XXX**

So it hadn't been a bird or a fox after all. Probably a late-night reveller, Cat thought, staggering home from a booze-up.

But, too hungry for distractions, she went to find some noodles.

CHAPTER
SIXTEEN

W HEN SHE GOT HOME, Cat turned on one of the TV news
channels to remind herself that her personal problems
didn't amount to a hill of beans. A disobedient country
somewhere was being bombed and starved into submission. The
billionaire founder of a famous telecommunications company
was scheming the tax system. The US Secretary of State was
eagerly anticipating the Rapture. A prominent MP had allegedly
murdered a rent boy who'd threatened to expose him. Scientists
were predicting that a catastrophic collapse of ecosystems owing to
aggressive farming techniques was 'all but inevitable'.

Cat absorbed it all absent-mindedly while drafting emails to the
soundproofing company, indicating that she was prepared to accept
the terms of their quotation, and to her solicitor Stuart, asking for a
rundown of procedures necessary for a property sale. Rummaging
her brain for the right words, she glanced upwards and noticed a
dark stain bruising the ceiling. She got up for a closer look.

No doubt about it. A brownish blotch, about the size of a dinner
plate, right above her globe lamp. And – now that she looked closer
– another one nearby. And a much smaller one near that.

Cat couldn't work it out. Maxine had spoken of Moyle's

overflowing bathtub when the previous owner, Connie, had been in residence, but this ceiling was nowhere near Moyle's bathroom. Maybe he'd just dropped something? A bottle of beer? Or wine? Or perhaps one of the radiator pipes, loaded with rusty water, had burst?

She returned to her emails, philosophical. If she went ahead with the installation of suspended ceilings then the stain would soon be concealed anyway. And if the problem persisted, the burst pipe dripping dirty water onto the lower ceiling . . . well, that would be the new owner's problem.

There you have it, Cat thought to herself – you've already managed to 'palm the problem off'.

For all that, she slept remarkably well that night, without a single interruption, and woke to the sight of an incredible sunrise – great flares of amber, peach and vermilion – bleeding out across the southern sky. She thought about going for an early swim, or a run, for the first time since those joyous first weeks in Edinburgh. But then she reminded herself that the serenity wouldn't last – it never did – and she rolled over for more sleep.

At the office that day she worked so fast and efficiently – beginning, among other things, a discreet investigation into the hierarchy of departments at ABC – that she started to feel that this enforced grounding might not be such a bad thing after all.

At lunchtime, word reached her that Agnes had again phoned in sick.

Arriving home that evening – she'd walked all the way – Cat noticed that a brown-paper envelope addressed to Moyle – a tax notice or some such thing – had still not been collected from the mailbox. And in her living room the brownish ceiling stain had darkened and spread. She wondered for the first time if it might be blood. The possibility was both appalling and exciting – because of what it suggested – but she chose not to take it seriously. She tried not to think about it at all.

That night she lay exhausted in bed – she'd been for a punishing run through leafy north-west Edinburgh – and listened intently for any noises from upstairs. But there was nothing. Not a single *creak*. Not a muffled *nnnnnnhhhhhhrrrrrrr*. And certainly no *plonks*, *ka-lunks* or *twangs*. She was so alarmed – and intrigued – that she couldn't relax until close to midnight, amused, for what it was worth, that it was now *tranquillity* that was keeping her awake.

On Thursday Agnes returned to the office and first had to submit to a dressing-down from Wing Commander Bellamy. Cat, at Jenny's desk with her back turned, heard the sort of protests that she herself had avoided. Then the slam of the cockpit door. She refrained from looking up, however, convinced that any sisters-in-arms camaraderie would be counterproductive at this stage.

But at lunch she caught up with Agnes at a tourist-crowded Forrest Road pub.

'That Sassenach cunt,' Agnes whined. 'Sorry, fud, Sassenach fud. I told you he had a problem with women. If you'd ever met his wife, you'd know why.'

'I heard they were divorcing,' Cat said.

'Really?'

'That's the whisper in the lunchroom.'

'Ha!' said Agnes. 'Did you know he had a fling a couple of years ago with some tart from Transaction Processing? Said he was the worst shag in history. And when that leaked out he was so humiliated he took it out on us. Well, looks like we're all gonna pay, yet again, because he feels emasculated. Do you know he's still pretending he's got Type-1 diabetes?'

'He hasn't?'

'Of course not. That's just an excuse he dreamed up to explain his failure to get into the RAF.'

'Sure about that?'

'Of course. Ever seen him injecting himself? Testing his blood sugar? It's bullshit. Everything about him's bullshit. He's especially scared of women who turn him on – that's why he doesn't like you.'

'I didn't sense that.'

'Trust me, I know what I'm talking about.'

Cat made an ambivalent noise. 'He had me in for one of his chats too, you know. He told me you'd claimed a couple of dinners I paid for as a business expense.'

'Aye, well.' Agnes giggled. 'The expense account is one of our few kickbacks in this profession – I was gonna mention it to you sooner or later.'

'I covered for you,' Cat said. 'I told him the meals were on business time.'

'You're a pet. I owe you one. Well' – Agnes reconsidered – 'I *would* owe you one, except of course that it's actually you who owes me.'

'I do?'

'Aye, you know. For all I've done for you.'

'Which is?'

'The problem. Has it been taken care of yet?'

'I'm not sure what you mean.'

'You know exactly what I mean.'

'You mean Moyle?'

'I don't mean Thomas the fucking Tank Engine.'

Cat shrugged. 'I'm not sure where he is.'

'Ha!' Agnes leaned in and lowered her voice. 'He's *gone*, isn't he!'

'He hasn't been collecting his mail.'

'Of course he hasn't.'

'But his car's still in its space.'

'Of course it is.'

Cat stopped herself from mentioning the stain on the ceiling. 'But that doesn't necessarily mean anything. He might have gone off somewhere.'

'Leaving his car behind?'

'People don't always take their cars when they travel.'

Agnes guffawed. 'The only place that Moyle's travelled to is the other side. He's been taken care of, Cat – I told you it would happen. He liked you. He really liked you.'

Cat wanted to point out that Agnes had never said explicitly *how* the problem would be 'taken care of'. Or who it was who 'really liked' her. But at just that moment Wing Commander Bellamy entered the pub, looking around for someone, and they both clammed up and bowed their heads, pretending they weren't there.

The following evening, Friday, 10 November, Cat was standing on a wooden chair, examining the ceiling stain at closer range – there was a line of congealed blood on the fitting above her globe light – when she heard the buzz of the intercom upstairs. Someone was calling up to Moyle. But Moyle wasn't answering.

More buzzing. Insistent.

Cat moved to her bedroom window, seeing a car parked at an angle behind hers, its doors wide open. She couldn't be sure, but it looked like the Hyundai belonging to the straggly-haired rocker – the guy who'd thought it was such a riot to call her Shania Twain.

Then her own intercom buzzed.

For a moment she thought about pretending she wasn't home. But she relented and answered the phone.

'Hello?'

'Aye' – a familiar Scottish voice; she was convinced now it was the rocker dude – 'can you open this door? I need to get up to Number Six.'

Cat wondered if she should resist – there was a warning downstairs about letting strangers into the common stair – but she gave in again.

'OK.' She hit the release button.

Kah-lunk.

Clapclapclapclapclapclap. More than one person was coming up the stairs. They were passing her flat. Cat backed into her living room, looking at the ceiling stain.

BANG BANG BANG BANG. They were knocking on Moyle's door.

'Bawbag! Bawbag! Open up! Bawbag!'

BANG BANG BANG BANG BANG BANG.

No response from Bawbag. Cat glanced again at the ceiling.

BANG BANG BANG BANG BANG BANG.

Eventually the visitors filed back down the stairs, defeated.

Clapclapclapclapclapclapclapclap.

Cat thought that might be the end of it. But when she went to the window she saw even more rockers standing next to the Hyundai, engaged in a sort of ragtag conference. One of them was talking earnestly on a mobile phone. When he looked up and spotted Cat she retreated, none too swiftly.

She returned to the living area. Put down a drop sheet. Dragged a can of white paint out of the box room. Popped open the lid with a flathead screwdriver and stirred the paint. Then – without even changing out of her business clothes – she climbed back onto the chair and started painting over the stain.

Even she, the student of human nature, wasn't sure why this was so important.

When she'd finished she was alarmed by the smell. Maybe

someone would come in and ask what she'd been doing. She washed the paintbrush in white spirits, dried it with an old cloth and replaced the can back in the box room. Then she noticed a drop of white paint on the shoulder of her jacket. *Dammit.* She tried to dab it out but now the jacket reeked of turpentine. The whole apartment did. Panicking, she tossed the jacket in the washing machine, along with the rest of her clothes and cleaning cloths, and put it all on an intense spin cycle.

She changed into her Lycra and even wondered if she should go out for a run, to prove how nonchalant she was. But when she went back to the window she noticed a locksmith's van had parked beside the Hyundai. The locksmith seemed to be chatting with Moyle's friends and occasionally glancing up at the building. Why weren't they coming up? Then Cat saw a police car pulling up as well. But of course – they needed official supervision to open the place.

Cat drew back again. She threw open a window and sprayed some perfume around.

CLAPclapCLAPclapCLAPclapCLAPclapCLAP. A whole posse was coming up the stairs.

Arriving at Moyle's door.

BANG BANG BANG BANG BANG. As if one last attempt might finally rouse Moyle.

Muffled voices. The squawk of a police radio. Firecrackers going off in the distance – leftovers from Bonfire Night.

Then the clink of tools. Scraping. More clinking. The locksmith doing his thing.

Kee-wah!

The door had been sprung.

CreakCreakCreakCreakCreak. The men were entering Moyle's flat.

Cat's heart was hammering.

CreakCreakCreak.

The men stopped.

Cat, standing directly beneath, was rigid, listening intently for some sort of reaction.

Which, it turned out, was a chilling exclamation flanked by two protracted periods of awestruck silence.

'. . . . . . . FUCKING *HELL!* . . . .'

A firework exploded in the distance.

CHAPTER

SEVENTEEN

T HERE WERE COMINGS AND GOINGS all night. Cat, still in her running gear, spent much of her time peeking out the window of her darkened bedroom, watching the new arrivals, recoiling at first whenever someone looked her way, then figuring that she had every right to be curious – anything else would be suspect. She even got a text message from Maxine:

Jesus, do you know what's going on?

To which she replied:

Not sure.

Before adding impulsively:

And my name's not Jesus.

Then she became ashamed of her own levity.

There were more police vehicles, and cops donning forensic suits, and a sober-looking guy in a crumpled grey suit and a plaid tie who everyone seemed to be deferring to. And finally a crane of a man who couldn't have looked more like a coroner if he was carrying a bone saw. All these in turn clopped up and down the stairs and into the flat above. The noises now were an odd mix of the everyday and the unfamiliar.

Creak creak creak creak.

Thonk!

Twik twik twik. Like equipment being set up.

Schwit schwit schwit. Like scraping.

Hhhhhhhhhmmmmmmmmm. Like a small motor.

And numerous guarded voices, saying nothing distinct.

Shortly after midnight most of the crew departed, but there remained three police cars downstairs and at least two officers above (Cat could hear them shuffling and chatting). When she finally risked opening her door, she saw crime scene tape strung across the stairwell – and that seemed to make it official.

Moyle – TurMoyle – was dead.

Cat indulged in a sleeping tablet that night simply because she knew she'd be questioned sooner or later and didn't want to be tired and confused. Or worse, to *look* tired and confused. But as it happened she barely slept anyway, trying to block from her mind any memories of the ritual at Aileanach Castle. Refusing to accept that she might be somehow accountable. And wary of some dreadful debt that she might now have to pay. While all the time, in the back of her mind, working out how much money she'd save by not installing the soundproofing; by not moving; by not paying sales tax and agency fees; by not spending a couple of nights a week in the hotel; by altogether being more rested, fitter and alert; by simply enjoying life again – by revelling in her wonderful new life in Edinburgh.

First thing in the morning the full posse of cops was back again, along with an elderly bewigged lady whom Cat assumed was Moyle's aunt. There was more clattering up and down the stairs and murmuring in sombre tones. The aunt was assisted back to a taxi and spirited away, looking pale as a corpse. Then the cops were back making measurements, using their strange equipment, finally extracting something – a body? crime scene evidence? – in a big black bag. A multitude of big black bags.

Cat's landline rang.

She'd been expecting a knock on the door but now she had to consider the possibility that the police were phoning her instead.

She answered tensely. 'Hello?'

'Well *done*! Well *done*, girl! I told you you wouldn't regret it.'

Cat – fearful she might be overheard by the cops upstairs – spoke in a whisper. 'I don't know what you're talking about.'

'Oh, come on, girl. I read all about it in the press! "Dead body found in Dean Village"!'

'It's in the newspapers? Already?'

Agnes laughed with unrestrained glee. 'If a dog shits on the pavement, it's news in Edinburgh.'

'But that's all they say? Just dead body?'

'Something about "mysterious circumstances".'

Cat lowered her voice even further. 'So he could have killed himself, right?'

'If that's what you need to believe, go for it.'

'I'm serious. He could have killed himself – I'm sure of it.'

'Aye right, whatever. The result is the same anyway. Rejoice! Wanna go out to celebrate?'

'I think it's best that I stay here.'

'Yup, I understand. We'll have a glass of bubbly later. This is a stormer of a day for you, Cat. You probably don't even realise it yet, but this is one fine day!'

When she hung up, Cat again contemplated the repainted ceiling. It was the quantity of blood that had made her suspect it was a suicide – as if someone had slit his wrists and slowly bled to death. Then again, if it had been an ordinary everyday suicide would there be so much police attention? Would it be reported on the news?

She threw down her drop sheet again and was painting the cornices – a means of accounting for the persistent paint smell

– when there was a commanding rap on the door. This was it.

She started taking off her paint-spattered DIY blouse – a chambray number she'd picked up at a charity shop – but then decided it looked OK and rebuttoned it. She took a deep breath, girded herself and answered the door.

'I'm Detective Inspector McReynolds.' It was the guy in the grey suit: balding, squinty-eyed, like the lead in some gritty BBC crime drama. He flipped open a warrant card and nodded to a younger guy with much better dress sense. 'And this is Detective Constable Purves.'

'Yes, yes, of course. I'm Cat Thomas. Come right in, officers. I've been painting today so you'll have to excuse the smell.'

The two men, looking appropriately grim, moved into her living room, where Cat invited them to sit down. 'Can I get you anything? Coffee? Herbal tea?'

'We've not got the stomach for anything right now,' McReynolds said gravely. 'Nice place you have here.'

'Thank you.'

'I had a schoolfriend once who lived down this neck of the woods.'

'Oh?'

'I used to come down the hill every weekend, stopping at the sweet shop. That's gone now.'

'I wish I'd been here to see it.'

'Beautiful place, the Dean. I'd love to be able to afford a place here now.'

'It's not that expensive, you know, if you've got American dollars.'

A paper-thin smile. 'Then I wish I'd the good fortune to be born in America.'

If this is your attempt at rapport building, Cat thought, you're laying it on a bit thick, buddy.

And McReynolds, to his credit, seemed to realise it. 'I take it you know why we're here?' he asked, stepping around the drop sheet and lowering himself onto the window-facing sofa. DC Purves was snapping open a notepad.

Cat, also sitting down, nodded. 'I've noticed all the activity, of course. And this morning I got a call from a friend, a work colleague of mine, telling me a body's been found – is that right?'

'I'm afraid so.'

'Mr Moyle?'

'That's correct.'

'I guessed that must be the case.' Cat made sure she maintained eye contact. 'And I expected you to call, you know. That's why I decided to wait here – and do some painting – instead of heading out.'

'You expected us to call?' McReynolds had tilted his head.

'As part of the investigation, I mean. I imagine you'll be inter- viewing all of the people in the building sooner or later, right?'

McReynolds didn't answer directly. 'Did you know Mr Moyle?' he asked. His irises, luminous with reflected sunlight, were the same colour as her blouse.

'Only as the guy who lived upstairs. We didn't socialise or anything.'

'Did you ever see him doing anything suspicious?'

'Suspicious? Such as?'

'Drug dealing? Criminal activity?'

'No,' said Cat, frowning. 'Criminal activity? No. I mean, I smelled some weed occasionally, but nothing really sinister – no.'

'You sound surprised by the question . . .'

'That's because I *am* surprised. Criminal activity? Is that what all this is about?' She was hoping it might explain everything.

But again McReynolds was evasive. 'Did you happen to notice if Mr Moyle ever had any unusual visitors?'

'Unusual?' Cat said. 'Well, he had some headbanging friends, but I wouldn't call them unusual.'

'You had direct contact with them?'

'Once. They came for a party upstairs.'

'Would you recognise them if called to do so?'

'I think they were the same guys who were here last night.' Cat saw no reason to lie. 'I saw them from the window. The guys who raised the alarm.'

McReynolds glanced at the younger cop, who was taking notes. 'DC Purves says you lodged a complaint about the noise of a party last month.'

'That's right – the one I just mentioned.'

'Apparently this led to some ill-feeling between you and Mr Moyle.'

'Ill-feeling? No – who said that? He was noisy, that's all.'

'He was noisy when he had parties or noisy all the time?'

'All the time.'

'How long have you lived here?'

'Since June. I moved here from Florida.'

'And he's been noisy since June?'

'When he's been upstairs, yes.'

At just that moment someone in Number Six – one of the cops – dropped something. *Ka-LONK!* Followed by a very audible 'Aw, shite!' and someone shouting, 'Don't touch that!' Then something rolling across the floor. *Kowok kowok kwok.* And footsteps. *Klonk klonk klonk.* And bending boards. *Creak creak creak.*

McReynolds was looking at the ceiling. He was staring directly at the patch that Cat had painted over. He seemed to be thinking. And eventually he dropped his luminous eyes to Cat again.

'Must have been a great disappointment to you, coming all the way from Florida and finding yourself lumped with such a noisy neighbour.'

'Well, it wasn't perfect, but then life rarely is.'

'So you won't be missing Mr Moyle, now that he's gone?'

'Let's just say I won't be sending any flowers to his funeral.' Cat wanted to make sure she wasn't completely Pollyannaish. 'I mean, he sure made his presence felt – in a bad way.'

McReynolds pursed his lips. 'Then would you say you'd have a good idea when he was home? When he was moving about?'

'I guess so, yes.'

'When was the last time you heard him, then?'

'Let me see – that would be last Saturday night, I guess, when I returned from . . . when I got back from a party with Agnes, my friend from work.'

'Mr Moyle was home that night?'

'He got home after four o'clock.'

'You're sure of that?'

'He'd been away for a few days. When he arrived home it was a bit of a disappointment for me, you know. So I checked the clock.'

'You're absolutely certain it was him?'

'As sure as you can be. He makes – *made* – some very distinctive noises.'

'Did you happen to hear him close his front door?'

'I think so.'

'But you can't be positive?'

'Well, he usually slammed the door, and he slammed it that night – why?'

Yet again McReynolds avoided answering. 'And you've had no reason to suspect that anyone else has been in the apartment since then?'

'I would've heard something, I think.'

DC Purves was scribbling furiously.

'So you didn't hear anyone visiting him? Acting suspiciously? Trying to break in?'

'Nothing of the sort,' Cat said. 'But I'm not usually here during the day, you understand.'

'You've been at work? All week?'

'Every day.'

'And you can verify this?'

'I can give you my office number, if you like.' Cat realised she had a chance to make a statement. 'I'm a fraud investigator at ABC Bank. Terry Grimes knows me.'

McReynolds looked surprised. 'You know Terry Grimes?'

'He's my police liaison in Scotland.'

'Oh aye?' McReynolds's expression had completely changed. 'Terry is a good man.'

'He's been very helpful.'

'That's Terry's way. Nothing is too much.'

'Uh-huh.'

'Sings in the choir at St Giles, you know.'

'I heard that.'

Cat wished she'd mentioned him earlier. The chill had completely left the air; the shift in McReynolds was palpable.

'I see you feed the tits,' he said.

'Sorry?'

'The birds,' he said, gesturing to the window, where a couple of blue tits were whirling about the seed bar. 'I feed them myself.'

'Oh yes, yes,' said Cat, relieved. 'The tits.'

'Cheeky devils.'

'They sure are.'

'Live in constant fear, though – of sparrowhawks, you know.'

'Is that right?'

'That's why they're always looking over their shoulders.'

McReynolds contemplated the twittering little birds until they flew off and then fixed Cat again with his chambray eyes. 'Let me be perfectly frank with you, Ms Thomas. I'm assuming I can rely on your discretion?'

'Of course.'

'We're in a bind here. All the usual signs in a case like this seem to be missing. Fingerprints. DNA traces. Evidence of tampering with the doors and windows. Everything. So we're relying entirely on witnesses. But there *are* no witnesses. And if the people in the building didn't hear anything, then nobody did.'

'I didn't hear anything,' Cat assured him. 'Nothing unusual, anyway. I wish I had, but I didn't.'

McReynolds nodded, clearly disappointed. 'Oh well, we're bound to be in touch.' He was already getting to his feet. 'This is my card. I'll be in charge of the case until further notice. So don't hesitate to contact me if you think of anything important. I'm available day and night – all hours.'

'Sure thing.' Cat looked at the card as she led the two men to the door. 'But "until further notice", you say?'

'I beg your pardon?' McReynolds had turned in the vestibule.

'You said you were in charge "until further notice".'

'Well, the case might be bucked upstairs to the MIT.'

'MIT?' To Cat that was a university.

'Major Investigation Team.'

'Oh.' Cat's curiosity got the better of her. 'So I take it . . . I mean, Moyle didn't slit his wrists or hang himself or anything, right? This is murder?'

McReynolds glanced at Constable Purves and back to Cat with an anguished expression. He seemed to consider for a moment. 'Ms Thomas,' he said, 'I hope you'll forgive me for speaking bluntly. But the victim wasn't just murdered.'

'No?'

'Mr Moyle was . . . well.' McReynolds sighed, clearly at a loss for words. 'I've never seen anything like it.'

'Oh?'

'*No one*'s seen anything like it. Not the forensic team, not the paramedics . . . *no one.*'

'Right.' Cat was aware that she wasn't breathing. 'Right.'

McReynolds looked like he wanted to say something else but couldn't bring himself to do so. 'Ms Thomas,' he said, nodding, 'good day to you, then.'

Cat closed the door and didn't exhale until she heard the two detectives rapping on the door of Maxine and Michael downstairs. Then she let out a long sigh and returned to her living room, slumping onto the sofa – it was still warm – and staring at the whirling tits, and feeling, just as she had when she'd bought the place, as though she were poised on a clifftop staring out over a sea of fog.

PART

—

TWO

CHAPTER

ONE

THE POLICE WERE IN AND OUT OF the place for another week. They brought in more forensic teams. They removed some of Moyle's furniture. They crawled over the roof. They put up ladders and inspected the windows from the outside. Whenever Cat saw them, they looked perplexed.

When they finally departed, the flat was locked tight for two weeks and then the movers came in. Later the renovation teams arrived. Cat heard hammering. Polishing. A new front door being installed. And finally, in mid-December, just in time for the season's first snowfall, a FOR SALE – UNIT 6 placard materialised on a post outside. Moyle's aunt had evidently decided to divest herself of the murder scene – the place where 'no one's ever seen anything like it'.

Notwithstanding her lingering uncertainty as to the extent of her own involvement, there was no question that Cat's life improved immeasurably. Night after night she slept so soundly that her energy reserves were rapidly restored. It was true, she suddenly became acutely conscious of other disruptions – birds, distant traffic, the rattling blind, the ticking clock – and was irritated by things she doubted she would have noticed if Moyle were still alive. But overall the change was dramatic. She resumed her morning swims at the

Drumsheugh Baths. She went for runs in the chilly late autumn evenings and virtually bounded up the leaf-cluttered sidewalks. Her skin cleared. The circles under her eyes faded. Her hair regained its lustre. Her complexion brightened. Her eyes sparkled.

'Hell's bells, Cat, you look *fantastic*.' It was Agnes, being ambiguous again.

'I feel better, that's for sure,' Cat admitted.

'I told you you wouldn't regret it. At this rate we'll be a team again in no time.'

Indeed, Cat was aiming to get back on the road as soon as possible. Her performance as departmental analyst had been immaculate. She was precise. She was focused. She anticipated all problems and attended to matters that even Jenny McLeish hadn't found time to complete. She was determined to make Wing Commander Bellamy acknowledge her improvement, even if it was against his own will.

'Let me know when I can get back on track,' she told him. 'There are a few things I'd like to look into.'

'Such as?'

'Our Credit Cards Department, for one.'

'Credit Cards isn't in your domain.'

'Not yet, but I'd like to look into it anyway.'

'Ambitious, aren't you?' Bellamy wasn't looking at her directly 'Your bank in Miami wasn't wrong about that.'

'Well, please consider it in any case. Those circumstances I mentioned – the matters that were holding me back – they're not a problem now.'

'Hmm.'

Cat wasn't sure if Bellamy had heard about 'the mysterious death in Dean Village'. But she sensed that he was disconcerted by her new radiance. And her directness. What she left unsaid was that she'd already commenced discreet investigations into the unwanted credit card, and – as a stalling gesture – had written to Mr Dennis Napier, the loyal customer from Dundee, promising that the matter would be 'comprehensively investigated and any developments forwarded at the appropriate time'.

It was Christmas now: the air stung her face, the sidewalks were slippery with ice, and the hours of daylight were absurdly contracted. But the wintry atmospheres – filtered light, skeletal trees, silhouetted tenements – combined to summon delightful memories of her first visit to the city when she was eight. She spent many evenings just strolling the streets, glorying in the Yuletide extravagance. She had never really cared for Christmas – the mandatory good cheer, the grotesque commercialisation – but she had to admit that this year she felt at peace with the world. Especially when it snowed. Especially when she heard carols being trilled in the parks. And most of all when she saw kids capering around with unequivocal joy.

But how long could it last? How long does the world allow *anything* unequivocal to last?

The very next night, as it happened, she heard footsteps upstairs. The oily voice of a solicitor or estate agent or whatever. Someone – a potential buyer or two – was enjoying a private viewing. When they departed, Cat rushed to the bedroom window for a look. A well-dressed middle-aged couple – investors, she guessed – were folding themselves into a silver Mercedes and gliding away.

It was an uncomfortable reminder that sooner or later there would be a new tenant. Someone who might even be worse – difficult as that was to imagine – than the unlamented Moyle. Maybe a whole hard-rock band this time, practising every night. Maybe an elderly couple who trundled to the bathroom every half-hour and played their TV at the highest possible volume. Maybe a homicidal maniac who shouted profanities and hurled things against the walls. Maybe a tap dancer. A salty old sailor with a wooden leg. An amateur boxer who liked to skip rope. Someone with a couple of boisterous dogs. A movie geek with a home cinema and a passion for war films. Maybe a whole hard-up family – kids running around squealing and rolling toys across the floor. There was even the terrible possibility that the place might be turned into a holiday let. Half the apartments in central Edinburgh were that way, apparently. Long-term residents were losing their minds. Unruly tourists dragging their wheeled luggage over the setts, buzzing the wrong flat, dropping keys and banging doors, crashing around as they looked for the heating controls, heading out late and coming home later, shagging each other silly, letting the kids go berserk, doing their laundry in the middle of the night, leaving piles of garbage in the hallway – you name it – before packing up and vanishing, never to be seen again.

Was it too much to ask for a Trappist monk? A mime artist? A retired ballerina? A reclusive millionaire who used the place for just a few weeks every year? Or would she have to go back to Aileanach Castle and put in another request?

During an open inspection the following weekend Cat, posing as an interested buyer, ventured into Number Six for the very first time. She saw the bathroom where Moyle had bumbled about and peed noisily into his toilet. The kitchenette where he'd banged his pots and dropped cutlery on the floor. The tiny box room where his washing machine had thumped and screeched through its cycles. The notorious bedroom, directly above her own, where he'd tossed his boots on the floor and *twanged* his electric guitar. The living area where he'd hauled chairs across the floorboards. She even thought she could discern the large blotch where he'd bled out . . . not unlike the bloodstain of David Rizzio, secretary to Mary Queen of Scots, that was supposedly visible in the Palace of Holyrood.

'Any idea why the place is being sold?' she asked, as casually as possible

The agent – a young guy in tortoiseshell glasses with lenses so thin and clear they could only be fake – looked taken aback. 'I think the old lady who owned the flat is liquidating some assets.'

'Then can you tell me who's shown the most interest in buying it?'

'We've had a good deal of interest.'

'I always like to have an idea of my competition, though.'

'Well, most of the interest has been from investors.'

'Investors . . .'

'Out of town investors. Mainly from the Asian market. This is a very popular area for investors.'

Cat's spirits drained. Unless the agent was just talking the property up, the 'holiday let' scenario was still very much alive. Definitely the rental property scenario. Which could easily mean a rolling succession of university students throwing twice-weekly parties – or something even worse.

She wished she had enough money to buy the place herself. She could swap it for her own flat, she guessed, but the place wasn't as roomy as hers (what with the slanted ceilings and all), and for that matter she didn't really fancy living in a murder scene. But that thought only made her wonder if she could scare potential buyers away with the place's history. By erecting a sign? Positioning herself at the bottom of the stairs and casually informing everybody who came for an inspection? Or could she get Maxine, the professional tour guide, to start a Ghost Walk that included the building in its itinerary?

Her best bet, she decided in the end, was to make herself known to the new buyer as soon as the place was sold, then lobby for some changes before any tenants moved in. Rugs for the floors?

New carpet? Maybe a tradesman could screw down the creaking floorboards? Or some sort of sound insulation could be installed under the floor? All to be financed out of her own bank account?

Then, two weeks into the new year, the dreaded UNDER OFFER sticker appeared across the FOR SALE sign.

According to Cat's still-limited knowledge of Scottish real estate procedures, this meant that an official bid had been received and accepted, pending legalities, but could still be gazumped by an even larger offer. The whole process could still take months – or so she hoped.

A few days later, however, the FOR SALE sign came down completely. And the listing disappeared from the property websites.

Oh well, Cat thought, there's still a settlement period – that could take months as well.

But then, in early February, on a Saturday afternoon so bright and cheery that it virtually commanded her to go for a stroll, she heard noises in Number Six.

Shifting to her bedroom window she saw a van parked outside. A couple of removal guys in overalls were unloading some stylish furniture: a mid-century sofa set, a standing lamp, some mahogany bookcases. She heard them going up and down the stairs and lowering everything into place. After such a long absence, the return of the *creaks* and *klonks* and *nnnnnnhhhhrrrrrrrrs* was particularly distressing.

But what about the new tenant(s)? Cat could see no sign of him/her/them. Just the removal guys. Feeling ridiculous, she got down on her knees and tried peering through one of the Chubb keyholes. But again, all she saw was the movers. She decided that the new owner must be preparing the flat for letting, and wondered if she should ask the moving guys for details. But no sooner had she resolved to approach them than their van disappeared.

She got a text message from Maxine:

Is that a new tenant moving in?

To which she replied:

Not sure, will let you know.

She waited half an hour but heard nothing more. She went out for a long walk along the Union Canal – which despite the sunlight wore a thin coat of ice – but was too keyed-up to enjoy herself. When she got home she thought she heard more squeaks and clicks from upstairs but wasn't sure – it might have been her imagination. She did her ironing. Scrubbed the bathroom floor. Read a book about the Kennedy assassination. Watched a David Attenborough documentary about warring chimpanzees. Cooked *spaghetti alla puttanesca*. Flipped through her folders on Scottish banking procedures.

She was trying to absorb the impenetrable jargon when she thought she heard movement – *creak creak creak* – but again decided she was imagining things. It sounded more like a mouse than a human being.

But that night she had a sense, close to a certainty, that there was someone in the bedroom directly over her head. She heard nothing until three a.m., however, when her hair-trigger senses detected a loud *shhhhhhhhhhhh,* like a tap being operated. She jolted awake and listened. But nothing after that.

In the morning she was surprised by a new text from Maxine:

Seen his MG? Stylish!

Cat had no idea what she was talking about until she heard an engine growling outside. She raced to the window and saw a canary-yellow roadster with wire-spoke wheels pulling out from Number Six's parking space. She couldn't make out the driver – the black canvas top was up – but the very fact that the car was heading out, rather than heading in, suggested that its owner had indeed slept upstairs.

But that didn't make sense. How could anyone, let alone a newcomer, spend a whole night in the flat and make such little noise?

She decided she must be mistaken – the sportscar must belong to an interior designer or something – and late in the afternoon she headed out to do some shopping. At the supermarket she loaded up on healthy foods – she'd long weaned herself off the coffee and microwave meals she'd favoured during Moyle's tenancy – and was returning home through the darkening streets when she noticed the MG back in the parking space of Number Six.

Disconcerted, she was halfway up the stairs, loaded shopping bag in one hand and keys in the other, when she heard someone closing a door above. And coming down the stairs. It could only be the new tenant. She braced herself – as for a catastrophic collision – and met him for the first time under the flickering stairwell light.

'Oh, hi there,' he said. 'You must be my new neighbour.'

He was tanned, black-and-silver-haired, honey-eyed, denim-shirted and English-accented – wickedly handsome and yet strangely, disturbingly familiar.

'Yes, yes,' Cat said. 'Pleased to meet you.'

'I'm Robin Boucher – delighted to meet you too. I hope I didn't disturb you last night?'

'Sorry?'

'Moving in, moving around – all that?'

'No, no, not at all.'

'Glad to hear it. I noticed one of the water pipes clangs like a bell. I'll get it fixed as soon as possible. And the floorboards need a little bit of adjustment – I'll get them fixed as well.'

'That's . . . that's very thoughtful of you.'

'Think nothing of it. I lived for a while under a noisy neighbour and it made my life hell. So it's the least I can do.'

'I must admit,' said Cat, 'that I've had some problems. There's virtually nothing between you and me, you see.'

'Then I'll do my best to tread softly. And in the meantime, if you have any complaints, just let me know and I'll see what I can do. This light needs replacing too, by the looks of it.'

'Oh yes' – she saw that he was indicating the malfunctioning stair light – 'I've tried fixing it myself but I can't get the cover off.'

'You need the right screwdriver. I'll have a look at it later. Where are the bins around here, by the way?'

'Sorry?'

'The rubbish bins,' he said. 'The recycling bins.'

'Oh yeah, yeah – there's a black Dumpster near the transmission box and the recycling bins are down on the corner, near the bridge.'

'Excellent,' said Boucher, with a dazzling smile. 'Well, I'll be seeing you around, I hope.'

'It's inevitable,' said Cat, smiling back.

He whisked past in a swirl of oaky cologne before wheeling around with a final thought.

'Must say, it's amazingly beautiful here,' he said. 'I feel so fortunate to have snared the place for such a reasonable price.'

'So you're the owner?' Cat said. 'Not a renter?'

'The owner, yes. Lucky I'm not superstitious, eh?'

'Superstitious?'

'You know, what with all that happened up there? To that poor fellow who was carved into a thousand pieces?'

He had a mischievous glint in his eyes. And Cat wondered how on earth he could have learned the details of Moyle's death. And why on earth he didn't seem remotely bothered about it. But she was too intoxicated – by his charisma, his cologne, his irresistible presence – to ask any questions, or feel anything but a recurring stab of guilt.

'Oh, that,' she said dismissively. 'Yeah, that was an odd story.'

'Well,' he said, still with a tawny gleam in his eyes, 'I'll catch you later. We must have a coffee sometime.'

'I'd like that,' said Cat, surprising herself by just how much she meant it.

And then he was down the stairs, out of sight, and the stair door was clicking neatly behind him.

Back in her flat Cat dumped her shopping on the kitchen table and had to pause for a few moments to deal with her feelings. The breathlessness. The constriction in her throat. The sense of weightlessness. It was as though she'd been electrocuted.

She couldn't remember the last time she'd felt that – if she'd *ever* felt that – and wasn't sure she liked it.

CHAPTER
TWO

'A YOUNGER GEORGE CLOONEY!' exclaimed Agnes, laughing delightedly. 'Well, then – it's a dream come true, right?'

Cat shook her head. 'I wouldn't say he looked *exactly* like Clooney. Just that he has the same little beard that Clooney sometimes has, the same haircut, the same twinkle in his eyes, the same sort of "sly observer" look. But that's all. He doesn't really look like *any* man I've seen before.'

It was 26 February and the two women were squeezed into a corner booth of a crowded Irish pub near Lauriston Place. Outside, a brutal horizontal sleet was raking down the street; inside, a fog of exhalations and effluvium had misted the already smoky windows.

'What colour are his eyes?' Agnes asked. 'His twinkling George Clooney eyes?'

'This weird amber colour, like autumn leaves in sunlight. I've never seen anything like it.'

Agnes guffawed. 'And his teeth? You can tell a lot about a man by his teeth.'

'Very neat, very white – and the sharpest canines I've ever seen.'

'All the better to bite you with.'

'*No*,' Cat said. 'I told you not to get the wrong idea. I'm only curious because there's something not quite right about him, that's all. Do you know he fixed the light?'

'What light?'

'There was this flickering light in the stairwell. It's been that way ever since I moved in. And he just looked it, said he'd fix it, and the next thing I knew he *did*.'

'Right,' said Agnes, 'and that's weird because—?'

'Well, it's unusual, that's all. Plus he's super quiet. So quiet it's uncanny. I mean, supernatural. I've never even heard him flush the toilet. Is that strange or not?'

'Maybe he pisses in his pot plants.'

'And he seems to know everything about me.'

'How so?'

'At our second meeting he was already calling me Cat – even though I'm sure I never told him my name.'

'He probably saw an envelope addressed to you – you said it was a communal mailbox, didn't you?'

'But I never get any mail addressed to "Cat".'

'Probably one of the neighbours mentioned you, then.'

'But he also made a sort-of reference to Florida – "You'd know all about heat, where you're from" – and I'm positive I've never told anyone in the building where I came from.'

'Maybe he just pinpointed you from your accent.'

'What is he, Henry Higgins?'

'Well, he probably just assumes that America is warmer than Scotland.' Agnes, reaching for her Guinness, sighed in frustration. 'I mean, shit, don't you think you're being a wee bit analytical, girl?'

'I prefer to think of it as common sense. He's living right above me, isn't he? And yet I know virtually nothing about him. He's neat, he's very well ordered, and he has great taste in décor, but—'

'*Décor*? How the hell do you know that?'

'I saw inside his apartment and—'

'You saw *inside* his apartment?'

'He invited me in for coffee.'

Agnes nearly snorted into her Guinness. 'For coffee? For *coffee*? You know what that means, don't you?'

'It means coffee,' Cat insisted. 'It *meant* coffee. I came up the stairs just as he was seeing some delivery guys out. He said, "Why not come in and have a look at what I've done to the place?" – and I did.'

'Was he wearing a silk dressing gown and smoking a pipe?'

'Nothing like that. I had a look around – the place is amazingly well-furnished, I don't know where all the stuff came from – and he served up a coffee, that's all.'

'From a Nespresso machine?'

'Look, I don't know what it was from – he already had something brewing.'

'I bet he did,' said Agnes, sniggering. 'He was doing some groundwork. Cat, I don't really need to tell you that, do I?'

'If that's his game, then he chose the wrong girl. I'm not suggestible. And I mean that. Hypnotists can tell it about me in twenty seconds. I'm not suggestible.'

'Being seduced isn't the same as being hypnotised, you know.'

'Of course it is – it's a complete loss of control. So is falling in love.'

'Have you ever been in love?'

'I'm not sure.'

'Then you've never been in love and you've no idea what you're talking about.'

'Possibly,' Cat conceded, not unhappily. 'Anyway, I tried to find out as much I could, as politely as possible, but he was evasive about everything. Didn't want to talk about himself and always turned the conversation back on to me. He was very good at it – better than anyone I've ever interviewed.'

'Where's he from – did he say that much?'

'From London somewhere.'

'With a posh accent?' Agnes affected a plummy voice: *'Oh, how charming it is to make your acquaintance.'*

'Nothing like that. Sounds regular upper middle-class to me. From his voice alone I'd have trouble saying where in England he comes from.'

'Not Oxbridge-educated, I hope?'

'You mean Oxford?'

'I mean Oxbridge – you've still got a lot to learn, girl. They hate us, you know.'

'Who does?'

'The born-to-rule crowd. The red trousers and raspberries set. Oh, they make the right noises but they always revert to type. The working classes, Northerners, Scots – they despise us. Boy, do we need another independence referendum.'

'Well, I know nothing about that,' said Cat, faintly annoyed by the digression. 'But I'm not convinced that anything he told me, even the stuff about London, is true. So I tried looking into his financial history and—'

Agnes laughed explosively. 'You looked into his financial history? You snake in the grass! You know what the Wing Commander would do if he found out?'

'I know, I know, I'm not proud of it. But my curiosity got the better of me.'

'Of course it did. Because you have no interest at all in this guy, right?'

'Call it a need-to-know thing,' Cat said. 'If he knows so much about me then it's only right that I should find out as much as possible about him.'

'Aye right. So, what did you find?'

'There are seven account holders in the UK named Robin Boucher, three of them in the London area. An author, an MD, a physiotherapist – but not one who matches the details of the guy upstairs.'

'Age, occupation, that type of thing?'

'Uh-huh. So I have to wonder if he's lying to me again. If he lies to everyone. But why?'

'Maybe he doesn't hold a bank account.'

'Possibly. I'd check his police record but I fear that's going too far.'

'Want me to do it?'

'Could you?' Cat asked. 'I'd ask Terry Grimes – I'm sure he'd help me out, no problem – but I don't want it getting back to Bellamy. It's taken me long enough to climb a few rungs on the ladder and I know he'd just love to kick me down again.'

'The fud. Sure, I can request a check for you, but are you sure you really want to know? I mean, this guy sounds like a dreamboat. Considerate, a handyman, movie-star looks – what more do you want?'

'I want a neighbour I can trust, that's all.'

'Jesus, girl, what's the matter with you? I know you had some awful experiences in your childhood, but why let that dominate your life? You've got to *live* a little, lassie.'

'I'm not at all sure what you're talking about, but this has got nothing to do with my past.'

'Well, don't tell me you wouldn't fancy a good shag? *Look* at you, girl – if I were you, I'd never stop shagging. I'd shag you myself if you'd only give me a chance.'

Cat was grateful that the pub's hubbub was drowning them out. 'If you're saying I look after myself physically—'

'That's exactly what I'm saying.'

'Well, that's only because I believe exercise and good nutrition are essential for your health.'

'Aye right, and it's purely for your health that you run around town in those sprayed-on tights.'

'You've seen me out running?'

'My spies are everywhere.'

Cat found the idea unnerving. 'I brought those pants from Florida, where they're about the only type of running pants you can buy. I'm not flaunting my glutes, whatever you might think.'

'Your glutes? Your *glutes*? Good grief, girl, can you not even bring yourself to say *arse*? Or *ass* or *butt* – or whatever it is you people say?'

Cat sighed. 'Just find out what you can, will you?'

'Your wish is my command,' Agnes said, laughing. 'But first I'm going to ring up Ladbrokes and see if they'll take a wager. A thousand to one that you're not under Cock Robin's duvet by the end of the next month.'

'Don't be absurd. Don't be absurd.'

Cat almost added that she'd accept the odds herself but at the last second decided against it.

★ ★ ★

Back home that night she again found it difficult to believe, despite the insistent presence of Boucher's MG, that anyone was home upstairs. There were no creaks, no hisses, no clanging pipes, no TV murmurings, nothing. Yet for some reason his *presence* was overwhelming. Cat even found herself lowering the volume on her TV and tiptoeing around so she would go unnoticed by *him*. It was absurd. When she dropped a pot while cooking she flinched like an assassin who'd accidentally snapped a twig.

Even in bed she couldn't shake the notion that he was lying prostrate on his own mattress, hovering over her, staring down at her. It was so discomfiting that she rolled onto her side and drew herself into a ball. But then, in the pin-drop silence close to midnight, she heard what sounded like the stair door being eased shut. And maybe footfall on the steps. And maybe a key turning in the lock upstairs (she had to strain to hear it). A maybe a door gently closing. And then – definitely – the sound of a board or two creaking ever so unobtrusively above.

So Boucher had been out after all.

This thought should have settled her. It should have given her cause for self-rebuke. But it only got her mind racing again. Where had he been? What had he been doing? Why was he so secretive? And how did he achieve such ungodly silence?

Her increasingly fantastical solutions – at one stage she had him pinned as a cat burglar, at another he had morphed into a vampire – kept her awake into the wee hours and eventually took root in her dreams.

CHAPTER

THREE

TWO WEEKS LATER CAT WAS RETURNING early from work when she caught a glimpse of Boucher, stylishly attired in a black knee-length coat with flared collar, striking out from Dean Village in the direction of the city centre.

It had already been, to say the least, an interesting day. Though officially she was still helming Jenny McLeish's desk, Cat had built up enough credibility to have Bellamy grudgingly allow her to check out ABC's Credit Cards Department. Along with the IT, Forex and Marketing departments, this was located in a charmless steel-and-glass cube in a business zone near the airport. She'd taken the tram – someone more important was using her VW – and identified the right building by a giant gnome in the ornamental pool outside (a moneybox in the shape of a gnome had been ABC's advertising symbol for decades). She introduced herself at reception and found the admin manager – a man bearing the improbable name of Carter Carterius – wearing a bow tie, a dress handkerchief and the fussy air of a museum curator. After just nine months in Edinburgh, Cat recognised him instantly as belonging to that curious sub-species of Scot more desperately British than the toffiest Pall Mall club man. Thus she knew that his persona – stiff, reserved and openly uncooperative – was a flimsy construct that would collapse under the slightest pressure. When, for instance, he pointed out that the department already had its internal investigation team she promptly laid on the charm, insisting that since the complaint in this instance – the letter from Mr Dennis Napier of Dundee – had first been lodged with Internal Fraud she was compelled to follow it through. There was simply no way around it. No way at all. She demanded to consult their files.

With conspicuous reluctance Carterius granted her access, by first entering his password, to the department's computer records. Here, after an intensive search through a labyrinth of irrelevancy, Cat confirmed that Mr Napier's account had been activated some seven months earlier, about the time the second card was sent to his former address in Glenrothes.

She turned to Carterius. 'I'm afraid this isn't much good to me. There's no record of who activated the credit card account I'm interested in.'

'What makes you think there would be a record?'

Cat blinked. 'I don't understand. Where I come from activation usually requires the authorisation of a senior officer.'

'I think you'll find there are many procedural differences between here and America.'

'You're saying that authorisation is just waved through?'

Carterius became defensive. 'Well, as you know, ABC only changed its credit card issuer four years ago.'

'Uh-huh.' She had no idea.

'And as part of the switchover process from Visa to Cosmos certain procedures were, shall we say, "loosened". To encourage customer take-up, you understand.'

'Right. So *anyone* in here could have activated this card?'

'Provided the customer has been with the bank for more than

two years and has a balance in excess of two thousand pounds, yes.'

'I see,' said Cat. 'May I use one of your phones?'

'I beg your pardon?'

'I need to make a call. And I'd prefer to use a landline.'

'Well . . . I can't stop you.'

'Excellent. I won't be long.'

Cat was directed to an empty desk in the corner, where she phoned the manager of the Glenrothes branch. But since he was tied up with a customer she had to settle for a senior accountant. She started by asking him if he was familiar with a customer services clerk called Violet Ross – the one who'd set up Mr Napier's savings account in the first place – and found him refreshingly blunt.

'Sure, I remember Violet. Dumb as a box of frogs.'

'She's no longer with you?'

'She got the flick last year. Nobody misses her.'

'Didn't pull her weight . . . shirked duties?'

'You could say that.'

'Any suggestion she had a history of pushing unwanted credit cards on customers?'

'Everyone did that. When Cosmos took over we were *encouraged* to do that.'

'So there's no reason to believe that Violet herself was crooked?'

'Violet Ross is too dumb to be crooked. You're from Frauds, did you say?'

'That's right.'

'And American?'

'That's right.'

'New to ABC?'

'Pretty new.'

'Then if I were you, I'd be looking at the Dunns, not some half-baked customer services clerk from Glenrothes.'

Cat frowned. 'The Dunns?'

The accountant made a sound of grim amusement. 'You don't know about His Satanic Majesty? And his junior demons?'

'Excuse me?'

'Alistair Dunn? Managing director of ABC? You must've seen his portrait in the lobby of the Aquarium?'

'I . . . think so,' Cat said.

'Sits in a throne room on the top floor. His son Craig Dunn is in Business Management. There's a daughter in HR. And another son in Credit Cards.'

'In Credit Cards?' Cat looked around the office but the staff didn't appear to be taking much notice of her.

'Sure. He's the one you should be investigating if you're looking for funny business.'

'I see.' She chose her words carefully. 'And do you remember the name of this gentleman, by any chance?'

'The one in Credit Cards? It's Mungo Dunn. Face like a slapped arse.'

Mungo Dunn. Sounded to Cat like a Flash Gordon villain. 'Well, I thank you for your cooperation. You've been unusually informative.'

'I'm leaving next week to manage an insecticide company, so I can afford to be.'

Cat experienced a brief, searing flashback to the day she had exterminated the insects in her cousins' backyard. She got off the phone and sat in place, pretending to consult something in the computer files. She hadn't felt her hair prickle like this since the hotel scam. But she needed to be cautious. She might have been too indiscreet already.

Finally she went back to Carterius's office and plonked herself in front of his desk.

'OK,' she said, 'here's what I want. A list of all your employees in this department for the past three years. Performance evaluations, responsibilities, authorisation levels, the works. There are hard copies of this, right? And before you say I should go to HR I'm telling you that I don't want to do that and I can't say why. And as to why I should trust you of all people, when you've been such a jerk to me, let me just say that it's exactly because you've been a jerk that I trust you. If you had something to hide you'd be unctuously ingratiating, at least initially – that's a given. And before you say, "Who do you think you are?" – I can see your jaw dropping right now – let's just say I have contacts in high places in this organisation, contacts that saw me invited from the US precisely to swoop into places like this and order people like you around. So let's get this ball bouncing, huh?'

She arched her eyebrows and flashed her incisors and generally hoped she hadn't overdone it – the last panoply of lies in particular – but her gung-ho performance seemed to do the trick. After he'd gained control of his jaw, Carterius swallowed, blinked several times and launched out of his chair.

'Give me a minute,' he said hoarsely. 'I'll fetch whatever we have.'

The records – old-fashioned printouts to prevent computer hacking – came in four cardboard box files. Cat retreated to the side of Carterius's office, snapped shut the venetians, and hunted for details on Mungo Dunn. And there he was. Twenty-nine years old, born in Edinburgh, clean but undistinguished performance record, currently chief supervisor of Credit Card Operations. On a hunch Cat leafed through the files of the previous chief supervisor – some guy fifty-five years old and distinctly better qualified.

She turned to Carterius. 'What level is chief supervisor here? Relative to you?'

'It's a different job entirely,' Carterius said stiffly. 'My job is to manage the department vis-à-vis the bank itself and its relationship with the credit card issuer.'

'And the chief supervisor?'

'Just day-to-day operations.'

'*Just* day-to-day operations?'

'That's correct – minutiae.' He made it sound like an insult.

'Minutiae such as credit card approvals, that sort of thing?'

'That sort of thing, yes.'

'Right,' Cat said. 'So where is he now? Mr Mungo Minutiae?'

Carterius seemed taken aback. 'If you mean Mr Dunn, well' – he glanced at his watch – 'I believe he should be back any moment now.'

'Out to lunch, is he?'

'I believe so.'

'OK, well' – Cat checked her own watch – 'it's now three thirty-five. When did this lunch begin?'

'I've no idea.'

Cat knew Carterius was lying. And she wondered who was really in charge of the department. But she chose not to prod him.

'Just one more thing. You said there'd been a switchover in credit card issuers. Can you tell me what sort of liability Cosmos shares with ABC? Equal, right?'

'Oh no,' Carterius said haughtily. 'That was part of the deal. A renegotiation of terms of liability.'

'So the answer is . . .'

'The bank has zero liability for ten years.'

'*Zero* liability?'

'Cosmos is a new issuer. That was part of their incentive.'

Cat was stunned. But it made sense all the same. Credit card issuers, especially new ones, have an insatiable appetite for sign-ups. But their security-slackening incentives make them vulnerable to all manner of fraud.

'Well,' said Cat, keeping her surprise to herself, 'it seems I've got a lot to work with, Mr Carterius, and thanks again for your cooperation. I'll call you directly if I have any need for further enquiries. In the meantime, I'll rely on you not to mention my investigation to anyone – here or anywhere else.'

'Naturally.'

When they parted at the office door, Carterius looked hopeful. 'Can I take it,' he asked hesitantly, 'that this investigation of yours involves some activity of Mr Dunn's?'

She almost laughed at the shine in his eyes. But it was good – it might even prove useful. 'And can I take it that wouldn't be the worst thing in the world to you?'

Carterius's expression told her everything she needed to know. 'Let me just say I'm happy to assist in any way,' he said. Then he opened the door.

On the way out Cat registered furtive glances from departmental staff and took a mental note of every face. When the elevator arrived, a pudgy red-headed fellow reeking of booze squeezed past, stifling a belch with a fist. Cat was about to enter the lift when a suspicion nailed her to the spot. She swung around.

'Mr Dunn? Mr Mungo Dunn?'

The red-haired man, a half smile on his florid face, fixed her with his gimlet eyes. 'Aye?'

'A pleasure to meet you,' she said, thrusting out a hand. 'I'm Cat Thomas from Internal Fraud.'

His grip was firm but moist. 'Nothing going on that I should know about?' he asked, still smiling.

'Oh no – I'm just new here and wanted to establish a good relationship with your department from the get-go.'

'Who did you meet with? Carter Carterius?'

'That's right.'

'Well, that's a good start, but if you have any queries relating to fraudulent activity I'm really the one to speak to.'

'Mr Carterius said something to that effect.'

'Did he now? Well then, we're on excellent terms already.' Dunn looked her up and down approvingly. 'I look forward to liaising with you, Ms – you'll forgive me?'

'Ms Thomas.'

'Aye.' A satisfied grunt. 'So we're hiring Americans now? That's an improvement, I must say.'

Cat chuckled. 'The circumstances were fairly unique.'

'I'll ask my sister about it – she's in HR, you know.'

'Really? Nice watch, by the way.'

'This thing?' He glanced at his chunky gold Patek Philippe. 'Just something my old man – Alistair Dunn, you know – gave to me.'

'I've only got a Swatch – see?' She angled her wrist.

'Well, it's Swiss, so you're off to a good start.'

Unctuously ingratiating, Cat thought in the elevator. A twenty-nine-year-old, boozy-lunchtime, unctuously ingratiating chief supervisor in a silk tie, a bespoke suit and sickly-sweet cologne. She didn't regret introducing herself – better that than letting him hear about her from others – but she wondered if she'd gone too far in admiring his watch. Not that she could do much about it now.

She rode the tram back to Queensferry Street and was still in a combative mood, yearning for answers, when she entered Dean Village via the Belford Road steps. Pausing on the riverside path to help a couple of beaming Italian-sounding tourists take a photo of the old Holy Trinity Church – which floated high over the village like some vision of Camelot – she noticed the darkly garbed Robin Boucher whisking across the old stone bridge not a hundred metres away. Cat felt an unusual frisson – which must have showed in her face, or her bearing, because the Italians tittered – and was on the verge of resuming progress to her flat when a new impulse seized her.

Submitting, yet again, to the compulsion to solve a mystery, she thrust the camera back to the tourists and headed up the riverside path, desperate to catch sight of Boucher before he slipped out of sight.

She had the curious impression that the Italians were snapping photos of her as she left.

CHAPTER

FOUR

OUCHER WAS ON THE PAVEMENT near the top of Bell's Brae, the steep incline leading east out of Dean Village. He had his hands buried in his pockets and was moving at a smooth but purposeful pace, almost gliding over the flagstones. Maintaining a distance of roughly eighty metres, Cat followed him up to Queensferry Road.

She knew it was crazy – literally stalking now – but she had never been so intrigued by a man. And she had to trust her instincts on the matter. Besides, Boucher had done everything imaginable to invite speculation about himself: through his evasiveness, his solicitousness, his supernatural unobtrusiveness – through the very fact that he seemed *too good to be true*.

In fact, when Cat had belatedly received a letter from Building Standards announcing that the acting surveyor had located enough time to pay her a visit, she felt obliged to respond that 'the matter in question has been resolved for now'. This was not without risk – she had no way of knowing how long Boucher would be so considerate – but at the same time she couldn't imagine presenting her neighbour with an order to attend to his flat's soundproofing just six weeks after he had taken ownership of it. Even if there was every possibility that he'd be just as accommodating as he'd always been.

Presently, having deftly weaved between the traffic on Lynedoch Place, Boucher curled into Randolph Crescent and the elegant environs of the New Town. This was a region of Georgian town-houses with ornate iron railings, glinting plaques and sparkling windows – the homes and offices of well-to-do lawyers, doctors, architects, bankers and sharp businesspeople. So Cat had to wonder if Boucher had a local destination in mind – something that might explain, finally, the mystery of his wealth and circumstances.

As Agnes had already established, no one matching his name, origin and description had a criminal record. No amount of internal investigation, by Cat herself, could uncover any hidden bank accounts. He rarely, if ever, received any correspondence in the mail. He seldom seemed to leave the building. And yet he had enough capital to purchase a not-inexpensive apartment, to maintain a classic MG, and to furnish his rooms with an impressive collection of antique furniture, original artworks, and bookcases bursting with priceless volumes.

When he turned up the hill towards Charlotte Square – a cheer-less sun painted the street behind him with a huge spidery shadow – Cat briefly wondered if he was about to visit the residence of the First Minister. If he had some secretive role at the highest levels of Scottish government. But even as she became increasingly excited – and daunted – by the prospect, he cut a right-angle through the square and headed for bustling Princes Street.

Perhaps he was on a shopping expedition, then. It was Thursday, after all, and the stores were open late. But as it happened Boucher did not digress into any of the shops. He did not even glance in their windows. He darted across the road to the Gardens side, under the Castle, and weaved between the workers lined up for peak-hour buses. He was so graceful in his movements, so swift of pace, that

Cat struggled to keep him in sight. But every time she thought he might have eluded her – purposely? – he appeared again: the winged black collar, the slick side-parted hair, the princely bearing.

When he ascended the Playfair Stairs into the Old Town and veered up the winding incline of Cockburn Street, Cat for the first time was struck by the notion that he might be making for a dinner engagement. With a business associate? A spymaster? A lover?

It was surprising how much the last prospect rattled her. And this when she assured herself constantly that she wasn't really into him. The fact that she had added a full mile to her nightly run and two hundred sit-ups to her exercise routine – that was only because she now had considerably more energy and endurance. The fact that she had become increasingly conscious of her calorie intake – well, such disciplines are easier to observe when one is otherwise content. And the way she dressed up as if for church simply to put out the rubbish – well, there were psychological benefits in always being presentable.

But she could hardly explain away the way she continued to listen intently for his movements upstairs. That she repeatedly contrived to run into him in the stairwell. That he regularly appeared in her dreams.

When Boucher turned left into the Royal Mile, Cat prepared herself for the sight of him turning into a cosy eatery or boutique pub and settling in for a romantic meal. Maybe she'd even spot him, through the window, taking someone into his arms. There was, after all, no obvious reason why he would be unattached. He was charming, thoughtful, tasteful, intelligent, stylish and clearly of independent means. Cat couldn't imagine a more perfect partner. And the idea that others hadn't thought likewise was preposterous. So why did he live alone? Why did no man, woman or beast climb the stairway to his apartment? Why did she never hear him hosting anyone? Cooking a meal for two? Playing a romantic ballad? Engaged in lovemaking? Was he recovering from a traumatic relationship? Was he 'between drinks'? Uncommonly choosy? A brothel creeper? Or was he, like her, so devoted to self-reliance that he didn't *need* to share his life with anyone?

Alas, the last notion only made him even more attractive – and frustrating – to Cat, who sighed so loudly that a passer-by shot her a quizzical glance.

When he went beyond the Royal Mile into Holyrood Park she started to wonder if he was merely enjoying an evening constitutional, very much as she sometimes liked to do. And though this notion endeared him to her even further, she feared that the wide-open spaces of the volcanic ruins – empty of all but dog-walkers, cyclists and a couple of hill-running clubs out for their evening training – would make it even more difficult to go unnoticed. She considered giving up. It was getting foolish now. And yet she continued following.

He skirted the park at top pace and started heading south around the Salisbury Crags. And downwards. He looked for all the world like he was heading for the Innocent Railway.

This path, which Cat had stumbled upon during one of her early rambles around Edinburgh, is a former train track incorporating a 520-metre tunnel just south of Arthur's Seat. Plying it for the first time in the middle of the day, Cat's only thought had been never to come back in the dark.

Did Boucher intend to head back into the city via the tunnel? Or continue down the open path toward Duddingston? Either direction would leave Cat painfully exposed. And night was encroaching rapidly.

But still she couldn't help herself. She counted off thirty seconds – giving him enough time to gain some ground – and then followed him down the incline.

When she came to the Innocent Railway, however, she found that he was nowhere to be seen. He was not in the gun-barrel tunnel itself. But neither was he visible anywhere on the walled-in path. And these were the only two directions possible. Unless he had sprouted wings? Or ducked into some hiding place she wasn't aware of?

She hesitated for a few moments – looking left, looking right, glancing up at the corrugated cliff face of Samson's Ribs – before deciding the time had come, finally, to concede defeat. A cyclist whizzed past and plunged into the tunnel.

Cat followed him in. Some of the sodium lamps in the ceiling had blown and she walked through alternating light and darkness. The walls were covered with lurid graffiti of huge phalluses and horned devil faces. She was still in her work shoes, low-heeled but nevertheless enough to create an echo.

Clack clack clack clack.

Plink plink plink – the slow drip of water leaking through cracks in the ceiling.

And the hiss of the cyclist passing through puddles ahead.

She was a third of the way through when she noticed something on the walls.

DER MENSCH IST GOTT.

And on the other side: GOTT IST DER MENSCH.

She had heard these same lines uttered aloud, she was sure, during her delirium at Castle Aileanach: *'Man is God! God is Man!'*

Ahead, the cyclist shot out of the tunnel, leaving her all alone.

Clack clack clack clack.

Plink plink plink.

And now, halfway through, another sound.

Shwee shwee schwee shwee.

It was a counterpointing footfall behind her. But whereas in other circumstances she would have glanced around to make certain, she was inhibited now by the notion that it belonged to Boucher.

Clack clack clack clack.

And *shwee shwee shwee shwee.*

The footfall was getting closer. She had the thrilling sense that he was playing a game with her. That he'd concealed himself some-where with the intention of doubling back on her, walking lockstep with her, tapping her on the shoulder, then grinning broadly when she turned – maybe even sweeping her off her feet.

Clack clack clack clack.

Shwee shwee shwee SHWEE.

She yearned to turn around but didn't want to spoil the 'surprise'. And because she hated the idea of appearing nervy, jumpy – to anyone.

Clack clack clack clack.

SHWEE SHWEE SHWEESHWEESHWEESCHWEE.

The footfall behind was accelerating. Her *pulse* was accelerating. She had almost reached the western end – there was a semicircle of blue light about fifty yards ahead – and it was now or never. But still she didn't turn.

SHWEEclackSHWEEclackSHWEEclackSHWEEclackSHWEE.

Finally a hand landed on her shoulder.

Cat swung around, just as she'd planned, with a guileless smile on her face.

And saw a long-haired devil glaring back at her.

'Well, well,' the devil snarled, 'if it ain't Shania Twain!'

For a moment – horrifyingly – she thought it was Dylan Moyle, back from the dead.

'Happy now, hen? That he's gone?'

Then it struck her. It was Moyle's friend, the straggly-bearded rocker.

'Who you gonna whine about now, cunt?' His hand was pinning her in place.

Cat saw genuine hatred in his eyes. As if he *knew* about Aileanach Castle. As if he *knew* she'd partaken in a Satanic ritual.

She tried to wriggle away but he was grappling with her, hauling her back – intent, it seemed, on inflicting damage.

For a moment she thought she was going to be struck – she could see ROCK STAR tattooed on his whitened knuckles – but then there was a *pulse* of energy. A formidable *swoosh*, like an electric wave.

And the rocker was thrown back. He was almost blown off his feet.

Unable to account for it – the *force* that had repulsed him – he glanced over Cat's shoulder, his face slackening and his eyes widening. He looked like a man who had peered into the Abyss. And then, in an instant, he was bolting. He was racing down the tunnel past a pair of tandem cyclists.

Cat was confounded. She turned, but there was no one behind her – not a soul. And yet clearly the rocker had seen something. Had someone – Boucher? – scared him away? Terrified him? She didn't understand.

The cyclists, both female, drew up beside her. 'You all right?' one of them asked.

'Yeah, yeah,' she breathed. 'It was nothing. Nothing.'

'You sure?'

'I'm sure.'

'Want us to call the police?' the other one asked.

'No, no, thanks.'

'Like an escort into town?'

'Thanks, I'll be OK.'

The cyclists looked disappointed with her but were on their way before she could ask them what they'd seen. She turned again and saw the rocker still hightailing down the tunnel, heading for the eastern exit and not looking back.

Perhaps, she speculated, he'd just glimpsed something overpowering in her eyes? Her fierce resistance? Her refusal to be intimidated?

Whatever. It had worked, anyway. The bastard was gone. She collected her bearings, straightened her jacket, and continued on her way.

Forty minutes later, still tingling with confusion and anger, she arrived home to find under her door a beautifully quilted envelope containing a handwritten invitation.

Dear Cat,

This evening on one of my aimless wanders around this sublime city I was seized by the notion that the two of us, both innocents in Edinburgh, should perhaps celebrate our arrival with a good meal.

Would you care to join me on Saturday night? My treat? At La Casa del Fuego? It's a Mexican restaurant I happened to notice tonight in the Old Town. I realise this is at short notice, however, so please don't feel under any obligation to accept if you have more important matters to pursue.

Sincerely,
Robin (Number Six)
'The bird a nest, the spider a web, man friendship.' William Blake

'Pursue'? 'Seize'? 'Innocent'? William Blake?
Was he toying with her?
It was Tuesday, 13 March.

CHAPTER
FIVE

I N THE MORNING CAT WAS CALLED in to Bellamy's cockpit, just as she had expected, for one of his infamous dressings-down.

'I've just had a call from HR, seeking clarification of your current role,' he said. 'Do you have anything to tell me?'

'I hope not,' Cat replied brightly. 'I'd like to think I've been doing pretty well at Jenny's job. Funnily enough I'm enjoying it, too, and think I've learned a lot quickly – just as I'm sure you planned.'

Bellamy looked unmoved. 'HR was referring specifically to your investigation at Credit Cards Department.'

'My investigation?' Cat made sure she looked puzzled. 'I'd hardly call it an investigation. Just following up on a complaint, as I said. All I did there, really, was shake a few hands and familiarise myself with their procedures.'

'That's not the impression they have at HR.'

'Well, I don't know where they're getting their information from. Was the officer you spoke to called Dunn, by any chance?'

Bellamy stiffened. 'That's of no relevance.'

'Uh-huh. Well, on the way out of the department I shook hands with some big cheese called Mungo Dunn. I think he took an instant dislike to me. He even snuck in a mention of his father. And a sister in HR. So he's probably marking his territory – you know what these guys are like.'

Bellamy sniffed. 'Then you didn't use the office to start phoning around? To the Glenrothes branch? And you didn't request files?'

'To be honest,' Cat said, 'I used the opportunity to chase up a few perfunctory things but I was unable to find any leads anyway. The employee in question – the one who forced the card on Mr Napier – has since resigned. I'm thinking of writing a letter to Mr Napier, implying that she was fired for incompetence. That will offer him some catharsis and everyone will be happy. He got his money back, after all.'

'Hmm.' Bellamy still looked unconvinced. 'Territory or not, I sincerely hope I shan't be getting any further queries about you, Ms Thomas. I always said it was a mistake to give you too much responsibility too soon. So take some free advice, if you will, from an old hand. It's not wise to step on big toes, especially when you're wearing new shoes. *Especially* when those toes belong to people called Dunn. I hope you'll keep that in mind.'

'I will,' said Cat. 'I will.'

As soon as Bellamy left the office, twenty minutes later, she got on the phone to her new friend at Credit Cards. 'Mr Carterius,' she said. 'I'm sure you know who it is. And here's what I'd like today. The names of former employees of your department who've since resigned or been moved to other departments. Specifically, I want names of those who worked closely with Mr Mungo Dunn. Even more specifically, I'd like you to single out the names of those you'd regard as people of integrity. Men or women of good character. Even better if they happen to live in Edinburgh.'

'May I ask why?' Carterius asked.

'Fallen branches.'

'I beg your pardon?'

'If a tree is diseased, you can learn a lot from fallen branches.'

Carterius told her he'd give it some thought and get back to her. Cat said she'd much prefer that she give him something now. Carterius sighed and, lowering his voice to a whisper, offered her two names. 'Karen Greeley was transferred to the branch in Leith. A loans officer, I think. And Poul Corneliussen – a Swedish fellow – was in line for the post that Mungo Dunn currently occupies. He took early retirement. Both are as honest as the day is long. Karen still lives in Edinburgh and so does Corneliussen, I'm sure of it. I saw him in Sainsbury's.'

'The Sainsbury's where, may I ask?'

'The one at Cameron Toll.'

'Remind me how to spell "Corneliussen".'

He told her.

'I'll look into it,' said Cat. 'And thanks.'

Deciding that the existing employee, Karen Greeley, might be unwilling to compromise her job in any way, Cat focused on the retired Scandinavian. And by happy coincidence the online directory offered up only one P. Corneliussen living anywhere near Cameron Toll.

It had been one of those curious Scottish days when the clouds seem permanently swollen with rain but never actually burst. Cat left the office at five o'clock sharp and headed for Corneliussen's listed address in Duddingston. It wasn't far from the Innocent Railway, so she had to resist thinking about the unsettling encounter with Moyle's buddy the previous evening. More to the point she had to distract herself from further concerns about the forthcoming dinner with Robin Boucher. Though she had not yet responded officially to his invitation, she had purchased some equally fancy writing paper and was intending to slip a reply under his door as soon as she got home.

Dear Robin,

Happy to accept your generous offer to accompany you to the suggested restaurant. Be warned, however, that being an American I have plenty of opinions about Mexican cuisine – and just about everything else – and I am not shy in sharing them.

Shall I come to your place or wait for you to come to mine?

Regards
Cat (Number Five)

It had taken her five drafts before she found a suitable tone – neither aloof nor overeager – and she still wasn't happy with it. But it would have to do.

Presently, using a map app, she arrived at Meadowfield Drive and a quaint bungalow half hidden behind a poorly pruned hedge. Pushing back the squeaking gate – a terrier started yapping behind the fence – she reached the door and pressed a cracked buzzer. When there was no sound of movement from inside, she jabbed it again. The dog next door was still growling. She was about to give up when the door drew back with a squeal. A wispy-haired man holding a canvas shopping bag stopped on the threshold.

Cat brightened. 'Mr Corneliussen?'

The man looked hesitant. 'Yes?'

'I'm sorry – I tried the buzzer.'

'It doesn't work.'

Cat nodded. 'Look, I don't want to hold you up, but I'm from ABC' – he tightened at once – 'and I'd just like to talk about your time in Credit Cards.'

'Who are you?' Corneliussen had narrowed his eyes.

'I'm from Internal Frauds.'

'Who told you I was in Credit Cards?'

'It's in the record, Mr Corneliussen. You worked closely with Mungo Dunn and—'

Corneliussen slammed the door.

Cat stood in place for a few moments, a trifle stunned, and then stabbed the buzzer again. Then she remembered that it didn't work. So she knocked. But Corneliussen clearly wasn't coming out – not while she was standing outside.

Cat, however, was nothing if not persistent. She feigned a retreat, raising the collar of her coat and making off down the street until she was out of sight. Then she crossed the road, marched up a grassy slope past some foraging crows, and came to the shelter of some leafless birch trees. Here she waited, rehearsing her lines while hoping it didn't start to rain (she hadn't brought an umbrella). Finally Corneliussen, still clutching his canvas bag, ventured out once more. Looking left and right – he was visible through a gap in the hedge – he had barely reached his front gate when Cat erupted from her hiding place. The crows took off with a start.

Corneliussen was unlocking the door of his ancient Volvo – a model so old that he was inserting a key in the lock – when Cat caught up with him again.

'Honesty and integrity never seem to pay, do they, Mr Corneliussen?'

Startled, Corneliussen seemed for a moment as though he was about to dive into his car and roar off. But something about Cat's comment immobilised him.

'I don't want to compromise you in any way,' Cat went on, catching her breath. 'And if you'd prefer I'll never mention your name to anyone. But it would help me immeasurably if you'd only let me know I'm on the right track.'

Corneliussen looked off into the distance for a moment, as if lost in some internal debate, then focused on Cat again – not exactly assenting but not retreating either.

Cat took a gulp of air. 'I suspect there's something very underhand going on in our Credit Cards Department. Maybe it's too discreet for others to see, but I've dealt with these sorts of things before.'

Corneliussen looked incongruously, bitterly amused for a moment. 'Dealt with this before, have you?' His lips had barely moved.

'I'm from America.'

Corneliussen again seemed to argue with himself. But finally he emitted a sigh. 'All right, then – tell me what you think is going on.'

'I think the Dunn family are running a scam at ABC with Mungo Dunn as the point man in Credit Cards,' said Cat. 'I think they have a system in place that takes full advantage of the zero liability and lax security arrangements with the current card issuer. I think that whenever an unwanted card is returned "NOT AT THIS ADDRESS" it's secretly activated and diverted to accomplices who rack up thousands of dollars of purchases before the original customer finds out. Across dozens, perhaps scores of accounts, the stolen amounts would be considerable.'

Corneliussen, still not looking at her, issued a barely audible chuckle. 'Pounds,' he said.

'Excuse me?'

'You mean pounds, not dollars.'

'Forgive me, pounds,' Cat said, nodding. 'But am I right or am I not?'

'Miss' – Corneliussen chortled bleakly – 'you've not even touched the tip of the iceberg.'

'I see. I see.' The clouds were so dark they were saturating all other colours by sheer contrast. 'Then can you give me some idea what I have to do to see the full iceberg?'

'Miss, you don't *want* to see the full iceberg.'

'Clearly you don't know me very well.'

Corneliussen studied her grimly, piteously, and seemed about to reveal something when a black four-wheel-drive breezed past on the road, the driver obscured by tinted windows. And he shook his head.

'"The best lack all conviction, while the worst are full of passionate intensity."'

'I'm sorry?'

Corneliussen smirked. 'Do you not know your Yeats?' he said. 'I'm telling you that I see little difference, sometimes, between the demon and the demon hunter. Between the devil and the exorcist.'

'I'm still not sure . . .'

'I'm saying that you'd have to be mad, dangerously mad, to pursue this. Because if you do, you'll inevitably end up – as I did – in the throne room of Alistair Dunn. And you can't defeat the King. No one can.'

'The King?'

'The King always wins. The house always wins. The *darkness* always wins.' Corneliussen's face was a picture of defeat. 'Don't delude yourself, young lady. "Hell is empty and all the devils are here." That's Shakespeare, you know. And he might well have been speaking about Edinburgh.'

Then he threw open the car door and swung himself inside.

'Mr Corneliussen—' Cat tried, but he was already turning the ignition.

He blurted off in a haze of diesel fumes, the Volvo coughing and backfiring as it rounded the bend.

Hell is empty and all the devils are here . . .

Cat stood on the edge of the pavement for a while, forlorn and unquenched, as the clouds rolled over and the crows wheeled home to roost. Then she started trudging back across town.

★   ★   ★

When Cat entered Dean Village she was surprised to find that the tourists had not yet departed. Despite the weather the little enclave seemed more popular than ever – many times more popular than when she had moved in – and it was becoming increasingly difficult just to cross its bridges without being bumped and jostled.

When she reached the stair door she sensed that some of the tourists – they looked disturbingly familiar – had even followed her up the street, just it seemed to watch her go inside. A figure loomed over her shoulder and she was about to shoot him a dirty look when she realised with a jolt that it was Robin Boucher.

'Just in time,' he said with a grin.

'Sorry,' she said. 'I thought you were one of the tourists.'

'Yeah, is it always this popular around here?'

'Not until you arrived,' she said – for the first time making the connection.

They eased awkwardly into the building's stairwell and checked the mail – a bill or something for Cat, nothing as usual for him – and then, with Boucher standing aside, they started the ascent of the spiral stairway.

'I trust I didn't offend you . . .' he said behind her.

'Offend me?' Cat said. 'About what?'

'The invitation . . .'

'Now why would that offend me?' she asked. 'I was about to slip a response under your door, as it happens.'

'Then you'll be joining me?'

'I'm looking forward to it.'

'Excellent,' he said, sounding genuinely relieved. '*Excellent.*'

They did the next two spirals in silence, Cat faintly amused by his schoolboy exuberance, before Boucher added, somewhat self-consciously, 'I hope you don't mind, but I've invited your friend along as well.'

'My friend?'

'Agnes,' he said, smiling. 'Agnes Sampson.'

Cat was almost speechless. '*Agnes,*' she managed, struggling to appear unfazed. 'What made you – well, how do you know Agnes?'

'She works at your office, does she not?'

'Of course.'

'She came around here the other night, looking for you.'

That didn't sound right. The only time Cat had been absent from her flat was when she had followed Boucher himself to the Innocent Railway. 'Did she really?'

'Really she did. She seems very much the live wire.'

'She sure is.'

'And I thought you might like to have her along.'

Cat couldn't work out if Boucher was buying distance from her or if he'd somehow gotten it into his head, possibly owing to her delayed response, that she was the type of girl who'd prefer a chaperone.

She settled on the latter and decided he was just being scrupulously considerate again.

'Sounds fabulous,' she said. 'Fabulous.'

'Excellent,' he said again. 'Well, the booking's at seven-thirty so I'll pick you up, so to speak, at six-thirty? I don't think we need to drive – it's difficult enough getting a car into that part of town – so we'll just enjoy the walk, eh?'

'Why not?'

'And Agnes can find her own way there, I imagine? She lives not far from the Old Town, doesn't she?'

'In Newington, that's right.'

'Well, then, everything sounds perfect.' With a serrated little grin.

When Cat had got inside her flat and closed her multitude of locks, she felt a vibration from her phone.

It was Maxine from downstairs, being cheeky:

Wow! Sounds like you and Mr Smooth are getting along FAMOUSLY!!!

The stairwell's acoustics, as Cat had already discovered, meant that conversations were piped into every apartment in the building.

She didn't respond immediately, but when she got around to preparing a meal – a bok choy recipe she'd found in a supermarket handout – it occurred to her that, for all the developments in the internal fraud investigation, and all the more pressing matters that should have been occupying her attention, she was now worrying almost exclusively about the forthcoming dinner with Robin Boucher, and conjecturing feverishly about his mysterious connection with goddammed Agnes.

CHAPTER
SIX

L A CASA DEL FUEGO TURNED OUT to be a spacious and well-patronised establishment with baked tiles depicting leaping flames and stained-glass lanterns casting kaleidoscopic hues. It was deep in the Cowgate – a notorious street that Cat hadn't seen Boucher enter on Tuesday evening – and, according to Agnes, whom they met in the foyer, was owned by 'a friend' of hers. In fact, Agnes, whose plunging purple frock exposed a staggering expanse of cleavage, claimed that she was the one who'd recommended it in the first place. Which only left Cat wondering how that chimed with Boucher's claims in his written invitation.

An oddly nervous waiter guided them through the crowd to a prominent table on the mezzanine, surrounded by volcanic imagery, where they enjoyed a magisterial view across the whole dining area. Boucher – who was wearing a corduroy jacket and plaid shirt which would have looked dorky on any other man, but on him seemed the height of retro *chic* – drew back the chairs for the two ladies before settling in and instructing them, 'Order whatever you like, and don't hold back.' Small-talk and menu-perusing ensued until their drinks arrived – a tejuino for Cat and tequilas for the others – and a tipsy Agnes commenced her presumptuous campaign.

'Cat never stops talking about you, you know.'

'*Well*,' said Cat.

'No, really – she talks about you *constantly*.'

Boucher, passing the menu back to the waiter, was courteously dismissive. 'I suspect she was merely wondering why I moved in so quickly,' he said, with a flicker of a smile at Cat. 'And why I seem untroubled by the flat's recent history.'

'That's a small part of it,' Agnes admitted.

'Well, the truth is that the area suits me perfectly. For professional reasons I need to be close to the facilities of a big city, yet I've always yearned for the peace and quiet of a sleepy little village. The Dean seemed to offer both.'

'If you get the right flat,' Cat put in.

'And the right neighbours,' Boucher said, with another indulgent little smile. 'And as for the flat's history, I leave it to others to be repulsed by such things. I can't imagine there's a property on this planet where some sort of grisly crime didn't take place. And if it helps to lower the price, so much the better.'

'It pays not to be superstitious,' Cat noted.

'I couldn't agree more,' said Boucher, as a fellow diner cackled wickedly in the background.

Agnes forged on. 'It's more than that, though. Cat has been wondering about everything. And I mean *everything*.' For a moment Cat thought she was about to say something unbearably crude. 'Like what you actually do. I mean actually *do* for a living.'

Boucher looked amused. 'Have I really been the cause of that much speculation?'

'How could you not?'

'I suppose it makes sense,' he said. 'I can be damnably secretive at times, I admit that, and I can only imagine what it looks like to others. In fact, I'd be surprised if there *weren't* a lot of misconceptions about me.'

He paused to savour the tequila like a fine wine.

'And?' said Agnes.

'And' – Boucher affected a sombre expression – 'well, I *still* can't talk about it. What I do, who employs me – it's going to have to remain a mystery. National security, you understand.'

Silence for a few seconds – just the general hubbub and mariachi music from the speaker system – then Agnes said in a whisper, 'So . . . *what*? You're with MI6 or something?'

'Would it bother you if that were true?'

'Not at all.'

'And if I were involved in international skulduggery, you wouldn't be concerned?'

'Of course not.'

'If I had a licence to kill . . .?'

'Well, do you? Do you?'

Boucher maintained his gravely serious expression for a few seconds and then snorted, shot a sly wink to Cat and shed the mask of solemnity entirely.

'No,' he said, chuckling. 'I'm not a spy. I'm not involved in counterespionage. I've nothing to do with national security at all. I wish I *did*, but I don't.'

Agnes kept glancing at Cat, as if to say, 'What a card this guy is!'

'I'm a chess player,' he said.

'A chess player!'

'A professional chess player.'

'Wow,' said Agnes, with another approving glance at Cat. 'As in tournaments and suchlike?'

'Not quite. Everything I do is online. But I do have a significant clientele.'

'Clientele?'

'Stock market traders, hedge fund managers, retired billionaires, princes, sheikhs, captains of industry, even a former prime minister – they all pay for my services.'

'Amazing,' said Agnes, like a private fan club. 'And we're talking good money here?'

'Enough to pay the bills. But some of my clients are rather unpleasant. Some of them take the game far too seriously. A few of them even make threats. It's another reason I find a monkish existence in a garret so agreeable. And why I generally prefer not to talk about it.'

To Cat this seemed highly unsatisfactory, even suspect, but she elected not to question him. 'You'll have to forgive us for being so inquisitive,' she said. 'It's just that the last guy in your garret was as far from a monk as you can imagine. And I guess I'm just relieved you're such a contrast.'

'It never hurts to follow a bad act,' he said.

'If you can contrive it.'

'If you can contrive it, indeed.'

Agnes said, 'You wouldn't believe how much Cat hated that last guy – the bad act.'

'Oh, come on,' Cat protested. 'I wouldn't say *hate* . . .'

'She dreamed of killing him. Actually *killing* him.'

'It's just human nature,' Cat said, shifting. 'It's hard sometimes, when someone is particularly obnoxious, to stop the imagination from wandering . . .'

'Oh, I agree entirely,' said Boucher. 'Every day, in fact, I kill probably a hundred people in my imagination.'

'Just a hundred?' Agnes joked.

'I often dream, for a start, of travelling back through time to assassinate the inventor of the leaf blower.'

'Before he could do any damage?' Agnes said, laughing. 'The inventor of the cream doughnut for me.'

'It was only fear of God,' Boucher went on, 'that used to prevent people acting on such whimsies. Now it's CCTV and CSI.'

'The new gods,' Agnes said, with an approving nod.

'So I hope,' Boucher said, looking in Cat's direction, 'that you didn't experience any sort of remorse – for what happened to him?'

'To the guy upstairs?' Cat felt oddly exposed. 'No, I don't think so – why?'

'Absurd as it is, people can sometimes experience guilt if they've wished ill upon someone who later suffers a misfortune. A sort of reverse *Schadenfreude* – the result, generally, of religious conditioning.'

'No,' Cat said, pointedly not looking at Agnes. 'That presupposes some sort of supernatural agency, and that's nothing more than magical thinking.'

'I wouldn't be so sure,' Boucher said mysteriously, and seemed about to elaborate when their meals arrived.

They were adjusting themselves – spreading out napkins, shifting glasses, selecting cutlery – when Cat noticed other diners in the restaurant staring at them. Some even seemed to be making guarded comments. Agnes, finely tuned to her attentions, chipped in with an explanation: 'They're all looking at you two,' she whispered. 'At what a gorgeous couple you make.'

Cat dearly hoped Boucher hadn't heard – he was spooning sour cream over his fajitas – and quickly changed the subject. 'Anyway,' she said to him, 'if I'm given to dark thoughts it's partly because I'm paid to. Sometimes I need to think like a fraudster – like the criminal mind, in general – just to imagine where an investigation might lead.'

'Cat cracked a big case in America that way,' Agnes explained. 'Organised crime, gangsters, the works.'

'Oh?'

'And she's got her teeth into something juicy here, too.'

'Anything I can help you with?' Boucher was lip-testing the heat of his meal. 'I have a lot of high-profile clients in the financial sector, you know.'

Cat started sawing into her spinach enchilada. 'At the moment it's just a credit cards issue. I suspect there's corruption involved in that department. Well, not suspect – I've been told it, straight out, by a former employee. But as for the details, it's still a matter of speculation.'

'And what is your speculation?'

She swallowed a bite. 'Fraudulent card activation. Redirection of credit cards to criminal elements. Probably misdirected statements as well. All that is possible if the systems are manipulated and the ethics are loose. But apparently that's just the tip of the iceberg.'

'And you hope to uncover the rest of the iceberg?'

'I'll get there eventually – or do my damnedest trying, anyway.'

Boucher ruminated for a moment, dabbed his lips with a napkin, and said, 'Rewards points.'

'Sorry?'

'Rewards points. All those credit card accounts come with incentives attached, don't they?'

'Sure.'

'Well, what if they're purposely misdirected?'

Cat reached for her drink – the meal was excessively spicy – and shook her head. 'Customers would notice if they're not getting their points.'

'I never bother checking mine,' Boucher said. 'In fact, I wouldn't have any earthly idea if I was getting any at all.'

'It only takes one . . .'

'What about corporate accounts, then?'

'Back-end software ensures that corporate accounts are ineligible.'

'And what's to stop that software being subverted? By someone inside? Considering the size of those accounts, the points involved would be massive, wouldn't they?'

'So massive that they'd be sure to draw attention.'

'Then what if the points were distributed over scores of individual accounts? Small business accounts? And what if those accounts were further modified to look like personal accounts? That would be possible from the inside, right?'

Cat was surprised by the depth of Boucher's insight. 'It's possible, I guess. Why – have you heard something similar, from one of your clients?'

Boucher returned to his meal. 'Not so much from a client as from my own imagination. Sometimes the mind of a chess player wanders into dark places. Sometimes, when it's particularly restless, it plots out complex scams and schemes – just to keep itself active and flexible.'

'Interesting,' said Cat, taking another sip to cool down. 'So you plotted that out all by yourself?'

'In the middle of the night, trying to lull myself to sleep. Though of course I've never acted on it – or any of the other schemes I've dreamed up. Out of civic responsibility, you understand.'

'Here's to civic responsibility,' Cat said, raising her tejuino.

Boucher lifted his tequila. 'And to those who are compelled to explore dark places.'

They clinked glasses – forgetting, for a moment, that anyone else was present – and Agnes issued a hearty guffaw.

'Look at you two. Just look at you. Fetch a fire extinguisher, someone! *Phew!* You're practically in flames here!' She fanned herself with her hands like a Victorian maiden.

Cat had to resist the urge to kick her under the table. But Boucher himself was admirably discreet. 'I hope you're both enjoying the meal, anyway. Though I must say the food's more *embellished* than I usually prefer.'

And the company, Cat thought.

At Boucher's insistence they indulged in dessert – a *crème brûlée* for Cat, who couldn't believe her own wickedness; churro bowls for the others – and then Boucher, who seemed to have mastered a multitude of languages (he had already addressed the waiter in fluent Spanish), regaled them with some other German words which he claimed 'deserve to be as familiar as *Schadenfreude*': *Backpfeifengesicht*, for a face that's just begging to be slapped; *Fuchsteufelswild* – 'fox devil wild' – for maniacal rage; *Weltschmerz*, for despair at the state of the world in general; and *Geborgenheit*, for a feeling of such emotional intensity that nothing else matters.

'I'm guessing you two are feeling a bit of *Geborgenheit* right now,' Agnes said – swiftly severing yet another strand of conversation.

When it came to settling the bill, Boucher flashed a wallet stuffed with an indecent amount of cash. 'I don't trust credit cards,' he said to Cat with a wink, and laid out a generous tip, adding, 'The food might be rich, but that doesn't mean the waiters are.'

As they headed for the exit other patrons seemed still to be glancing at them; in particular Cat noticed an aquiline gentleman in the shadows of the bar area.

'Absalón Salazar,' Agnes said at her side. 'The owner.'

'*Who?*'

'Absalón Salazar – you know, from the conclave?'

'Oh, yeah,' Cat said, vaguely remembering the angular face. 'Absalón Salazar. He owns this place?'

'You know he does. That's why I recommended it.'

It was another curious moment in an altogether curious evening.

Despite Boucher's obvious and effortless charm, Cat had the sneaking suspicion that everything – from the overspiced food to Agnes's salacious drunkenness – had been prearranged for a specific purpose. But as to what that purpose was – she and Boucher had still to get home, after all – she didn't care to contemplate.

CHAPTER
SEVEN

WHEN THEY PARTED A FEW DOORS up from the restaurant, a by-now thoroughly plastered Agnes assailed them with yet more unsolicited encouragement: 'Oh well, don't want to stand in your way any longer than necessary, eh?' Giving a sordid wink to Boucher. 'Just a warning, though – Cat doesn't enjoy being submissive.'

'Really, Agnes.'

'It's true. She had a traumatic experience in her youth that she doesn't like talking about. That's the real reason she moved to Edinburgh, you know.'

'Agnes . . .'

'But you'll know she's ripe when she starts babbling.'

Cat shot her the daggered look she'd been suppressing all evening.

'Uh oh! Better stop or she'll want me dead too!'

And with that Agnes headed off in the general direction of Newington, her laughter echoing fiendishly around the Cowgate.

Cat and Boucher themselves turned back past the restaurant – other patrons seemed to be retreating self-consciously from the window – and headed under the gloomy arches of the South and

George IV Bridges. When she judged a suitable distance had been covered, Cat coughed and said, 'I really should apologise for Agnes, I guess. I don't know what's gotten into her.'

'She's a character,' Boucher said. 'And I'm fond of characters.'

'There are limits, though.'

'She's a good laugh, and not at all malignant.'

'That stuff she said about trauma,' Cat went on. 'I'm not exactly sure what she's talking about. One night, possibly when I'd had a little too much to drink – and I don't normally drink – I must have mumbled about something that happened in my youth. She's seized upon it for some reason and blown it up into something earth-shattering.'

'She sounded genuinely concerned for you, for what it's worth.'

'Well, she has no reason to be. What happened is . . . irrelevant. I've been very disciplined about that. I never talk about it. I shouldn't be talking about it now. I think there was something in that drink. It had a strange taste.'

'Tejuinos can have added alcohol.'

'Yeah.' She felt surprisingly light-headed. 'I've noticed, by the way, that people are always looking for sinister psychological reasons to account for others who don't fit the mould. Self-reliance is seen as abnormal – threatening, somehow.'

'I think Agnes admires you more than anything. But it's true. People in general have puerile imaginations. Look at this bunch.' Approaching them was a cluster of middle-aged theatregoers. 'I guarantee that there are corners of their minds that are festering with malice, spite, sexual perversity . . . everything. Not that they'd never admit it, of course.'

'My mother was deeply religious,' Cat heard herself saying.

'Ahh.'

'And she used to compare the dark and light sides of the mind to two rooms side by side. She said that an unlit room would always become brighter by throwing open the door to a brightly lit room, but a brightly lit room would never become darker by opening the door to an unlit one.'

'An interesting metaphor,' Boucher said. 'Your mother's way of suggesting that the faithful should have no fear about peering into the dark?'

'I think' – and here Cat experienced an unsettling flashback to Aileanach Castle – 'she was trying to say that good is always more powerful than evil. But I prefer to interpret it as you've suggested. If you're confident of your own rationality, then you should have no fear about confronting your inner darkness. It won't harm you to throw open the door – and the door should always be open anyway.'

'So there's more room for the mind to wander, apart from anything else . . .'

'Exactly. I guess I was molested.'

Boucher looked at her for a moment, clearly doubting his ears. 'I'm sorry, Cat?'

'Yeah,' she said, not sure why she was suddenly admitting it. 'That thing that Agnes was referring to. It was in Philadelphia. I'm not sure how old I was. Nine, actually. My mother was ill and my father was in financial distress and we had some cousins who agreed to take me in. And their son – he was twenty-one at the time – cornered me in the garden shed one day and . . . you know.'

'My God, Cat . . . you don't have to talk about this, if you don't want to.'

'No, no, it's all right. I knew it was sick. But I'm not sure it surprised me. Angered me – really infuriated me – but it didn't surprise me. And there were circumstances – it's difficult to explain – that meant I didn't speak out, and neither did my father, and we both felt guilty about that.'

'*Guilty?* What on earth do you feel guilty about?'

'He – the cousin – went on to assault others, you see. And I could have saved them. Could have done something. But I didn't, and that haunted me.'

'Cat . . . you were a *child.*'

'Yeah, I know. I don't even know why I'm telling you this. It's all in the past. I was pretty messed up, but I've found my calling now. I've got a mission. I'm not "carrying any baggage", or whatever they say. I haven't been "running away" from anything. I'm a happy person. I'm not a victim. Not a victim, believe me.'

'It's *all right* to be a victim, Cat.'

'Of course it is. But I'm not a victim.'

They passed awkwardly through the open space of the Grassmarket, erstwhile scene of public hangings, where currently a group of aggressive hoons was chanting a football anthem. For a moment a confrontation seemed inevitable – some of the men were eyeing Cat suggestively – but Boucher swelled out – a remarkable physical transformation – and the hoons wilted, separating around them like flustered pigeons and reassembling only when they were well behind.

The incident sparked an oblique acknowledgment from Boucher. 'Just let me know if I can help you, Cat – any time at all. I'm always there for you.'

'No, no – I'm OK.'

'Any sort of trouble – personal or professional. Trust me, I know how to deal with such things.'

She wanted to ask him to elaborate. Had he been threatened over his chess playing? But she was feeling unusually woozy. They passed under the Castle Terrace Bridge and she stumbled briefly on the flagstones. He shot out a hand to prevent her falling.

'You might be right about those tejuinos,' she said, thinking for some reason of Absalón Salazar. 'I was confronted a couple of weeks ago, you know.' She was disentangling herself from his grip. 'By a friend of the guy who died upstairs. For a moment it looked like it might turn nasty.'

'Did he threaten you?'

'Not really. He swore at me and then ran off. It was very strange.'

'Strange or not, I wish I'd been there to deal with it.' Which seemed to Cat, even through her haze, to be a very awkward denial.

They climbed King's Stables Road towards the stately bulk of the Caledonian Hotel. At one of the windows a well-dressed couple seemed to be peering down at them with what looked like opera glasses.

'People really do seem to be staring at us around here,' Boucher noted, pausing at the corner to flip a coin to a rough sleeper.

'Good of you,' said Cat.

'Just paying the ferryman before the passage to Paradise.'

She tried to pretend she hadn't heard him. In Shandwick Place she stumbled again, on the tram tracks this time, and Boucher again seized her by the arm. By the time they entered Queensferry Street she was feeling fully inebriated and apologised for losing control.

'Losing control is good for you sometimes,' he said, and for the first time – she must have been in furious denial – she had a vision of what he must have had in mind. But surely, she thought, he wouldn't try anything tonight? After all the barbed wire she had just spun out?

To distract herself, she said, 'I think you were going to say something about negative energy . . .'

'I was?'

'Back at the restaurant, before the meals arrived.'

'Well, yes. Negative energy, mind viruses, the real nature of evil. I'd love to discuss it further, but I don't think tonight is the night.'

'I'm not shy . . .'

'Glad to hear it. But we've better things to do, have we not?'

They were passing under an amber streetlight and his eyes were flashing with reflected glow. His teeth, his dimples, his permanently amused expression – she thought he looked *demonic*. And what happened next would continue to disturb her for days afterwards.

When they took the Belford Road stairs deep into Dean Village a mist rose up and seemed to swallow them. She felt Boucher's arm slide around her, but she was too weak to resist. Then they were gliding – literally, it seemed to Cat, as though they were *gliding* – across the footbridge, over the rustling river, as darkly garbed people (tourists? even this late?) seemed to supplicate before them. They swept soundlessly up to their building and round and round the stairway and Cat saw her own red-painted door staring back at her with the number 5 pulsing in the sickly yellow light.

But did she go through that door? With Boucher?

Or did Boucher carry her higher into Number Six?

Whatever. Only fragments of dreamlike imagery would later survive. She was taking off her clothes. She was having a shower. She was drying herself. She was entering the bedroom, completely naked. She was heading for her bed – or his? – and reaching for the duvet, to peel it back, when muscled arms closed around her. Fur bristled against her back. Hot breath scorched the nape of her neck. And she was not resisting. She was losing control. She was being lifted off her feet and deposited on the bed. She was atop the duvet and her legs were being prised apart. She was staring, astonished, at Boucher, who beneath his luxuriant body hair had pronounced abs, pecs, deltoids, the works – even the sort of defined obliques you usually see only on body builders. But how could that be? This plainly was not the physique of a chess player. He seldom left his flat. And she'd never heard him doing exercise of any kind.

Then he was swinging himself onto the bed. He was positioning himself over her. His manhood looked as big as a rolling pin. And, without any sort of foreplay, he was guiding himself into her. He was thrusting in and out. It was excruciating. It was extraordinary. She heard herself moaning, squealing, and tried to stifle the sound lest it be heard by Michael and Maxine downstairs. Or Boucher upstairs. Then it occurred to her that the stranger *was* Boucher. But it still seemed impossible.

She heard the voice of Agnes Sampson:

'If you'd been had by him, you'd know, girl, you'd know.'

And then the impossibly deep voice of Boucher himself:

'Everything is going to be all right.'

His hands closed around her throat and his deep-flecked eyes were staring at her hypnotically. His nostrils were flared and his lips were curled back on wickedly sharp teeth. Her unstifled moans and gasps were now so loud that she feared she might wake the entire neighbourhood. At one point she heard herself shriek – either in agony or ecstasy, or possibly both.

And this might have been exactly what woke her up. Or maybe it was the sound of her phone purring. For when she came to her senses she saw her mobile illuminated on the bedside chest. The wind was moaning. Tree shadows were swirling across the ceiling. She reached over, plucked up the phone and found a message from Maxine.

That a nightmare you're having? You okay?

Cat felt obliged to answer promptly.

It was a nightmare, yeah. Thanks for ending it.

But it still made no sense. As dreams go it wasn't unwelcome, as distressingly debauched as it had been, and she wasn't sure she had really wanted it to end.

She switched on the beside light, pulled down the blind, and, exactly as she had after returning from the conclave, examined herself thoroughly. But there were no signs that Boucher, or anyone else, had had his way with her. She scolded herself for even imagining it. And decided to blame everything on the tejuinos.

She cracked open her bottle of sleeping tablets – untouched since Moyle had been permanently silenced – and swallowed two pills, washing them down with tap water. Then she dived under the duvet, waiting for sleep to overcome her again. But for the life of her all she could think about was Boucher's godlike physique, at least in her imagination . . . and his extraordinary prowess . . . at least in her imagination . . . and the flames of devilish lust in his eyes . . . at least in her imagination . . . and the unruly emotions that his physique had invoked in her through its very bestial magnificence. But in the end she consoled herself with the thought – indeed, the indisputable logic – that his real body would be considerably paunchier, droopier and unthreatening . . . and all the more comforting for that.

Assuming she ever got to see it, of course.

CHAPTER
EIGHT

A T THE AQUARIUM ON MONDAY MORNING, with Bellamy at the mandatory interdepartmental briefing, Cat got on the line to the liaison officer at Cosmos's UK head office in London. Since she preferred not to be overheard, she was using Agnes's figurine-cluttered office.

'You don't know me,' she told the officer, who was called Peggy and had a cut-glass accent, 'but I'd like to hit you with a hypothetical. And all I want you to do is to tell me if it's possible.'

She proceeded to outline Boucher's theory about rewards points being activated on corporate accounts by disabling the backend inhibitors and redirecting the proceeds.

'It's certainly plausible,' Peggy said in her precise tone. 'We had a very similar case at a regional bank in Kent recently. A staff member in their IT department was funnelling rewards points from a storage company.'

'Is it possible on a much larger scale, though? Across many different accounts?'

'It would require high-level corruption. Why? Are you suggesting something?'

'I don't know what I'm suggesting,' Cat admitted, glancing at

Agnes. 'But tell me, how are corporate accounts monitored? How would you know if an account was fraudulently accruing points?'

'To be perfectly honest, it's difficult for us to monitor such things from London. We're as chronically understaffed as you are. And the multitude of new banks, regional banks, foreign banks, credit unions and so on makes it doubly difficult. We're largely reliant on the integrity of our partners.'

'There's a liability-versus-legality calculation as well?'

'Of course, though that's officially off the record. But if you have anything at all – especially if it's large scale – we'd be more than happy to discuss it with you.'

'Then I might get back to you,' said Cat, hanging up.

Agnes said, 'He's on the money, isn't he?'

'Who's on the money?'

'You know exactly who I mean. He's on to something with those rewards points, isn't he?'

'Possibly.'

'Of course he is. He's as sharp as a tack, Cat. As sharp as you – up top, I mean.'

'Sharp, maybe, but does he ever tell the truth? I couldn't find his name anywhere on the chess websites, you know.'

Agnes smirked. 'Oh?'

'The World Chess Federation publishes an annual list of the world's top two hundred players. But there's no mention of anyone called Robin Boucher. There's hardly anyone from Britain, period.'

'He said he wasn't into tournaments.'

'But he claimed that he made a good living out of it. And how would anyone but a grandmaster profit out of playing chess online?'

'Maybe he uses his "twinkling amber eyes"?'

Cat ignored her. 'Do you mind if I make another call?'

'Make it snappy, will you? Wing Commander is overdue.'

Cat called Carter Carterius at Credit Cards, only to be told that he was unavailable.

'Oh,' she said, disappointed. 'Can I call back later?'

'Mr Carterius is absent from the office today,' a stern secretary told her. 'Can I take your details? Or get someone else to assist you?'

'That won't be necessary.'

Cat's discomfort must have been evident because when she hung up Agnes said, 'Shit – you look like you swallowed an ashtray.'

'I've sure got some thinking to do.'

'Do it at your own desk, can you? Wing Commander's got us in his gunsights, you know.' And before Cat left the office she called out: 'Did you fuck him, by the way?'

'Sorry?'

'Stop playing innocent – it doesn't suit you. And don't tell me you didn't want to.'

'No, I didn't . . . *do anything* to him. Nothing. Didn't even kiss him.'

'Why the hell not? You were so hot for him you were sweating – it was literally dripping off your face.'

'That was just the meal.'

'Aye right,' said Agnes. 'What's stopping you, anyway? Give it a whirl, girl. A bairn or two would be good for you.'

'Seriously? You're talking babies now?'

'Why not? Not barren, are you?'

'No, I'm not *barren* – as far as I know.'

'Good to hear.' Agnes sniggered. 'There will be no miracles here.'

It was the *other* illuminated sign in the Modern Art Gallery gardens: **THERE WILL BE NO MIRACLES HERE**. But Cat couldn't work out exactly why Agnes had said it.

Back at her desk, after sorting through the mail, she spent some time further contemplating Boucher's suggestions about internal credit card fraud. She was staring absent-mindedly out the window – there was a billboard across the street advertising the 'new' John Lewis store – when a devious new possibility occurred to her. Preferring not to wait until Bellamy left the office again, she risked another call to Peggy in London.

'It's Cat Thomas from Edinburgh again. Listen, I don't know if this is possible but could you send me a full list of credit card account holders at ABC? Just the ones earning rewards points?'

'A full list? That's really something your own department should be doing.'

'I know, and I apologise. My contact there is indisposed.'

Peggy made an ambivalent noise. 'It might take an hour or so. It's bound to be a long list.'

'I'd be extremely grateful.'

Cat's desktop monitor had gone to sleep and she was able to see a reflection of Bellamy, back in his cockpit, staring at her contemplatively but talking on his phone. She doubted he had overhead anything.

When the list of account holders came through, Cat was gobsmacked. It was exactly as she had suspected. And it took only a few search engine clicks to confirm it. She stared at the list for two minutes, her heart thumping, then deleted everything as a precaution and headed out for lunch.

But she had no appetite for food. She took the bus down to portside Leith – a ten-minute journey – and found the local ABC branch on Bernard Street. Here she asked to see Karen Greeley, the former Credit Cards employee whom Carter Carterius had described as 'honest as the day is long'.

Greeley, just as she had hoped, was out at lunch. Cat asked where. The desk clerk told her she should try one of the eateries at the local shopping mall, and gave her a concise physical description as well: 'Spitting image of Susan Boyle.'

'Susan Boyle?'

'The singer, you know. *Who's Got Talent* or whatever?'

'Oh yeah – Susan Boyle. Do you know where she'll be dining, by any chance?'

The clerk had a mischievous streak. 'Let's just say that garlic is her perfume.'

Glancing repeatedly at her watch – she had twenty-five minutes of lunchtime left – Cat did a brisk march to the shopping centre past the survey vessels at Leith Docks. Racing around the food court, she found Greeley, who indeed looked like Susan Boyle, sitting alone at a Greek outlet. With no time to be anything but direct, Cat went straight up to the table – Greely was dining alone – and placed her hands on the back of a wooden chair.

'Karen Greeley? I'm Cat Thomas from the Internal Fraud Department. Can I have a word with you, off the record?'

Greeley, who'd been in the process of squeezing lemon over a slab of fried cheese, squinted up at Cat, appraised her for a few moments, and in the end just nodded. 'Take a seat,' she said. 'I've been expecting this.'

Lowering herself gratefully into the chair, Cat said, 'I want to assure you that this isn't about you and I don't want to comp—'

'I know, I know.' Greeley was still squeezing the lemon. 'It's about Credit Cards. It's about Mungo Dunn.'

Cat hesitated. 'Well, I can't say with any accuracy—'

'Just go for broke and if I don't agree then I'll say so.' Greeley started slicing the cheese into quarters. 'It's best to get this over as fast as possible, don't you think?'

Cat nodded, tried to work out the best way to ease into it, then filled her lungs. 'I think the Dunn family is manipulating its power within ABC for personal gain. I think all the Dunns are involved. I think Mungo Dunn was – *is* – the kingpin in Credit Cards.'

'This is excellent saganaki,' Greeley said. 'Very authentic.'

'I think part of the scam involves rewards points on corporate credit cards. I think the changeover to Cosmos and the zero-liability clause opened up a new opportunity for internal fraud, specifically relating to the submission of details for credit card accounts that fit certain criteria.'

'The dips are even better,' said Greeley. 'The tzatziki especially.'

'That criteria being companies with personal names in their titles. S.D. Watts, an accounting firm in Aberdeen. J.P. McLeven, a publishing company in Glasgow. Ross Gibson Delivery Services in Perth. Campbell Diesel in Ayr. Emily Brown Clothing and Accessories in Edinburgh. And so on. Not huge accounts in themselves but collectively amassing a huge amount of corporate rewards points – points to which they're not officially entitled.'

'The baklava's not bad either.'

'All such accounts are presented to Cosmos in London via conveniently shorthanded titles. J.P. McLeven. Campbell Diesel. Emily Brown. As far as the issuer is concerned, these look like standard personal accounts. They haven't got time to check up every account, especially when they're from Scotland. The companies themselves are none the wiser – assuming undoctored correspondence gets through to them – as the abbreviated account titles are technically accurate.'

'I'm no great fan of their coffee here, mind, but there are plenty of other places if coffee's your thing.'

Cat stared at Greeley and felt a rush of affection. She was right. Boucher was right. It was both thrilling and terrifying. 'Then – what can I say?' she said. 'I thank you. I truly thank you.'

'Thank me for what?' Greeley was dabbing her lips. 'I said nothing.'

'Then I thank you for saying nothing.'

'There's a whole lot more I *didn't* say,' Greeley said. 'But I like my job. I really like my job. I like my *life*, for that matter.' She took a sip of her cola. 'So I'll thank you for not mentioning me in dispatches. Especially to the Laird.'

'The Laird?'

'Alistair Dunn. The Laird of Lucre.'

Cat nodded with relief. 'Treat it as a given.'

With just fifteen minutes left, she took a taxi from outside the shopping centre to Police Scotland Headquarters near the Gothic bulk of Fettes College. It was ambitious, even reckless – she knew by now she was going to overrun her lunchtime – but she needed to register her findings while she could.

At reception she asked for DS Terry Grimes of the fraud team. When Grimes appeared – cherubic, sandy-haired, bright-eyed – he looked stunned.

'My word,' he said with a half-grin. 'I must say you're looking well.'

'Everyone is telling me that,' Cat said, wondering if she should deglamorise. 'Do you have time to talk?'

'For you, of course. Step in. My office is being renovated but—'

'Actually, would you mind if we walk while we talk? I'm sort of pressed for time.'

'Not a problem,' said Grimes. 'Let me grab my coat.'

Outside it was chilly, rain-flecked and windy, but Cat hadn't even noticed. She curved into Comely Bank Road.

'Look,' she said, 'I'm still new here, so I don't know much about the hierarchy of crime in this country. I don't even know much about the hierarchy at ABC. But I'd like to mention a few names to you and see if I get a reaction.'

'Go ahead,' said Grimes.

'Mungo Dunn. Craig Dunn. Alistair Dunn. The whole Dunn family.'

She was watching Grimes and his face tightened visibly. 'The whole Dunn family,' he repeated. 'Now that's very interesting.'

'I take it the names are familiar with you?'

'Well, they keep . . . *appearing*, yes.'

'Appearing?'

'Look, Cat – are you saying that you have something on Alistair Dunn? Something solid?'

'I don't know at this stage. I really don't know. I need to probe further. But I've been here before, in Florida, and I was explicitly warned not to go digging "where the worms got teeth".'

'If you're asking me if the worms have teeth in Scotland,' Grimes said, 'then I'd have to say you should be wary of where you stick your shovel. High-level internal fraud in the Scottish banking system is as old as the City of Glasgow Bank.'

'The City of Glasgow—?'

'A famous case in the Victorian era. The directors got rich on falsified statements and profit reports, but the bank went bust. Thousands of innocent investors got dragged down with them. I can lend you a book about it if you like.'

'That's OK,' said Cat, wondering if he was hitting on her.

'At any rate,' he said, 'that's the sort of worms we have in Scotland. They're deep, they're many, and they bite. Are you sure you don't want to leave this to me?'

'I just want you to know I've been digging. And I'll keep on digging.'

'Then you'll need to be careful – extremely careful.'

'I will be.'

'And you'll need to know your limitations. With Alistair Dunn in particular.'

'I do.'

They stopped under some early cherry blossoms and Grimes ran a hand over his choirboy quiff. 'How are you getting on, by the way?'

'Getting on?'

'Well' – Grimes seemed uncomfortable all of a sudden – 'you've been through an awful lot here, what with that Moyle business and everything.'

'Yes, of course.' Cat thought about it. 'Can I ask if there are any leads in that case?'

'As far as I know it's still a complete mystery. One of his chums turned up dead, though.'

'*Oh?*' said Cat. 'Who?'

'Fellow named Blair Griffon.'

Cat frowned. 'A suspect?'

'Don't believe so. The manner of death was highly unusual, though.'

Something horrible occurred to Cat and her frown deepened. 'Is this by any chance the same guy who was there when they found Moyle's body? Tall, long-haired, bearded?'

'I'm not sure – the body has only just been discovered.'

'Where?'

'I'm not sure.'

'Was he murdered?'

'Again, I'm not sure. Why?' Grimes had noticed her reaction. 'You don't have anything to offer us?'

'Nothing,' she said, working hard to keep her voice steady. 'Not really. But you say he died in some unusual way?'

'I don't know the full details yet but yeah, I've been assured it's very weird.' Grimes was still watching her closely. 'You positive, Cat, that you don't know anything about it?'

'No – but it's a bit of a shock. I mean, if this is the guy I'm thinking of, then I met him once. And Moyle, of course – I met him too.'

'Then you might be interviewed about it.'

'Of course. Of course. Not a problem. But for now' – she glanced distractedly at her Swatch – 'I've got to get back. I've got to return to work. I'm late enough already.'

She thanked Grimes profusely and then raced up Raeburn Place, past the trendy cafés and boutique trinket shops of Stockbridge. Forty per cent of her mind was revisiting the night in the Innocent Railway, another forty per cent was preoccupied with the Dunn dynasty, and twenty per cent was deep in mourning for her once-immaculate record for punctuality.

CHAPTER
NINE

I T WAS IN THIS FRAME OF MIND – wary, suspicious, unable to
distinguish one devil from another – that Cat went for her
nightly run. It was now 20 March, and while the daylight
hours were lengthening appreciably the roads were still prone to
be slippery with ice and compacted snow. A couple of times she'd
ended up sprawled across the asphalt with bleeding palms, torn
pants and injured dignity. So she had every reason to reconsider
her routine – perhaps exercise at home, do crunches and sit-ups
or whatever – but she needed to feel cold air on her face and the
ground under her feet. She needed the ruthless clarity of running.

Upon her return from the extended lunch hour, Bellamy – who
was idling with malignant purpose near her desk – had glanced
very pointedly at the wall clock. She'd affected her most disarming
smile.

'I know, I know – I can still get lost around town without my GPS
and—'

'Kindly step into my office, Ms Thomas.'

Inside he told her not to bother taking a seat. Leaning back
against his desk and folding his arms, he said, 'I believe you know a
man called Carter Carterius?'

'Of course.' Cat hadn't been expecting this. 'The admin manager at Credit Cards.'

'He was your personal contact there?'

'He was.'

'Do you know he's been reassigned to branch manager – effective immediately?'

'He has?' Cat blinked. 'To where?'

'To Musselburgh. To take over from a manager who's retired due to illness.'

'Well' – Cat gulped, feeling of rush of claustrophobia – 'that's interesting.'

Bellamy's nostrils dilated. 'Are you absolutely sure, Ms Thomas, that you've put to bed the Napier credit card case?'

'I can guarantee it,' she said – truthfully, because she'd long moved on from that.

He strained all the muscles of his face. 'You know, I want to believe you, I dearly want to . . . and yet something makes me sceptical.'

Cat made sure she didn't even blink.

He thrust himself off the desk and glided past her, uncomfortably close. 'Never mind. Just remember that I only need an excuse, any excuse. Because let me tell you' – he was holding the door open with a sadistic grimace – 'I *enjoy* clearing out the troublemakers in my department.'

There was something specifically sexual about the way he said it that Cat would later find troubling. But that wasn't to say he wasn't right. It *was* enjoyable overturning old stones and exterminating insects. It was, in fact, her calling. Her destiny. The very reason for her existence.

Presently she ran up and down the hilly side streets of sleepy Ravelston. In Miami she had very nearly been run over by a car backing recklessly out of a driveway, purposely or not, and afterwards she had taken to running in the middle of the road wherever possible. She was doing it now, constantly on the alert for strange people, menacing faces, 'operators' sent out to 'deliver a message'. It had happened in Florida and there was no reason why it couldn't happen here.

In Blinkbonny Avenue a woman straightening a wheelie bin glared at her. Towards the bridge underpass on Craigleith Drive a four-by-four squealed to a halt behind her. Hammering up the incline of Ravelston House Road, she noticed a hedge rustling and was preparing to change course when a scrawny fox bolted across the road. Pounding down the slope on the other side she flinched at what she thought was a rifle shot, but it was only a man slamming the rear door of his hatchback. She reprimanded herself for being oversensitive.

She was three-quarters of the way through the run, passing through the inky shade on Ravelston Dykes, when she noticed a shawled woman standing on the verge holding a dog by the leash. The dog – yet another Border Terrier – was snarling at her defensively. Cat, vaguely amused, was transferring from the road to the pavement when she thought she heard the woman bark something.

'Cat.'

Perhaps she was taunting the dog for some reason.

'Cat Thomas.'

The woman had spoken louder than strictly necessary. Caught up in the impetus of running, Cat considered not altering her stride, but curiosity got the better of her. She drew up in her tracks and looked back, panting.

'Excuse me?'

The woman was about thirty feet away, standing in the shadow of an elm tree, an orange streetlamp casting an ungodly nimbus behind her. It was difficult to make out anything but a wizened face under an old-style cloche. She resembled Miss Marple. The Border Terrier was still growling.

'You should be wary of the company you keep,' the old woman said in a phlegmy voice.

Cat assumed at first the warning had something to with her investigation. 'Say again?'

'I said you should be very careful of the people you associate with. They have plans for you.'

Cat stared at the woman. As far as she could tell the two of them, plus dog, were entirely alone for hundreds of metres.

'How do you know my name?'

'I made it my business to discover your name.'

'Who are you?'

'I only want to protect you.'

'Protect me from who?'

The old woman glanced at her Border Terrier. 'From the dark ones,' she said, with a sibilant hiss.

Cat started to get angry. 'Who sent you? Was it the Dunns?'

'I know of no Dunns.'

'Then why are you here?'

'I've made it my duty to watch those who consort with witches.'

Cat narrowed her eyes and the woman seemed to read her mind.

'That's right, dear – I know of which I speak. And I say again, they have great plans for you.'

'Is that some sort of joke?' The sweat was freezing on Cat's skin.

'You know very well it is not.'

The Border Terrier was still *grrrrrrr*ing. Meanwhile a shadowy figure was emerging from a house across the road with a brace of eager hounds on leashes. Their presence seemed to put the old hag – and her terrier – further on edge.

'Come to me when you need to know more,' she said. 'And in the meantime consider your every step.'

'Why should I come to you?'

'Because you will want answers. You will *need* answers. You have my address.'

Then the old hag turned, jerking the dog's chain, and hobbled up the sidewalk. The hounds across the road were undulating like a seven-headed hydra.

Cat watched for a few moments, trying to raise an objection. Or a chuckle. But the hag, moving up the sidewalk with great alacrity despite a pronounced hobble, soon disappeared around a corner. And Cat got back to finishing her run – frowning, freezing, and wondering how the hell she was meant to know the old woman's address.

When she reached Dean Village she was so distracted she barely noticed the now-familiar crowd of shadowy tourists. But when she got closer to her building she certainly noticed Boucher – he was leaning into the engine cavity of his MG with a flashlight – and she swung around impulsively before he could spot her.

She had barely taken two steps, however, when she found herself being wrenched around – a muscular movement that sucked the air from her lungs.

An ogre with a buzzcut and a flattened nose had a hand the size of a baseball mitt clamped around her upper arm. He waited just long enough for her to recover from her shock, then he leaned in.

'It's a warning,' he spat. 'Don't end up like the—'

Then: *the force.*

Cat had no time to react. She could only watch, breathless, as the ogre was ripped away from her. As he was propelled against the wall of a neighbouring building. As the back of his head was slammed against the sandstone blocks.

It took her a moment to register that the surge, this time, was most definitely Robin Boucher.

'Keep your fucking hands off her!' he was yelling. 'Don't ever touch her! *You hear?*'

The ogre – looking as stunned as Cat – seemed not to know what to do. He stared up at Boucher, who was *towering* over him.

'*Do you hear?*'

The ogre couldn't counter Boucher's intensity. And he wilted. All two hundred and fifty pounds of him wilted. He squirmed away, like a chastened dog, and with one last terrified glance at Cat – as if she were somehow responsible – he disengaged from Boucher and loped off, picking up pace as he gained distance.

Boucher, whom Cat had never realised had such *heft*, looked across at her. 'Are you all right?'

'Yes, thank you,' she said.

'A friend of yours?'

'No, I've got no idea who he is.'

'Something to do with your work?'

'Probably.'

'The investigation?'

'I guess so.'

'I told you to be careful.'

'You did. You did at that.'

They took a final lingering look down the street, where the ogre was being swallowed up by a cluster of disapproving tourists.

'Anyway,' Boucher said, drawing a chamois cloth from his pocket, 'it's good to see you again.'

'You too,' managed Cat, almost laughing at the tone shift.

In truth, she was still shaken by his thrilling performance. It had been pulsating. Erotic, even. And just quite possibly contrived.

'Just one second.' As Cat continued to the stair door, Boucher diverted to the car and gently closed the bonnet. He was wearing what passed for his down-and-dirty clothes – oil-stained jeans and sleeveless jacket – and yet still looked impossibly stylish. 'Haven't seen you since that overspiced dinner,' he noted, joining her again.

'That's right,' she said, getting the key out of the lock. Her breath was still coming in gasps. 'I should've thanked you for that.'

'And I should've thanked you for being there.' When he raised an arm to hold back the door, she got an intoxicating whiff of heated engine grease – he seemed almost to be *smoking*. 'No mail for me?'

'Doesn't look like it, no.' She withdrew from the mailbox a brown envelope and a padded envelope.

'Oh,' he said, as if he *ever* got any mail. 'After you.'

As they ascended the stairs, Cat, still reeling, was painfully conscious that her pert Lycra-bound glutes were practically in his face. 'I'm a little sweaty,' she said.

'I don't mind. I hope you had a good time anyway – at the restaurant?'

'It was great, thanks.'

'You were a bit under the weather at the end.'

'I was, I apologise. I disgraced myself.' They whirled upwards. 'I hope I didn't say anything stupid?'

'Nothing of the sort.'

'I ended up having a nightmare,' she admitted.

'Did you? I didn't hear anything.' Which didn't sound remotely convincing. 'But really, I'm the one who should apologise. It wasn't right of me to leave you in that way.'

Cat was startled. Was he saying he'd been in her flat after all? She fumbled for her keys.

'You know, Cat,' he went on, as they reached her landing, 'if you don't mind my saying, you look a bit shaken up.'

'I *am* shaken up,' she said, still trying to open the door. 'That guy – well, it brought back bad memories.'

'No doubt,' he said, as smooth as ever. 'I expect you could do with a distraction.'

'Always.'

'Then I was wondering' – he sounded almost tentative – 'if next time you might join me for dinner upstairs.'

The lock finally clicked. Cat looked at him. 'You want to . . . cook me a meal?'

'I'm rather proud of my culinary prowess, you know.'

'Is that right?'

'And you didn't speak highly of the Mexican food.'

'I didn't?'

'"Bobo" or something, you called it.'

'There you go, I did embarrass myself – "bobo" is a Floridian term.'

'No, you were right to criticise. But what I can cook upstairs, I promise, will be a perfect Italian pasta.'

'Uh-huh.' She had all the locks open now.

'Even though I'm not remotely Italian.'

She pushed open the door and finally dared to look at him. 'Uh . . . Italian? Pasta? Yes, of course, that sounds fine.'

He arched his eyebrows, smiling. 'Well, then – say, seven-thirty on Friday night?'

'Sounds great,' said Cat, but immediately she had second thoughts. Because she was *submitting* again. 'Hang on,' she said, before he could turn. 'Hang on. I've got an even better idea. How about *you* come to *my* place? And I cook *you* an Italian meal?'

'Really?'

'It's my turn, yeah? The Mexican meal was your treat, after all.'

'That's true – and it's very thoughtful of you.'

'I fancy my hand at Italian cuisine too, you know.'

'Indeed?' He sounded amused. 'Then I'd be delighted to come down.'

'Just knock whenever you feel like it.'

'And I'll bring a bottle of something – non-alcoholic, of course.'

'OK.'

'There's still a great deal I'd like to clarify about myself, you know.'

'OK.'

She stepped across her threshold and closed the door. Chained it. And turned the Chubb locks.

Still a great deal I'd like to clarify about myself.

And that would be very much in order, Cat thought.

When she had settled enough to open the mail she was surprised to find nothing inside the brown-paper envelope but an elegant business card.

MADAM MORGANACH

OCCULT RESEARCH

13A Featherhall Close, Corstorphine
Edinburgh

She was so disturbed by this – the idea that Miss Marple had traced her somehow to her residence – that she barely noticed herself tearing open the padded envelope. It was only belatedly that she remembered the growl – the *threat* – of the ogre: '*It's a warning.*'

Looking down, she flung the envelope on the table in disgust.

Inside, bound in cling film, was an enormous maggot-ridden rat.

CHAPTER

TEN

THE NEXT DAY, AS SOON AS BELLAMY departed the office for points unknown, Cat ducked into Agnes's and called the Musselburgh branch, hoping that Carter Carterius had already assumed his new role there. But, after being kept on hold for an indecent amount of time, she was told that the manager was unavailable.

'But he's there, right – he's taken up his appointment?'

'As I say, miss, he's out of reach.'

Cat considered invoking her rights as a fraud investigator but thought better of it. She hung up.

'That was quick,' noted Agnes.

'I don't like where this is going,' Cat admitted. 'What do you know about the Dunn family? Alistair Dunn in particular?'

'Alistair Dunn? As in Dunn and Dusted?'

'I've no idea what that means.'

Agnes, who was slouched in her chair eating a Bakewell tart, shoved a chunk of icing into her mouth. 'Alistair Dunn is the closest thing we have to royalty at ABC. And that means something, believe me, because we Scots aren't good at royalty.'

Cat remembered the tacky portrait in the foyer. 'Royal or not, is he crooked?'

'Of course he is.'

'Do you know that for sure?'

'You know what Rabbie Burns said – "Behind every great fortune is a crime."'

'I'm pretty sure that was someone else.* But he's rich, anyway?'

'Wickedly rich. Got a castle in Morningside that's as big as your building.'

'And that's unusual in Edinburgh?'

'Let's just say J.K. Rowling made an offer and he gave her the *who-are-you-again?* treatment. And he's ruthless. Psychopathic. Every time he takes down a rival he shoots a stag in the Highlands and mounts the head on his wall. Or so they say.'

'Surely that's just a myth?'

'Well, he's ruthless anyway. Got tentacles everywhere. Claws too. Don't poke that bear if you don't wanna get scratched.'

'"Don't go digging where the worms got teeth"?'

'Eh?' Agnes washed down the tart with a sip of coffee. 'You're not pitting yourself against Alistair Dunn, are you?'

'Is that suicidal, career-wise?'

'It might be suicidal, period. You sure you want to get mixed up in that type of thing?'

'I've got to see it through now, regardless of what happens.'

'In for the kill, huh? Blood on your tongue?'

Cat baulked, for intimate reasons, at the expression. 'It's got nothing to do with my personal inclinations. But—'

'Listen to you.' Agnes had put her coffee down. 'Just listen to you, Cat. You're a hunter, accept it. You're a tigress – a true cat. You like sinking your teeth into flesh.'

* Balzac.

Cat winced again. 'But do you know of *anyone* absolutely trustworthy in this bank? Anyone I can approach with full confidence?'

'I don't know if anyone is absolutely trustworthy, do you?'

'What about whoever it was that accepted my transfer from Florida? Someone upstairs? They must have known about my record?'

'Don't kid yourself,' Agnes said. 'If your appointment was ticked off by someone upstairs, it was probably Alistair Dunn himself – and then only because he thought it'd be handy to have someone in Frauds who knew nothing about him. Or Scottish crime in general. Maybe he just liked the look of you. Did you send a photo of your glutes?' She smirked, but her face abruptly froze. 'Uh-oh.'

'What's the matter?'

'Wing Commander is staring at us.' Agnes was glancing over Cat's shoulder.

'He's back?'

'Looking as sexually frustrated as ever.'

Cat, who was holding a sheet of paper as though consulting Agnes about some technical matter, made a show of studying the figures. 'Well, thanks for your help. See you at lunch, maybe?'

'If I'm still here.'

Back at her desk Cat concentrated on her menial duties while considering her peculiar catch-22: trying to save her job by pursuing an investigation that might well get her fired. But why, she wondered, was she making life so difficult for herself? Because she needed to prove her moral superiority? Or was it because, as Agnes had suggested, she was a born predator? One thing was for sure: it wouldn't be easy to get a new job in Edinburgh if she'd been perceived to fail miserably in her first Scottish appointment. She needed to make a decisive move before it was too late.

She was heading out to lunch when she noticed Agnes sitting in Bellamy's office, her arms folded in disgust. Bellamy himself was leaning back in his chair, one hand pressed on the desk – the old 'repulse' posture. When his eyes flicked in Cat's direction, she quickly averted her gaze.

At the pub, waiting for Agnes, she took out her phone and did a private search on the Dunn family. There were scattered news items linking them all in innocuous ways to crime. The *Daily Record* had Craig Dunn from Business Banking warning about the dangers of 'fly-by-night banks vis-à-vis established financial institutions such as ABC'. In *The National* Mungo Dunn was quoted about credit card security: 'I can honestly say that the safeguards we have in place at ABC are among the most stringent in the world.' In *The Scotsman* Alistair Dunn himself warned of the 'increasing sophistication' of crime gangs and the 'duty of financial institutions like ABC to be constantly on our guard'. The accompanying photos featured all of them wearing squinted eyes and smug grins, as though taunting someone to take a swing at them. *Backpfeifengesicht*, as the Germans said – the eminently punchable face. And that was a fatal weakness of white-collar crooks, Cat thought – they revel just a little too much in their guile and duplicity.

Agnes didn't show up at the pub and wasn't anywhere in the office when Cat returned. Reminding herself that they had never quite confirmed their lunch date, Cat got back to her spreadsheets. When Agnes still hadn't shown up by three o'clock, however, she started to wonder if something had gone wrong. There was a distinctly unsettled atmosphere throughout the office: people button-lipped and barely looking up from their desks. Venturing past Agnes's office, Cat noticed that all the silly little knick-knacks – a cartoonish voodoo doll, a goat's head figurine, a sign saying LIVE IS EVIL BACKWARDS – were gone. With mounting alarm she went to Bellamy's cockpit and rapped on the glass. Looking annoyed – he was doing some two-fingered typing – he nodded to her to come in.

'Agnes,' Cat said promptly. 'What happened to Agnes?'

He didn't look up from the computer screen. 'What should have happened a long time ago.'

'You've fired her?'

'I did what I had to do.'

'Why?'

'That should be obvious.'

'I'm afraid it's not obvious to me.'

Bellamy fixed her with a glare. 'You'd be well advised not to take that tone with me, Ms Thomas.'

'All right then, why was Agnes dismissed? I'd like to know.'

'Unacceptable standards. Deviation from established protocols. Improper lifestyle choices.'

'Improper *lifestyle* choices?'

Bellamy's brows knitted. 'She claims to be a *witch*, Ms Thomas. An actual witch.'

'So?'

'*So?*' He issued an incredulous snort. 'It might mean nothing to you, but ABC doesn't need a devil worshipper in the workplace. It doesn't need those who rally around them either. That used to be grounds for execution itself, in better days.'

'*In better days . . .*' Cat hissed.

'In better days, yes.' Bellamy was wearing his very own *Backpfeifengesicht*. 'In any case, I'm rather busy here, as you can see. Have you anything important you wish to see me about?'

'No,' said Cat, feeling a wave of contempt rush over her. 'I'll be back at my desk. Sorting through the mail.'

She counted down the minutes until five o'clock and then headed purposefully through the chiaroscuro streets – the gorse on Arthur's Seat had spontaneously combusted, apparently, and the air was choked with fragrant smoke – all the way to

Newington, where she found Agnes half-tanked in her stuffy top-floor flat with its purple-painted walls and menagerie of demonic figurines.

'Can I pour you a glass of whisky?' Agnes slurred, waving the bottle. 'It's the Laird of Howgate's own brand, can you believe that? I got it at Aldi.'

'Do you want to talk about it?' Cat asked, settling into the sofa beside a cardboard box of Agnes's office decorations.

'My sacking? I told you it was inevitable. That fud's had it in for me from day one.'

'But there are procedures, surely? You need fair notice.'

'I've had enough notice. I walked out in the end.'

'But he told me you were a witch. As if that were some basis for a sacking.'

'I *am* a witch . . .'

'Metaphorically speaking.'

'Nothing metaphorical about it at all. I *am* a witch. I'm from a long line of witches. You're not still kidding yourself that the conclave was just some kind of parlour game, are you?'

Cat ignored her. 'So what are you going to do?'

'What do you recommend? Invoke the Laird?'

'I'm not sure what you mean.'

'Well, I won't be getting my job back while that Sassenach fud is in charge, that's for sure.' Agnes surveyed Cat with a roguish expression. 'Maybe you can fix the problem for me?'

'Now I'm *really* not sure what you mean.'

'Oh, I think you are. Or you will be soon enough.'

'If there was any way I could genuinely get your job back, you know I'd do it.'

'OK, then, we have a deal. How is the King, by the way?'

'The King?'

'Cock Robin, remember him? The grandmaster? Has he check-mated you yet? Exposed his bishop?'

'You really are drunk.'

'Sure I am. *In vino veritas*, eh? You needn't worry your gorgeous wee head about me, Catriona Thomas. I'll be back quicker than you can say *shenhamforash*. And meanwhile I'll just bide my time. Paint the walls black, maybe – this purple shite really makes me wanna puke sometimes.'

Cat got to her feet. 'Just let me know if you need any help. I've always appreciated everything you've done for me, you know.'

'Now, now, Cat, sentimentality doesn't become you. Besides, you've got more important things to do, haven't you? Dinners to cook? Cocks to stroke? Pests to exterminate? And we still wanna cuddle some bairns now, don't we?'

Cat shook her head. 'You really need some rest.'

'And yet the wicked get none,' Agnes returned puckishly, raising her glass of Howgate Scotch and draining it all in one fiery gulp.

CHAPTER

ELEVEN

B Y FRIDAY EVENING'S DINNER DATE – if indeed it was a date – Cat had good reason to feel flustered. She was increasingly isolated at work. Her only friend – if indeed she was a friend – was gone. Others in the department were sneaking pitying glances at her. Bellamy was circling like a Spitfire. She suspected it was only a matter of time before she was called into his cockpit for the 'Sadly, I've come to a decision' talk.

Neither had she found enough time to collate the evidence she felt was necessary for official presentation to the ABC Board or the fraud unit at Police Scotland. In fact, Bellamy had piled extra duties on her precisely in a bid, she suspected, to keep her from doing anything out of order. She needed to speak to Carter Carterius but every time she phoned the branch he was 'unavailable'. She considered heading out to Musselburgh to confront him in person, but she could scarcely afford to overrun her lunch hour again.

On top of this, she had begun to feel as though she were being watched – hunted as though by a sparrowhawk. She knew very well the propensity of people under pressure to manufacture perils – and would have been happy to admit she was in such a hyper-neurotic state – except for one salient point. She had experienced the same suspicions in Florida, and they had very much been *not* a figment of her imagination.

'My radar is finely tuned,' she said to Boucher. 'Maybe too finely tuned, but it's tuned. So when I open up the departmental mail and there's nothing inside but a blank sheet of paper spattered with blood, I'm prone to think it's someone sending me a message.'

'My God,' said Boucher, taking a seat at her kitchen table. 'Are you saying you actually received a bloodstained page?'

'Well, it's not entirely unusual. It's our job to take out fraudsters, remember, so the sender could have been anyone currently under investigation. Or someone whose career we've already shot down, excuse the metaphor. For that matter, it could be entirely unrelated to me personally. But my radar is saying the opposite.' She stirred black pepper into the chopped tomatoes.

'Have you reported it to anyone?'

'I passed it to my boss Nick Bellamy, but of course he said it wasn't important enough to record officially. And he's right – it's *not*. But when you put it together with some other things, like the dead rat in the mail, it—'

'The *dead rat* in the mail?'

'That came in the padded envelope. The one I picked up the other night – after you roughed up that guy. He must have delivered it himself.'

'You mean to say he personally shoved it through the slot?'

'I assume so – you didn't see him do it?'

'Can't say I did,' Boucher said, thinking about it. 'Have you reported *that* to anyone?'

'Not yet. Maybe never. How much salt do you like?'

'As much as you're comfortable with,' Boucher replied, before adding, 'I must say, Cat, you seem to be taking it all with remarkable indifference.'

'Oh, I'm not taking it well at all, I assure you. I'm about to rile up a real hornets' nest, if I haven't already. My boss Bellamy is on my tail. I'm in danger of losing my job. I've been told it's suicidal to go after the Dunns. So I'm taking refuge in routine, just as I did when I went through the same thing in Florida. It's all I can do. But I'm frustrated, believe me. I shouldn't even be mentioning this to you. But I think it's important to put it on the record with as many people as possible. How much parmesan do you prefer?'

'Whatever you think is best, Cat. But really' – Boucher shifted in his chair – 'are you absolutely sure you know what you're up against? As I've mentioned in the past, I know a good deal about organised crime in this country. I know exactly how the system operates. I even know Alistair Dunn.'

Cat turned. 'You know Alistair Dunn?'

'Not well – I've met him just once or twice; he's been a client of mine – but I know all about his connections. And I can assure you that he has influence everywhere. In parliament, the press, even in the police. So you can't rely on *anyone* if you go after someone like that. Except me, of course – I can make things go away.'

Glancing at him again, Cat wondered exactly how he might 'make things go away'. Using his supernatural powers? His own muscle? He was wearing a light tweed jacket and a check shirt – the attire of a county squire – and couldn't have looked less like an enforcer. Yet she had seen him effortlessly overpower the ogre. She had felt his power – or something – in the Innocent Railway. And she had seen his Herculean body – at least in her imagination.

'I'll summon you if I need to,' Cat said, and served up the meal.

They sat at opposite ends of her Heart Foundation table and he reached for the bottle he'd brought with him. 'Have some of my Pimento – it's great with pasta.'

'That's OK. Look' – Cat raised her hand in front of her mouth as she chewed – 'I've been meaning to ask you about something, I hope you don't mind.'

'And I've already indicated that I have something to explain to you.'

'Then perhaps we're talking about the same thing?'

'Let me tell you and we'll find out.' He poured himself some Pimento. 'At Casa del Fuego on Saturday evening I mentioned something about being a chess player, without going into much detail. So I'd be surprised if you didn't prove curious about that. And even more surprised if you hadn't checked out my credentials, so to speak, on the Internet.'

'Uh huh.' Cat tried not to blush.

'No need to be embarrassed – I would certainly have done the same thing. But the truth is that I'm not a traditional chess player. I certainly play it, and I'm rather good at it, though not nearly accomplished enough to go professional. What I've done, though, is applied its disciplines – what might be called a certain algorithmic way of thinking – to much more important matters. But it's all very complex and sensitive, and I invariably reveal only as much as I need to.'

'If you're trying to tell me you're still unable to talk about it, then that's OK.'

'No, that's not what I mean.' He put the bottle down. 'I'm willing to tell you – and you alone – because I think you deserve it.'

She guessed she was supposed to be flattered.

'The truth is' – he paused so long she almost heard a drumroll – 'I'm a fortune teller.'

'A fortune teller.'

'A tea-leaf reader.'

'A tea-leaf reader.'

'A social meteorologist, you might say.'

221

'A social meteorologist.'

He smiled. 'What I do is collate a vast amount of information from across the world's newsfeeds – I have access to thousands of sites – and lay that over a matrix of recorded history and the psychology of the main players to help identify certain trajectories.'

'Trajectories indicating what?'

'Voting results, uprisings, wars, stock market crashes, revolutions. I don't wish to boast – and in many cases I dearly wish I'd been wrong – but I've predicted most of the shocks to the system of the last twenty years.'

'Such as?'

'The Dot.Com collapse, the Sub-Prime Housing Crisis, the Iraq War, and most of the major terrorist attacks in a roundabout sort of way.'

'Interesting,' said Cat. 'And what are you predicting now, for the future?'

'A fair question, but do you really want to know?'

'I'm not sure – do I?'

'Let's just say I see nothing to be optimistic about,' he said. 'Failing, of course, the arrival of a black swan – and as it happens I increasingly suspect we're about to see one.'

'And why would a catastrophic event be a good thing, exactly?'

'Well, black swans aren't always unwelcome. And they're not always events, for that matter. They can be people as well. Which is exactly the sort of black swan I'm predicting right now.'

'A messiah?'

'Let's just say certain confluences are currently in motion. And powerful confluences in themselves often invoke a flesh-and-blood personification. Sometimes a messiah, sometimes a monster. Sometimes a monster who's greeted as a messiah, sometimes a messiah who's treated as a monster – both paradigms are depressingly common. As to which one we'll see in the next few years, that's what my clients are counting on me to identify.'

'I see.' Cat wondered if he was spinning a tale. 'And this, you say, is the way you make your living?'

'My reputation as a fortune teller means that many unpleasant people – disaster capitalists, hedge fund managers and weapons manufacturers among them – are prepared to pay highly for my wisdom. Ah.' Something amusing seemed to have occurred to him. 'You're still suspicious of me, aren't you, Cat?'

'I'd be happier if you offered some evidence.'

'But of course.' He looked around. 'Do you have a laptop here, by any chance?'

'In the next room.'

'Your own laptop – not something belonging to work?'

'Uh-huh.' She wondered why that was important.

'Well, let's finish this splendid meal and then I'll show you my website.' He tapped the bottle. 'Are you sure you won't try this Pimento?'

'I'm OK.'

When the dinner was fully eaten – barring a couple of lemon sorbets Cat had whipped up – she slipped into the living area and returned with her laptop. 'What am I looking for?' she asked, opening a search engine.

'The Augur's Well,' he said, and when she looked up: 'It's just a name.'

After a few minutes of frustration – the laptop was busy updating itself – she brought up a stylised homepage showing crows erupting from a well. 'Got it.'

'You'll need to log in,' he said, and provided the password: 'Morgenstern.'

'Two words?'

'One word,' he said. 'Again, just a name.'

The login opened a new page of PDF documents of what looked like pie-charts, projections and profiles of various world leaders. Titles included: SOUTH AMERICA: RHYMING WITH ASSONANCE, THE POPULATION ULTIMATUM, MONITORING PROPAGANDA AS A HARBINGER OF WAR, and TRENDS IN POPULAR CULTURE AS INDICATORS OF IMMINENT TRAUMA.

'Choose one,' he said.

She selected a document entitled THE MOST DANGEROUS MAN ON THE PLANET – fascinated, as always, by hazardous men – and found herself looking at a wretchedly familiar face above a page of text. 'OK,' she said. 'What now?'

Boucher, leaning back in his chair and staring upwards, recited the opening paragraph as though reading the words off the ceiling.

'In a crowded field of sociopathic, mendacious, Machiavellian and Strangelovian officials who currently populate our corridors of power, there is one man whose resistance to shame and self-reflection, brazen pursuit of his cult-like ideology, and total disregard for the consequences of his actions, marks him at the very top of the list of the most dangerous people on the planet. Since he currently occupies a post integrally connected to the fate of nations, since his hunger for wars of conquest is without equal, and especially because he has an unerring habit of "failing upwards" despite his disastrous misjudgements, it is incumbent upon me to study his education, career trajectory, personality traits and moral conditioning in order to identify likely timeframes and locations of future conflict.'

He dropped his head and broke into a semi-apologetic grin. 'From that little diatribe you'd be forgiven for thinking that I *like* the fellow.'

Cat wasn't sure what to make of it. He had recited the paragraph verbatim, true, but that didn't necessarily mean he had written it. He could have memorised a few opening paragraphs for later usage. The proper thing to do now would be to open another document, find a random page, and ask him to quote something from that as well. But that might cross a barrier – it might officially offend him.

And there was something else. Something unexpected. The passage he'd recited, though a trifle earnest, had *turned her on*. It might have been his senatorial voice; it might have been the dreamy look on his face; or it might have been the sheer novelty of having someone in her kitchen use words like 'mendacious' and 'Machiavellian'. Whatever. She saw in Boucher something of a kindred spirit, and that ripped a rug from under her.

'Okey-dokey, then – I'm pleased we've got that established.' She launched to her feet to fetch the sorbets (wondering if she had ever in her life said 'okey-dokey').

'You don't look convinced,' Boucher said, sounding remarkably unoffended.

'No, it's not that at all.'

'You can choose another passage, if you like.'

'No, really.' She transferred the sorbets to the table. 'I *rarely* sound convinced. It's my nature, I guess. I'm hopelessly sceptical and cynical. I think perhaps I was born that way.' She settled back into her chair and started scooping into the dessert with a spoon. 'I remember when I was five years old being taken to see the Thanksgiving parade in New York. And I was freezing cold and I had sticky soda on my hands and I was watching it all – all the floats and marching bands – saying to myself, "Is this supposed to be fun? We came all this way to see this?" At five years old. I remember, even earlier, there was a magician at a friend's birthday party and I told my parents not to waste any money hiring him for my own birthday because he was such a lemon. I hated magicians. In fact, I hated birthday parties in general. I hated Disney movies. I hated family vacations. I hated getting hugged. I hated dolls and teddy bears. I hated everything except cats. So it's hardly as though any "traumatic experience" later made me cynical. *More* cynical, maybe. But I don't know.'

She was babbling – she knew it – but couldn't stop.

'There are huge advantages, of course, to being cynical. You're rarely disappointed, for one. But great disadvantages as well. It's easy to become alienated. It's hard to maintain relationships – serious relationships – because you're always expecting them to unravel.' She was carving into the icy sides of the sorbet now. 'People often ask me, in fact, why I'm not married – why I've never been married. And I have to assure them it's not because I don't like the idea, the institution of marriage – not at all. But I'm too cynical to trust romantic love. I don't trust it because it's based on things that are hopelessly ephemeral. The foundations are shaky. Worse than shaky, they're pinned together with bestial instincts. And, as powerful as bestial instincts are, they should always be treated with caution. I mean, I've been with men and I've seen the lies in their eyes. They don't even have to speak, they don't even have to lie to me, because I can sense it, I can read people's subtitles. And while that gives me some advantage as a fraud investigator, it makes me a terrible life partner. I mean, I'm even ambivalent about sex. I mean, if you stand back from it, survey it critically – the act of physical coupling, I mean – it's bizarre, it's demeaning, and it's like a mass delusion, this whole idea that it's desirable, it's essential, it's the source of all happiness. To *not* need it is liberating. Really, when you consider the sheer volume of time and money and mental energy that is squandered just preparing for sex, pursuing it, talking your way into it, performing it, and dealing with all the frustration and disappointments that come with it – not to mention the *diseases* – well, what's wrong with some healthy prudishness? Alienation? Why persist with the madness? Are people really frightened of what might happen if they snap out of the trance? People need to get real. Some deep soul searching, reviewing what's really important, scraping away all the baked-in grime with cynicism – that's a cleansing process. And it makes life a thousand times better. You have to overturn everything you know, rip up the underpinnings, rewire all the cables, and then reconstruct everything from the ground up, but you're stronger, you're more efficient, you're not straitjacketed by tradition or societal pressures or your own unreasonable expectations. What's that, if not freedom? What's that, if not a superior, liberated, rational existence? And total mastery of the self? I ask you. I ask you. I ask you.'

Cat almost slammed the dessert bowl on the table and was surprised – astonished – to see that it was scraped clean. She'd been stuffing her mouth with sorbet even as she spoke. Boucher, as usual, looked tremendously amused and approving, with delightful crinkles at the corners of his eyes. He waited until he was sure that she was finished speaking – that she was inviting him to contribute – and then he chuckled appreciatively.

'Cat,' he said quietly, 'I couldn't agree more.'

'I'm glad,' said Cat, meaning it. 'I'm glad. No, really – I'm glad.'

She nodded, and nodded again, then looked him dead in the eyes.

'Would you like to fuck me, by the way?'

He paused to furrow his brow and purse his lips, as though mocking the whole idea that he needed time to consider.

'Uhhhhh,' he mused, frowned some more, and narrowed his eyes. 'Well, yes . . . yes, I suppose . . . yes . . . indeed.' As if the reality had only just occurred to him. 'You know . . . yes . . . I can't imagine anything I'd like more.'

'Good,' she said with finality. 'Good.' And they sat there at her Heart Foundation table for what seemed like sixty seconds, coming to grips with what they'd both agreed to, before Cat pushed herself back, the chair scraping across the boards, and got to her feet.

'In that case,' she said, 'let's get on with it.'

Later she told herself that the real reason she'd set the whole process in motion was curiosity – that she needed to assure herself once and for all that he was not the same ludicrously muscled and over-endowed demon that had visited her in her dream.

But when he disrobed at the foot of her bed – she was already naked on top of her duvet, waiting for him – she saw bristling fur, biceps, triceps, abs, pecs, trapezoids, deltoids, obliques, and a throbbing member that already looked the size of a rolling pin. He must have seen she was aghast – she'd stopped breathing, her eyes widening in horror – but he swiftly swung into position anyway, wrapping his huge hands around her throat and forcing his immensity into her while staring down at her with snarling lips and flared nostrils and pointed teeth and eyes that were positively demonic.

'Everything is going to be all right,' he kept hissing as he thrust and thrust into her, again and again like some piston-operated machine, and Cat, with her heart hammering around her ribcage, could only shudder in terror, because it was true, oh dear God it was true.

She was getting fucked by the Devil.

PART
THREE

CHAPTER

ONE

C AT EXPECTED THE HOME OF Madam Morganach to be intensely dark and cluttered with occult mementoes and arcane texts, much like Agnes's flat, but instead it was bright, exceptionally warm and decorated only with a few sticks of mismatched furniture. The whole effect – like the set of an avant-garde play – seemed to Cat curiously artificial, not to be trusted, and made her further ill at ease when she could least afford to be. She had been struggling for two days to get a grip on herself and scarcely needed more complications now.

After their extraordinary intercourse Boucher had transformed instantly, magically, into the most charming and sympathetic of lovers. His whole body seemed to deflate. But Cat herself was nauseous. She told him he was great, marvellous, then whisked off to the bathroom, locked herself inside, and in a blind panic tried to douche out what seemed a half-pint of his essence. She had a scalding hot shower. She almost threw up. But at the same time she became determined not to betray her feelings. Part of her feared Boucher would think she was mad. Another part feared she *was* mad. She climbed back into bed and turned her back on him and bunched the sheets to her throat and tried to sleep even as he caressed her hip as if, for the love of God, he was anticipating another session. She was unmoving as the Sphinx, however, and eventually Boucher rolled over and fell asleep, snoring in barely audible exhalations. He had kissed her in the morning – she had slept barely a wink – and they had shared some breakfast and a smattering of small-talk, but everything about her body language communicated to him the folly of trying to mark out new territory. She had ignored an ambiguous text from Maxine downstairs:

Not another nightmare, I hope?

And, through a distinct aura of petulance, had compelled Boucher to retreat to his own flat upstairs. But it wasn't until she heard the reassuring creak of his floorboards that she finally exhaled. And resolved to visit Madam Morganach as soon as possible.

'I should warn you now,' Cat said, still clinging desperately to reason, 'that I don't believe in Satan.'

'Oh,' Morganach twittered with weary amusement, 'that matters not, dear, if *he* believes in *you*.'

The old woman was seated on a damask chair, balancing a flower-patterned teacup (Cat had declined a drink of her own), and in the cold light of day – and it *was* cold, and it *was* light, with the sun blazing through the conservatory and airing the room with a foggy luminescence – she appeared much statelier and more elegant than how Cat remembered her from the night in the street. But that only made her seem even more at odds with the minimalist décor.

'Tell me,' Cat asked, 'why you said you've been keeping an eye on me.'

'I regard it as my duty to do so,' Morganach told her, 'because I was once very much like you. I once turned to the black arts too, you see, and I also consorted with witches.'

'What witches?'

'Some of the very witches you yourself have met.'

'Who exactly?'

'Elspeth Ross, Maggie Balfour, George Pickingill, Zara Mashasha . . .'

Cat recognised some of the names from the conclave. 'Agnes Sampson?'

'She is not of my generation, dear, but I know of her well enough. I know all of them in one way or another. They claim to be direct descendants of witches past, but in truth their names are rarely those that they were born with.'

'They change their names?'

'To honour famous witches, dear. Allison 'Maggie' Balfour – tortured in Edinburgh Castle in 1596. Agnes Sampson – tortured in Holyrood Palace in 1591. Both were later burned at the stake.'

Cat shook her head. 'Just because they were burned at the stake doesn't mean that they *were* witches.'

'Again, it matters not, dear. For their imaginations alone – for the strength it took to fabricate outrageous confessions in the face of death – the witches of old are worshipped by today's covens. There are scores of Maggie Balfours and Agnes Sampsons out there.'

Cat, nodding now, saw a glimmer of reason. 'So you're effectively admitting they worship a myth, right?'

'Of course they worship myths. The Satanic community is as prone as any cult to nurture their fantastical stories, to revere their martyrs, and to revel in a sense of persecution. But the witch trials of history require little exaggeration. They are evidence enough of the madness at the heart of piety. Are you sure you wouldn't like a cup of tea?'

'I'll be OK.'

'Then excuse me a moment while I fetch Sirius – he frets when I have company.'

Now that she thought about it, Cat had registered the persistent snarling of a dog somewhere. And when Morganach returned she was holding the hostile Border Terrier, which glared at Cat with its flews curling.

'I once was deeply religious,' said Morganach, settling back into her chair. 'A devout Baptist. But then mother was diagnosed with liver cancer and my prayers went unanswered. My own daughter died in infancy after my prayers went unanswered. My husband died of malignant mesothelioma after my prayers went unanswered. So when my son fell ill with pleurisy, I turned to a different power. I attended a séance. I implored Lucifer for help because the traditional deities had ignored me. And I learned the founding myth of modern Satanism.'

'Which is?'

Morganach spoke in warbly voice. 'Lucifer broke with the Creator over the right of mortal human beings to supernatural deliverance. The Creator is – and has always been – an arrogant, disinterested, even contemptuous deity. He cares not for even his most devout followers and refuses to meddle in their affairs. If the human race is damned, He believes, it's because it has damned itself. His hands are off. But Lucifer, who adored humanity with all its warts and weaknesses, was moved to tears by the suffering of the mortal masses and pleaded with the Creator to change His mind. When the Creator refused, Lucifer absconded from Heaven, vowing to share his powers with the beleaguered souls of Earth.'

'Uh-huh,' Cat said. 'You're not telling me you really believe that?'

'No more than the acolytes of any religion really believe their foundation myths,' Morganach admitted, a little defensively. 'It's the sentiment that's important and the sentiment is enough to constitute a truth. But I will say this, dear.' She was stroking the dog furiously. 'More unaccountable happenings occur under the aegis of Satanism than any other religion. My son was saved, I can tell you that, and he recovered fully. I too prospered in many other ways. It was a genuine miracle.'

Cat thought again of the illuminated sign around the corner from Dean Village: **THERE WILL BE NO MIRACLES HERE**. 'Then I don't understand,' she said. 'You're trying to tell me that Satan *helped* you?'

'He will do that when he sees fit.'

'Then' – Cat frowned – 'you'll have to forgive me, but I'm still confused. Are you a Satanist?'

'A former Satanist. A former witch.'

'Then why did you leave?'

'Because Satanism is evolving, dear. It has ambitions, very grandiose ambitions. Too grand for the likes of me.'

'What sort of ambitions?'

'Satanists now see themselves as the saviours of the world.'

'You'll have to explain that.'

A wan smile and another *grrrrrr* from the dog. 'Look around you. The history of humankind long ago reached a point where certain ideologies became not just life threatening but world threatening. And still the Creator – the distrustful deity – remains aloof and disinterested. Because He cares not if the whole planet is reduced to ash.'

'And Satan?'

'Is the only one prepared to act.'

'How?'

'By removing malignancies.'

'What malignancies?'

'Enemies of humankind.'

'What enemies?'

'Enemies that don't even know they are enemies.'

'Such as who?'

Morganach offered the faintest of smiles. 'Have you never encountered a human being who offers nothing to the world but trouble? Whose only purpose seems to be to create misery?'

Cat felt her blood heating. 'Perhaps.'

'And have you ever thought about killing that person?'

'I guess I have. I guess we all have. But it's not to us to make such judgements.'

'Of course not. God will sort it out, will he not?'

'We have processes in place, processes that—'

'Yes, yes, yes.' Morganach gave an impatient frown. 'There are always processes, aren't there? Always laws and regulations and adherence to codified principles. As the hawks soar and the sparrows cower. As the sociopathic, mendacious and psychotically greedy continue to pilot us towards destruction.'

Cat was startled: Morganach seemed almost to be quoting from Boucher's website.

Morganach shifted in her seat, as if belatedly realising she'd gone too far. 'The point is that Satanism is not just about liberation, dear, or freedom from shame and intellectual oppression – it's about realistic answers to existential problems. It's about taking action when conventional morality inhibits us from acting, using powers not usually at our disposal.'

'Now I'm *really* confused,' Cat said, shaking her head. 'Because – you'll forgive me if I say this – you sound like you're proselytising. Like you're *promoting* Satanism. I can't see what your issue is with it at all.'

Morganach grunted self-consciously and her face softened. Sirius seemed to be daring Cat to move.

'My issue is with the way they go about things,' she said. 'The way they seek out those who share their world view and recruit newcomers into the fold. The way they charm them, manipulate them, make them beholden to them. And yes, in certain cases, where a person is particularly attractive to them – when a person wins the approval of Lucifer himself – the way that person is groomed.'

'*Groomed.*' The very word sounded like a curse.

'Groomed for a very special role.' Morganach's watery eyes were barely blinking. 'They once tried to groom me, you know. Because I was very much like you back then – pretty, intelligent, scathing about corruption.'

'I'm *not* scathing about anything. I'm cynical, that's all.'

'Atheistic, self-reliant, sexually liberated.'

'Sexually liberated? Who told you all this?'

Morganach's eyes narrowed. 'Can I ask, dear, if you went to Lucifer with a request?'

'I went to a meeting, that's all – a conclave.'

'At which Lucifer was invoked?'

'I don't know – I didn't see anyone. Just the . . . the . . .'

'The?'

'The Laird of Howgate.'

'The Laird of Howgate.' Amusement flashed across Morganach's eyes. 'And did the Laird agree to intercede on your behalf?'

'As far as I know, nothing was ever agreed.'

'But you went there with a need, a wish? A desire they knew about?'

'I don't know. I don't know what they knew.'

In the silence that followed, as Morganach studied Cat, there came creaking from upstairs. Someone in the flat above – it was a two-storey house – was shifting furniture.

Nnnnnnnhhhhhhhhrrrrrrrrrr.

Creak creak creak.

Ka-LONK.

Cat felt as though she were being deviously mocked. And she could not hold Morganach's gaze. Even as the woman reiterated the awful truth.

'They groomed you, my dear. Because you fit a certain profile. Because you have certain values that make you useful to them. They groomed you as they tried to groom me. But you still have time, if you wish, to extricate yourself . . .'

In a flood of rapid-fire memories Cat heard Agnes saying, '*He liked you, Cat, he really liked you.*' And '*We want to see plenty of bairns now, don't we?*' And she saw the admiring face of the Laird of Howgate in the darkness of Aileanach Castle. And Boucher poised over her with his ripped physique and his demonic eyes. '*Everything is going to be all right.*' **THERE WILL BE NO MIRACLES HERE.** And repeatedly she relived the extraordinary moment when her own body had convulsed and trembled and she had lost control. No man had ever done that to her before. And the mere idea that it had taken the Devil to bring her to orgasm, for the very first time, nauseated her all over again.

She shook her head with despair. One moment of weakness and whimsy, one reckless acquiescence, one mysterious night in a Scottish castle, and one night of submission had led to the demolition of her belief system, the pollution of her body, and endlessly horrifying complications she could not bear to contemplate.

'But how do I extricate myself,' she asked, raising her eyes to Morganach, 'if it's already too late?'

'Is it too late, dear?'

'I fear it is,' whispered Cat. 'He conquered me, you know. Because I allowed him to. Because I *let him inside.*'

Morganach leaned back in her creaking chair, looking fatalistic.

'Then you must do your duty, dear, to the best of your ability,' she said. 'My only mission was to avail you of the facts. And that I have done, as well as I can. But if it is already too late, as you now claim, then the time for chatter is over. Also the time for regrets and tears. Destiny commands that you take up your crown and march forth into the great city. I bow to you, offer you my fealty, and humbly seek your clemency. *Shenhamforash!'*

Cat was wordless. The dog was growling. The uncooperative sun was still flooding the room with shafts of heavenly light.

CHAPTER

TWO

A CHAIN OF EMERGENCY VEHICLES howled down the street. A page of newspaper flapped past, bearing photos of tanks and aircraft carriers. A flock of ravens swayed on the bare branches of a sycamore tree. Cat lowered her head but otherwise saw very little, immersed in her own turmoil, oscillating wildly between acceptance and rejection, between a conviction that everything made too much sense to be denied and an equally adamant commitment to reason she was unwilling to sacrifice, even for a moment's whimsy. Robin Boucher, said one side of her mind, was the Laird of Howgate. More than that, he was Lucifer himself. At Aileanach Castle he had become so smitten with her that he had moved swiftly to eliminate Moyle and install himself in the flat upstairs. To work his devilish charm on her. To infiltrate her dreams. To impregnate her. And make her his Princess of Darkness.

Yet, even as such thoughts swirled like dead leaves through her mind, Cat scolded herself all over again. For bothering to listen to an eccentric old crone who clearly believed too much of what she should have been debunking. A mad hag who clearly couldn't decide if she was promoting or denouncing Satanism. Or if Cat was cursed or blessed.

Why had she visited her in the first place? Was it genuine fatigue or just fear of conventional happiness? Some mysterious and ongoing legacy of her early trauma? In the end Cat wondered if she had simply set a test for herself – to challenge the structural integrity of her reason – and the act of rejecting it all, blowing it clear out of her head, was now a matter of principle.

She was so emboldened by this new resolve that she barely noticed a car swerve across Murrayfield Road and almost clip her as she reached the kerb. She took the stairs down to the Water of Leith walkway and gained speed as she negotiated the winding path, under old stone bridges and soaring branches, all the way to Dean Village. But here she encountered even more tourists than usual – as if half a dozen coaches had disgorged them all at once – and they were more brazen than ever. They crowded around Cat, speaking a whole babel of tongues, gasping, snapping photos, pointing from afar, even presenting her with trinkets and strange figurines.

They were treating her like a princess.

She was almost panting when she spilled into the common stair. Halfway up to her flat she heard a squeak which could only be Boucher opening his door. She raced up the steps, struggling to get her keys out, like a scream-queen eluding a masked killer in a slasher movie.

She had not even made it to the fifth level when she saw his shadow sprayed across her door. Boucher was standing on the granite steps above, one arm hidden behind his back.

'*Cat*,' he said, looking like a game-show host concealing a prize.

'Hi there,' she returned.

'I just want to apologise to you.'

'Apologise?'

'For being so insensitive.'

She was stabbing her key at the lock. 'I don't know what you're talking about.'

'I was rather *enthusiastic* on Friday night,' he said. 'Perhaps a bit too much so. But I trust you understand?'

Inserting the key. 'Don't be silly, you've got nothing to apologise about.'

'In any case, I thought I should make it up to you.'

'Oh?'

His smile broadened. 'A Cat really should have a cat, don't you think?'

She was trying to engineer another chuckle when he produced something from behind his back. It was black. It was furry. It had yellow eyes. And yet it took her a few seconds to realise that what he was offering to her was a cat. An honest-to-god, living, breathing cat.

'He's twelve months old, they tell me. Fully neutered and vaccinated – I picked him up from the animal shelter.'

Cat was speechless. She loved cats, of course, but she didn't need a pet. And at any other time she would have told him to keep it for himself, or take it back, or give it to some kid down the street. But these were not normal times. These were moments when one acted antithetically to one's first impulses.

'Oh my,' she said finally. 'You shouldn't have.' Even while accepting the little critter – velvety, curious – into her own hands. Even while Boucher continued to grin.

'I hope it's not an imposition?'

'No, no – I love cats. I said that, didn't I? I love cats.'

'You did say that. And I couldn't resist.' He smirked. 'Thomas Cat – the obvious name, eh?'

'Yeah, yeah.' With an affected laugh, as if no one had ever said that before. While standing awkwardly on her threshold, trying to reject his implicit request to follow her inside.

The door buzzer saved her. The sound was coming from within her apartment.

'Oh – do you mind? Sounds like I'm wanted.'

'Indeed. Well, I'm so glad the gift is not unwelcome. I'll be seeing you around, then?'

'Yes, I'll see you around.'

He headed down the stairs, still wearing his grin, as Cat forced her way into her flat, dropped the cat to the floor and picked up the intercom phone.

'Hello?'

'Ms Thomas – it's Detective Inspector McReynolds. May I speak to you for a few moments?'

'Down there?'

'I'd prefer to come up.'

'Yes, of course.' She buzzed him through. Then heard him saying something to Boucher – or Boucher saying something to him – as the two men passed each other in the stairwell. Cat looked down at the cat, which was staring up at her with its diamond irises.

Knock knock knock.

She went back to the door. 'Yes, come in, please.' McReynolds moved past her, reeking of a tobacco-scented deodorant. Or perhaps tobacco. 'Nice cat,' he said, glancing down.

'He's new,' said Cat.

McReynolds wasn't really interested in cats. 'I've not seen you since the business with the Moyle fellow.'

'I guess so,' she said. 'Is this something to do with that?'

'Not exactly. Not exactly.' But he was looking at the ceiling. And running fingers over his powder-burn bristles. 'I should explain, for a start, that I'm no longer leading the official investigation. It's been bucked upstairs.'

'To the MIT?'

'That's right,' he said, 'to the MIT. I'm only working the fringes now. Running on my own gas, as you Americans say.'

She wondered if she was supposed to be sympathetic.

He straightened his shoulders. 'Are you familiar with a fellow called Blair Griffon?'

'Moyle's friend?' She thought it best not to lie. 'Yes, I heard something from Terry Grimes. He was found dead, too – is that right?'

McReynolds had been watching her closely and seemed pleased – or disappointed – with her reaction. 'In the reeds beside Duddingston Loch, aye. You know the reeds around there? They grow as high as a man.'

'I think so . . . I don't know.'

'Well, that's where his body was found. Or at least what was left of him.'

'He was . . .?'

'Ripped apart. Butchered. Exactly like Mr Moyle.'

'Uh-huh.'

'And again there are no evidentiary traces whatsoever.'

Cat was intensely aware of the need to act natural. And equally aware that people like McReynolds – people like herself – knew exactly how people did *not* act natural.

'I see . . .' she said. All the time thinking that the loch was not far from the Innocent Railway. And if Griffon had found his way there after fleeing down the tunnel, then there was every possibility that she and the tandem cyclists were the last people to see him alive.

'So do you have anything to offer us?' McReynolds asked. 'Anything that might connect the two incidents?'

In a flash Cat considered the possibility the cyclists had already been questioned; that lying now might only implicate her later. But ultimately she could not bring herself to admit anything

– certainly not the possibility that Boucher had driven Griffon off with a pulse of energy. And possibly murdered him in the same way.

'I wish I could help,' she said. 'But I really don't know what's going on.'

He paused before nodding. 'Well, you're not the only one.' His eyes were fastened on her. 'Can I show you a photograph?'

'Of course.' She had a terrible suspicion it would show Griffon's body.

'Fellow named Angus Blinny.' From his breast pocket, McReynolds had produced a mug shot. 'An underworld hitman.'

Cat recognised the ogre who'd seized her after her run. But again she wasn't sure how to react. 'Uh-huh,' she said, not looking up.

'You don't know him?'

'Can't say I do.'

'A witness said he attacked you.'

'Oh?' Cat made a show of squinting at the photo.

'Recognise him now?'

'It was dark. I really don't know.'

'So you *were* attacked?'

'I don't know if I'd call it an attack. A man grabbed my arm – when I was coming back from my run.'

'Why?'

'I don't know. He bolted away before he explained himself.'

'He didn't say anything at all?'

'I didn't hear him properly.'

'And then he just fled?'

'Not from me.'

'Then who?'

Cat again felt disinclined to mention Boucher. But why wasn't McReynolds himself mentioning him? She raised her head to look at him. *Natural*, she reminded herself. 'I don't know . . . he just ran away. Why? Has he lodged a complaint or something?'

McReynolds sniffed and repocketed the photo. 'Mr Blinny won't be lodging any complaints.'

'You mean . . .?'

A flutter of the chambray eyes. 'His body was found in the Water of Leith, about three hundred metres from here.'

'My God.' Cat didn't need to feign surprise. 'He wasn't . . .' She wanted to ask if he'd died the same way as Moyle and Griffon.

'Stabbed, beaten around the head with a blunt instrument . . .'

Cat remembered the tourists closing around him. 'And this happened – when?'

'Same night as he assaulted you.'

Cat suppressed a shudder. And with great effort she kept her voice steady. 'But he didn't assault me, as I said. He just tried to get my attention. And I don't know why he did that – honestly, I don't know.' She didn't mention the dead rat. 'Something to do with my job, possibly.'

'Your job.' McReynolds glanced at the black cat, which had climbed onto an arm of the sofa and was watching them blankly. 'Yes, Terry Grimes told me he saw you in the street.'

'That's right.'

'Apparently you've had some problems recently at your work.'

'That's true. It's very complex.'

'Nothing you want to tell me about?'

'Not really. Not yet, anyway. It's all rather messy.'

As he had at their first meeting, McReynolds looked as though he was struggling not to say something. 'Well, just look after yourself,' he said in the end. 'I know Alistair Dunn. I know the men, high and low, that he associates with. And I know exactly what he's capable of. You still have my card?'

'Uh-huh.'

'Then I'm still contactable if necessary.' An apologetic smile. 'If I come back here – if I'm *allowed* to come back here – I'd just like to make sure it's not for the wrong reasons.'

When she was alone, Cat rushed to the bathroom and retched into the basin. Then stood staring at herself in the mirror as vomit dribbled down her chin. Moyle. His friend Griffon. The ogre who'd seized her. And: 'I don't want to come back here for the wrong reasons.' Unless she was mistaken McReynolds was telling her he couldn't protect her any more. That no one could.

Her newfound resolve, not thirty minutes old, had already shattered into a thousand shards.

A movement at the corner of her eye startled her and she whirled around defensively. But it was only Thomas Cat, standing at the bathroom door and staring at her icily.

CHAPTER

THREE

C AT KNEW VERY WELL THAT OLD-TIME witches and warlocks kept cats as malevolent servants and bodyguards. She knew it because once, when she been particularly argumentative in Literature class, her exasperated teacher had exclaimed, 'Catriona Thomas, I swear you're the Devil's own familiar!' And it had stuck. Whenever she was being difficult or argumentative she was called 'the Devil's familiar'. Now, surveying the newly acquired Thomas Cat, which continued to look remarkably sly for something barely older than a kitten, she started to wonder if he too was meant to be a familiar – for her – or some sort of monitoring device for Boucher himself.

Hearing her own thoughts aloud, she chided herself again for entertaining such absurdities.

But then, remembering the gruesome and unexplained murders of Dylan Moyle, Blair Griffon and Angus Blinny, she decided that Boucher might indeed wield supernatural powers.

Then she started to contemplate the possibility that she was losing her mind. She paced restlessly around the flat for twenty minutes and the cat followed her everywhere.

There was a knock on her door.

She knew immediately it was Boucher because no one else could climb the stairs so unobtrusively. She considered pretending she wasn't home before deciding it wouldn't wash. She opened up.

He was bearing a big sack of eco-friendly cat food, a bag of kitty litter and a tartan cat bed.

'The least I could do,' he said, oozing charm. 'Oh, there he is now.'

The cat had worked its way between her legs. Boucher dropped to his haunches to give it a stroke. And Cat, standing astride the thing, very nearly kicked it into his face. But once again she was inhibited by the possibility that she was submitting to her self-destructive impulses.

'Thanks,' she said. 'He's already settled in nicely.'

'They told me he was fully house trained.'

'Then we'll suit each other perfectly.' She closed the door before he had risen fully to his feet.

Inside, still watched attentively by the cat, she considered fleeing for the hills. Because she doubted she could live like this. Even now, Boucher's barely audible movements in Number Six grated on her as much as Moyle's aggressive clatter.

But if she fled, would she not become the prime suspect in the mysterious murders of Moyle, Griffon and Blinny? And what, for that matter, would Boucher himself make of it? Would he become enraged? And *prevent* her from running? Strike her down, even?

She settled on writing up a list of essential items and prized possessions – objects and mementoes she would prefer not to leave behind – but even this raised more questions than it answered. How, for instance, would she organise a sale of her property from afar? What about all the garden birds that had come to depend on her feeders? And Thomas Cat, for that matter, who was even now nudging her legs as though demanding more food?

She barely slept that night, twisting and turning and waking up feeling as seedy and ragged as she had during the height of Moyle's campaign. The cat was sitting on the end of her bed, staring at her. She got up and sprayed a heap of Boucher's pet food onto a dish, put out a bowl of water, had a scorching hot shower – the cat, having wolfed down its food, wormed into the bathroom to watch her – and headed off to work, where she was promptly called into the cockpit.

She entered with leaden feet, assuming the hour of her dismissal had come.

'Ms Thomas.' Bellamy had his right arm clenched around the back of his chair this time – clearly a need for anchorage. 'I thought I understood that you'd shelved your rogue investigation. You assured me that you'd moved on. Is that not what you told me?'

'If you're saying that Mr Napier has not yet received that letter it's only because I judged it best—'

'No, Ms Thomas, I don't give an actual toss about Mr Napier.' Bellamy's teeth were shimmering with saliva. 'But I've now received word – from upstairs, no less – that an officer in my department has been making unauthorised probes. Demanding account information, customer names, logs of staff authorisations. Now, I was given no indication of who that officer might be, but what name do you think popped instantly into my head? Joshua Walsh?'

Josh Walsh was a mistake-prone temp whom Bellamy had once reduced to tears.

'I honestly don't know,' Cat replied. 'But I assure you that that investigation is the last thing on my mind right now.'

'Then you admit the investigation has been going on behind my back?'

'Only in the sense that I needed to clear up some loose ends.'

'Clear up some loose ends . . .'

'More a case of, you know, letting the air out of the balloon slowly so no one notices the noise. Always best to walk away backwards from a shit show, huh?'

Bellamy contemplated her a while before unclamping his arm from the seat. 'You know,' he said, 'I hope you're not still communicating with Ms Sampson.'

'I've not seen her since . . . I don't know when.'

'Is that right? If I didn't know better, I'd say her influence was rubbing off on you.'

'I can't comment on that.'

'Of course not,' Bellamy said. 'Well, next time you happen to see her, please give her my kind regards. I have a feeling she'll soon try to invoke the powers of the FSU' – the Financial Services Union – 'so our paths are bound to cross again.'

'She's given no indications . . .'

'Not that it will do her any good. I had everything – everything – signed off by senior management. And I'm meeting with them again this very afternoon. With any luck your name won't come up this time.'

He'd tilted his head upwards, as though to give her a sneak preview of his plans. And Cat realised at that moment that Agnes was right – this guy was a right royal bastard.

'Dismissed for now,' he said, exactly like a Wing Commander to a fighter pilot, and got back to consulting his diary.

Cat had not been long back at her desk, feeling increasingly desultory, when a call came through from the switchboard.

'The manager at Musselburgh wants a word with you.'

'Carter Carterius?'

'That's right.'

He was the last person Cat needed to speak to right now. 'OK,' she said, sighing inwardly, 'put him through.'

'Dear Ms Thomas.' Even Carterius's voice wore a bow tie. 'I believe you've been attempting to contact me.'

'That was some while ago . . .'

'Well, I can see you now. The sooner the better.'

Cat wasn't sure if this was a test. On her monitor she could see a reflection of Bellamy in his office, staring at her. 'I don't know, Mr Carterius. I've sort of been *moved on*, you see, and now—'

'You said you wanted to take this to the top, didn't you?'

She winced. 'I might have.'

'Then meet me this evening. I can't overstate the importance of this. Meet me this evening. Can I count on you to be there? Six o'clock on the seventh floor?'

'The seventh floor?' Cat had a vague memory of someone saying Alistair Dunn reigned from there.

'Six o'clock. It's in your interests to come, Ms Thomas, trust me.'

He hung up.

To Cat, he sounded very forced and unnatural. And it seemed manifestly imprudent to phone her at the office to arrange such a rendezvous. But then she saw Bellamy heading off to his meeting, smugly re-knotting his tie like a scheming MP off to plot a cabinet coup, and she figured she had nothing to lose. This might be her final chance to hurdle Bellamy, save her job, boost her status in ABC, and bring a little retribution to the world. As unlikely as all that seemed now.

By the time she stepped into the elevator most of the staff had departed. Standing at the console, a maintenance guy in overalls asked her for her floor. When she told him, he gave her a onceover and smirked. He got out at the fifth.

On the seventh, Cat found Carterius standing with hands steepled like a vicar leading a group prayer. He said, not looking at her directly, 'Ms Thomas – you made it.' As if hoping she hadn't.

'What's this about?' she asked.

'Just come with me, please.' Wearing a pained expression, he led her down a corridor decorated with paintings of old ABC buildings.

'I say again, what's this about?'

Carterius looked as though he was hardly breathing. 'It's out of my hands now,' he said.

'What is?'

They arrived at a reception desk, where Carterius muttered something to a sleek male secretary. The secretary asked for their phones. Carterius promptly handed over his Samsung and indicated that Cat should do the same. 'Just a formality,' he assured her. Then he guided Cat to an imposing door and knocked. When someone inside yelled 'Aye!' Carterius opened up and, as Cat whisked past, whispered as discreetly as possible, 'I'm truly sorry about this.' Then he drew the door closed behind her.

Cat found herself in an office that seemed transplanted from one of the buildings in the paintings. Wainscoted walls. Ranks of stag heads. Furniture that was all rosewood and buttoned leather. A stunning view across the Old Town to the Castle on its rock. And, seated behind a desk in a haze of cigar smoke, a ruddy-faced, pock-marked gentleman with neat coils of grey hair raked across a sun-blotched scalp. Cat recognised him immediately, from both the newspaper photo and the portrait in the lobby, as Alistair Dunn, patrician of the Dunn family. He waved her into a seat while still speaking on the phone.

'—two hundred and fifty million in sales and forward contracts and fifteen million to the bottom line.' He had a smoker's voice burred even further by alcohol (there were half-empty bottles on the sideboard). 'Well, I want to know why the node failed. I want to know why automated recovery didn't kick in. And most importantly I want a cast-iron guarantee that there's been no security breach. It's bad enough that you've fucked up on one of the busiest sales days of the year. But there'll be hell to pay if the market gets spooked. So get out there and deal with it, or I'll nail your head to my fucking wall.'

He slammed the phone down, took one last pull on his cigar, ground the butt into an ashtray, glanced at his watch – something with a high-end strap and a gold bezel – and then glanced in Cat's direction with an irritated sigh.

'Very well,' he said. 'I've got exactly thirty-five minutes before I'm due across town for dinner with the Justice Minister. And I desperately need to have a dump. So I'm not going to mince words. Your name is Catriona Thomas. You come from Miami. You live in Dean Village. You own a black cat. You're fucking the guy upstairs.'

Cat opened her mouth to interject but Dunn's voice cleaved the air.

'Don't even try to speak, lassie. This isn't a two-way conversation.' He paused just long enough to give her a look of paint-stripping disdain. 'Now apparently my youngest and dumbest son, Mungo, has a little thing going on in Credit Cards. Something involving rewards points. And apparently you found out about it. And apparently you've been sitting on your discovery until you decide what to do. And meanwhile you've been getting "warnings" from my son to back off. And apparently you still haven't decided what to do. Maybe now, even now, you're wondering if I'm going to reward you. If you're in a position to bargain with me. If I'm going to sacrifice my own fucking son. I can see it in your eyes, that you're still wondering.'

Cat shook her head. 'I assure you that—'

'Shut up, lassie. I told you not to speak.' Dunn sucked air through yellowed teeth. 'Now let me explain something to you. I know all about you and your history – the hotel scam in Miami. And I know all about your record here, too. Nick Bellamy has told me all about you. Your insolence. Your slutty ways. The way you bat your eyelashes, lick your lips, bend over at every opportunity. But you shouldn't delude yourself. You're not as irresistible as you think. You're not even as smart as you think. And you weren't as popular as you think in Florida, either – not at all. Your little exposé cost the bank dearly. Six per cent off the share price overnight. Millions off the balance sheets. Hundreds of thousands off annual bonuses. So don't think you're *admired* there. You were a nuisance. A cockroach. You were *tolerated*, but only because you were too much trouble to exterminate. Because your bank hasn't cultivated the sort of *connections* we have here.'

Over his shoulder dark clouds were massing around the Castle.

'You know, lassie' – Dunn's lower lip had curled – 'I personally signed off on your appointment here. As a favour to my opposite number, you know – just to get you out of the way. For your own sake as much as anyone's. But we never thought you'd stumble upon anything damaging. More than that, we didn't think you'd have the inclination. The fucking *gall*. I mean, we knew you had a fucking American puritanical mind-set. But we didn't think you'd import that same mentality over here. We didn't think you'd get the *opportunity*. I mean, hell, what was it that set this thing off again? A letter from a customer in Dundee? My God. My fucking God. From little things big things grow, eh? And so it's come to this.'

There was a flicker of lightning in the clouds.

'Now listen closely, lassie, because I won't be repeating myself.' A minor tremble as the thunder reached the office. 'You're going to resign from your job. Effective immediately. Before we *make* you resign. You're going to pack up and leave – not just ABC but the whole fucking country. And you're gonna forget everything you tried to investigate, every single thing that ever passed before your eyes. And if this matter ever crosses my desk again we'll *assume* it was you and we'll be forced to take action, do you understand? Because this isn't your playground, you've stepped beyond your boundaries, and if you think America is the only country where stool pigeons sleep with the fishes then you don't know much about Scottish culture. Consider yourself lucky that we're such a hospitable people. And don't think for a second – not a single second – that you'll get anywhere by pouting your lips at me. Or that it will do you any good running to the cops. Or the media. Or the unions. That we're *scared* of what might happen if you do that. That it troubles us for a millisecond. Do you understand what I'm saying?'

Cat was staring at the incoming storm. It was really beautiful. She missed the Florida thunderstorms.

'*Understand?*' It was Dunn again.

She nodded, refocused on him, and said, 'I understand.' Hoarsely.

'Just as well.' Dunn grunted. 'Just as well.' He leaned back in his chair and took another glance at his watch. 'Now get yourself out of my sight, you bony-arsed bitch. Dunn and dusted. Go back to your boutique little apartment in Dean Village and start packing. This is *Scotland*, for fuck's sake.'

Cat rose wearily, as if wading through quicksand, but by the time she reached the door she couldn't resist an afterthought.

'How do you like the Devil's whisky, by the way?'

He followed her glance to a bottle of Howgate Scotch on the sideboard. Then looked back with snarling eyes. 'I haven't the foggiest what you're talking about.'

'Never mind,' said Cat, closing the door with a thunderous boom.

CHAPTER
FOUR

S HE WOKE UP WITH A START. In a strange bed, in a strange room. With people talking loudly outside her door. 'And don't forget the cookies!'

She blinked, dragging herself out of a dream

'The cookies – the ones on the tray!'

In her dream she was a tigress on a blood-soaked veldt.

'Next to the coffee pot. The coffee pot!'

The dream had been so satisfying – so *purifying* – that it was difficult for Cat now to abandon it.

'We can eat them on the way to the airport!'

Then reality caught up to her with a thud.

'Take the sachets too!'

She was in the budget hotel. The one that overlooked Dean Village.

'The coffee sachets – and the milk things!'

And it all flooded back.

After leaving the Aquarium she'd wandered through the rainswept streets, her defence mechanisms crumbling under waves of mounting despair. She'd tried so hard, after departing Dunn's office, to keep her spirits up. She'd thought about his ludicrous Mob

Boss delivery and not-so-veiled threats. She'd remembered – and tried to chuckle over – his claim that Scotland had nothing to learn from America about organised crime. She'd recalled her stoicism in Miami when dealing with even greater levels of hostility. And her lack of surprise, even at nine years old in a garden shed, at being confronted by the workings of demons.

But such steely defiance hadn't lasted long. Because she had to consider the possibility that Alistair Dunn really did have strong links to the local constabulary. She had to wonder if he'd learned about her intimacy with Robin Boucher through Boucher himself. And she had to take seriously the possibility that if his offer – allowing her to pack up and retreat – was an act of genuine Scottish hospitality.

She had cast herself adrift, that was the truth of it. She had come to Edinburgh hoping to burn a bridge to the past, but the perfidy of men had chased her across the ocean. And all the pressure, all the dismay, all the disillusionment was now magnified to biblical proportions. It was too much. She was a victim. She had to accept it now – she was a victim.

Overflowing with *Weltschmerz*, she had started weeping. The rain camouflaged her tears. She huddled into her coat, avoiding all human contact, and ploughed into the deluge through New Town lanes slick with rain and flaring reflections. At the last moment she decided she could not return to her flat and instead took refuge in a basement pub, trying to prolong the moment by ordering two courses, even though she barely had an appetite. On the wall-mounted television the seven o'clock news was typically dismal: a boat carrying three hundred refugees had sunk in the Mediterranean, a wedding party somewhere had been blown apart by a missile, a river in Asia had been poisoned by a chemical dump: dead fish, choking children, weeping women. At one point Cat, her lips trembling, heard a voice.

'Cheer up, lass.'

She came out of her trance to find a whisky-reddened fellow at a nearby table hoisting a glass.

'God will look after you,' the man said, and Cat couldn't decide if he was an angel or a satanic apparition sent to mock her.

She left the rest of her meal untouched and went to a movie – something about a lone yachtsman trying to survive a hurricane – but hardly registered any of it. When she came out it was close to midnight and rain was still sweeping across the streets. Deciding she could still not go home – not while Robin Boucher was sleeping upstairs – she headed for the budget hotel and sobbed out the last of her tears. And finally – forlorn and alienated, conquered and defeated, fearing for her life, and bursting with *Fuchsteufelswild* – she had fallen asleep. Dreaming of Boucher, Bellamy, Alistair Dunn, and all the devils upstairs.

In the morning she forced herself out of bed and called down to the desk.

'Mohammed,' she croaked. 'I made a request last night for Room 406.'

'It's still occupied, Ms Thomas. I'll let you know as soon as it's free.'

'I'd be grateful.'

Room 406 had the hotel's best vantage point over Dean Village. Cat's plan was to watch until Boucher left the building and then race over to her flat, fetch her US and UK passports and her most treasured valuables – not forgetting Thomas Cat, whom she planned to take back to the shelter – and then flee Edinburgh entirely. Perhaps go back to Florida until things settled. And pray that Boucher wouldn't find her there.

But as it happened it took until after midday before Room 406 was free. And by that stage Dean Village was cloaked in a fog so dense she could see nothing from the windows but the outline of the squat office block across the street. She called down to the desk for a weather update.

'I'm afraid the fog is going to be around for a while,' Mohammed admitted, as though personally responsible. 'Would you like to order some food or drink?'

'I've had the complimentary stuff, thanks,' said Cat.

She decided to head into ABC to collect her possessions, copy her complete files to a USB, and then officially tender her resignation. If this too represented a defeat, a surrender to powers of darkness, then so be it. She'd done enough resisting to last a lifetime.

When she arrived at the office, however, she found it curiously empty. Apart from Josh Walsh, who was printing out new tabs for the filing cabinets (one of the few tasks that Bellamy still permitted him to do), everyone seemed to be crammed into the lunchroom. She wondered if they were fielding a stern lecture from the Wing Commander, with herself and Agnes used as scare stories. For a long time, in fact, she'd suspected that her colleagues – Ross, Fergus, Lesley, Skye and Isla – were content to 'go along with things' just to ensure survival, when in truth they hated Bellamy as much as anyone else. Well, they were probably 'going along with things' now.

Alone at Jenny McLeish's computer, Cat called up her files only to find that everything was missing. She looked everywhere, including the Recycle Bin, but all her documents and spreadsheets seemed to have been permanently deleted. And to do that would have required her password. She glanced suspiciously across the office – chatter was still floating from the lunchroom – and was about to rise when an ABC security guard appeared, escorting a uniformed policeman. For a heart-stopping moment she feared they were coming for her – that she'd been framed for something

– but instead the cop was ushered directly to Bellamy's office. Here he spent some considerable time – Cat was watching in the monitor – poking around Bellamy's desk, examining the diary, taking a couple of photos.

Then he departed, looking very grim, and the office was largely empty again.

Cat forced herself to the lunchroom, where she saw a huge box of doughnuts on the table. Cartons of takeaway coffee. Everyone present – about seven people – seemed glued to the little TV monitor. The atmosphere was one of flimsily camouflaged excitement.

The live news feed seemed to be showing a turreted mansion somewhere – a drone camera was sweeping over a well-groomed back yard and a lichen-coated roof – with police cars crowding the street outside and crime scene tape strung up like streamers at a kid's party. It resembled her own building when Moyle's corpse was discovered. Some slick senior detective – the chyron at the bottom of the screen said DCI Gordon Brewer, MIT – was muttering through vinegar-sucking lips.

But Cat couldn't hear what he was saying.

'What's going on?' she said.

Beside her, Fergus grappled for an appropriately sombre expression. 'It's Alistair Dunn – he's been found dead, apparently.'

'Dead?'

'Murdered, they think.'

Cat felt her throat swell. '*Murdered?*'

'That's what they think.'

Cat, her mind spinning, remembered Dunn's last words to her: 'I haven't the foggiest what you're talking about.' She remembered McReynolds talking about his sinister connections. And Boucher saying he could protect her. Then she looked back at the TV screen to see DCI Brewer staring straight into the camera – directly at *her*

– just as her phone vibrated. Dizzy, she hauled it out and discovered a triumphant message from Agnes.

DING DONG THE FUD IS DEAD!!!!

She shoved the phone back in her pocket and was still trying to make sense of it when Fergus added mysteriously, 'Talk about two birds with one stone.'

She wasn't inclined to question him at first. But then a strange suspicion seized her.

'Two birds?'

'You didn't hear about Biggles?' The other nickname for Bellamy.

Cat was almost breathless. 'What about him?'

'Had a massive heart attack last night.'

'He did?'

'In a sauna, they say.'

'A sauna?' In Scotland that meant a brothel.

'His heart exploded, they reckon – what a way to go, eh?'

Cat, feeling utterly drained, glanced again at Agnes's message, looked again at the TV – where DCI Brewer was still staring at her – and withdrew swiftly and wordlessly from the room, collected the keys to her company VW and headed downstairs to the underground car park. There, in the little metal cocoon of the Golf, she sat for a long time, fogging the windows with her breath, attempting to get a grip on herself, trying to assure herself repeatedly that this was all some sort of organised crime clean-up, and nothing at all to do with her or Robin Boucher. But again and again her mind returned to the night at Aileanach Castle, the distinguished face behind the black mosquito nets, and the smirking message from her friend Agnes Sampson the witch:

DING DONG THE FUD IS DEAD!!!!

Cat gunned the motor and boomed up the ramp, erupting into the late afternoon mist and heading around the corner for Newington. But finding a parking spot near Agnes's place proved difficult – even in an emergency she couldn't bring herself to occupy a disabled space – and by the time she'd entered the street for the third time Agnes was emerging from her stair door and plunging into what looked like a third-hand Clio. Cat had to complete another circuit of the block and by the time she'd returned the Clio was taking the corner into Dalkeith Road.

With great difficulty she followed Agnes through the fog-choked streets of peak hour Edinburgh, at first thinking that she was heading to the scene of Bellamy's death – to gloat? – and then following her past the city bypass and the Ikea store. And now she knew exactly where Agnes was going. The Clio, sure enough, turned into the blackened pine forests, where the trees were sporting early spring foliage, weaved around the serpentine road and then swung through the open gates of the Aileanach estate. Cat followed her down the foggy drive.

When she arrived at the castle she found Agnes being greeted at the door by doddery Maggie Balfour. Both women turned to watch Cat screech to a halt and fling open the VW door. They were still beaming when she marched towards them, furious.

'You did it!' Cat exclaimed. 'You put a curse on Bellamy!'

Agnes chortled. 'What are you talking about, Cat?'

'Did you put a curse on him or not?'

'Listen to yourself! Did *I* put a curse on him?'

'All of you!'

'All of us!' Agnes was delighted. 'What's the matter with you, Cat? This is another red-letter day!'

'People have *died*,' Cat said. 'People have been *killed*.'

'Aye! Torn apart! Eviscerated! In the middle of the night!'

Cat wondered if everyone had lost their minds. Maggie was

looking at Cat with something like awe. And there were others behind her, jostling about, coming forward for a look.

'Bellamy . . . Alistair Dunn . . . Blair Griffon,' Cat cried. 'Who killed them, if not you?'

'Who do you think, Cat?' Agnes's great bosom was heaving.

'Who?' Cat demanded hysterically. A crowd of shadowy figures was shifting and pressing behind Maggie. 'Tell me *who*.'

'The one upstairs, Cat.'

'*The one upstairs.*' It was exactly what she didn't want to hear.

'Aye,' said Agnes, sniggering. 'The one up top. Everything is going to be all right! Now is the time for the reckoning! *Die Frau ist Gott!*'

'*Gott ist die Frau!*' hissed Maggie.

'*Shenhamforash!*' chimed the people in the room behind her.

Cat stared at Agnes – her caterpillar eyelashes, her kidney-red lipstick – and almost slapped her. But there was something about the whole nightmare – the swirling fog, the palpable sense of evil – that she could no longer tolerate.

She marched back to the VW, ignoring Agnes's cries – 'Cat! Cat! Don't do anything daft now!' – and wrenched the engine into gear and took off in a haze of fumes and back-spun gravel, heading for Dean Village or Hell, whichever came first.

CHAPTER

FIVE

B Y THE TIME CAT CROSSED THE city bypass the fog had become practically impenetrable. Twice she came close to rear-ending vehicles before remembering to activate the high beams. And even then it was difficult to keep her focus on the road while coming to terms with her new reality.

The reckoning, Agnes had called it. And if Cat had had any lingering doubts, they were now demolished. Robin Boucher had 'taken care' of things, all right. Dylan Moyle and Blair Griffon, torn to shreds. Her malignant senior officers Alistair Dunn and Nick Bellamy, also struck down. Who would be next? How far would he go to 'protect' her? Had he ever stopped to consider that he might be turning her into a prime suspect? Mysterious deaths in Edinburgh were not common to begin with, but to have four of them directly related to her was too much for anyone to overlook. What should she do now? Go on the offensive? Call the police? When she'd been explicitly warned she couldn't trust them – or anyone else?

She swung into the kerb of a Liberton side street and phoned DI McReynolds but terminated the call before he could answer. She needed to be realistic. She couldn't just *imply* things. Imply that she'd had some involvement in a Satanic ritual and that things had gotten out of control. Imply that Robin Boucher, the guy upstairs, was directly responsible for four murders while implying, for the love of God, that he was the Devil himself.

She needed to speak to Madam Morganach, the self-proclaimed occult expert. Maybe the old hag would be able to provide some advice – maybe even some refuge until things worked out.

Thirty minutes later, however, when she arrived outside the Corstorphine house – she'd used the car's GPS – Morganach was not answering the door. Cat was backing into the fog, looking for some signs of life, when a pixie-like woman wearing a high-vis vest halted on her way past.

'Can I help you, dear?'

Cat wheeled around. 'I'm looking for the lady who lives here – Madam Morganach.'

The pixie shook her head. 'She's gone, whoever she was. I'm the next-door neighbour.'

'*Gone?*' whispered Cat, fearing for Morganach's fate as well.

'Packed up and left,' the pixie said. 'She was only there for a month or two.'

Cat stared at her for so long that the pixie seemed alarmed.

'Best get out of this fog!' she said, hastening for her own front door.

Back in the VW, Cat could make no sense of it. What was going on? If Madam Morganach had been a transient, then who was she working for? Was she part of the game too? Cat gunned the motor again and steered through the mist to the budget hotel.

'Melanie,' she asked at the desk, 'can I ask you another favour, off the record?'

'Of course.'

Cat lowered her voice, even though the only person in the lobby was an old guy tussling with the revolving door. 'If anyone enquires about my presence here, can you give them the run-around, tell them I'm not here? And then let me know about it as soon as possible? I'd be grateful.'

'Of course, Ms Thomas.' Melanie sounded as though such requests were commonplace. 'And do you want me to record you under a different name, perhaps?'

'Please,' said Cat, 'that would be excellent. Try – uh – Stella Vidales.' Her friendly sister's married name. 'And do you know a place where I can conceal my car? Out of sight, you know?'

'Oh' – Melanie leaned halfway over the counter to point, as if asked the same question every day – 'there's a spot there beside the maintenance shed that's never used.'

'Fabulous,' Cat said again, and went back into the fog to shift the VW. When she returned a group of Slavic-sounding tourists were bustling out of the elevator. Seeing Cat they stopped in their tracks, stared at her and chattered excitedly among themselves. Chilled by the thought that they might be part of Boucher's fan club – that they might inform their king of her presence – Cat dived into the elevator, hammered the buttons and tried not to think about it.

From the window of Room 406 she could still see little through the mist but the building across the road. And when she dragged out her phone she noticed that someone had been trying to call her from a suppressed number – almost certainly DI McReynolds. *Shit.* She turned the thing off at once, hoping the cops hadn't already triangulated her location.

She hauled out the hotel's instruction book – a folder of plastic-sheathed pages – and worked out how to make an international call. Then, using the room phone, she rang through to her sister.

'Cat, it's great to hear from you.' Her sister sounded distracted.

'Stella, you wouldn't believe how good it is to hear your voice.'

'Is something wrong? I didn't recognise the number you're calling from.'

'It's too difficult to explain. I just want you to know I miss you. Hell, that I love you.'

'Seriously, Cat, what's wrong?' It was as if affection, coming from the black sheep of the family, was itself cause for alarm.

'If I told you what was going on here, you wouldn't believe it. All I want you to know is that I'm completely innocent. If something happens to me, just remember that. I'm completely innocent.'

'Innocent? Cat, what are you talking about?'

'Look, there are things going on here for which I might get the blame. That's all I can say.'

'Something to do with your work again?'

'Partly.'

'I told you, Cat, you should have gotten out of that business long ago.'

'You might be right. Also, I don't want to sound melodramatic – I *really* don't want to sound melodramatic – but I might end up dead.'

'Jesus, Cat, now you're scaring me.'

'I'm sorry, but that's the way it is.'

'Are you sure you shouldn't be talking to the police?'

'I wish I could trust them. Or even trust them to believe me.' Cat released an anguished sigh. 'And there's one other thing. Would it be OK if I decide to come home?'

'Here? To Fort Lauderdale?'

'Uh-huh.'

'But of course – of course you can come here.'

'I might effectively be hiding out there, I don't know. Would that be OK with you?'

'The spare room's yours whenever you want it. I've been meaning to call you, you know. I was going to phone you today. There've been some developments you should know about.'

'Oh?'

'You know that crime boss who was threatening you? Paul Scicuna or whatever he was called?'

'Paulie Scicluna, yeah.'

'He's been murdered – in prison, it was – so you don't have to worry about him any more.'

Cat almost said 'Good' but settled for 'Oh'. Scicluna had been the head of the syndicate that orchestrated the hotel scam. Even after being sent to the Miami Correctional Facility he'd represented a credible threat to Cat's safety. So naturally she had wanted him dead.

'Also' – Stella hesitated – 'I don't know how you'll take this, Cat, but it's about Scottie.'

'Scottie . . .' Cat instinctively tightened. 'What about him?'

'I'm sorry I have to mention him at all, you know, but—'

'Just say it.'

'He's . . . he's dead too, Cat.'

'Dead.'

'Found dead in prison, just like Scicluna.'

Cat closed her eyes. And for a second she felt overwhelmed, as though all her circuits were going to blow at once.

'Cat – are you OK?'

Nothing from Cat.

'Cat, are you all right?'

Everything is going to be all right.

'When' – Cat had to force the words out – 'when did this happen?'

'Scottie's death? Why, just yesterday evening. We only got the news this—'

Cat dropped the phone and slammed her hands around her head.

CHAPTER

SIX

O
H JESUS, SHE THOUGHT. *Boucher's not just killing men I've told him about – he's killing everyone I've ever wanted dead.* It was as if he'd raided the darkest fissures of her memory and, with a few bloody strokes, sterilised the world for her – cleaned up the world for his princess.

Scottie was her cousin from Philadelphia. The one who'd watched her from his upstairs window. The one who'd cornered her in the garden shed and asked her why she was exterminating the insects when 'all God's creatures have their duties, Cat – even the slugs'.

The one who'd then lowered his pants and presented to Cat his own pulsing slug.

The one who'd moaned with delight when he forced himself into her mouth.

The one who'd shrieked in agony when Cat bit him in half.

Oh, it was a terrible, terrible thing. And things were already so complicated, what with Cat's mother fatally ill and her father knee-deep in financial problems. So, in an atmosphere of heated claims and counterclaims, everyone in the end agreed not to talk about it. The two families had gone their separate ways, acrimonious and shrouded in shame. And in the way of such things the monstrous secret had festered. And when the delayed impact of anger and trauma finally walloped Cat, she had naturally dreamed of crushing Scottie like a centipede.

Presently she spent another fraught night in her hotel bed, shredded by anxiety and uncertainty, remembering things that ought to have been quarantined, imagining things she wasn't supposed to think about, her emotions wheeling wildly between satisfaction, confusion and disgust. When she awoke in the morning she was shocked she had slept at all.

But at least the fog had lifted.

The view from the window was even better than she remembered. Through leafless tress she could see deep into Dean Village: the winding river, the gables, the slate roof tiles, her own building with Boucher's MG in its parking space. She could even see a few of the acolytes, or whatever they were, milling around with cameras. When a couple of them looked in her direction, she shrank back into the darkness, unlikely as it seemed that they could have spotted her from such a distance.

She wanted to witness Boucher leaving the building but that meant a constant vigil without pause. She could not afford to visit the bathroom or go out for lunch. Or to draw up a chair because she could not see the stair door from sitting level. But for a full three hours, barely blinking, she stood in vain. She thought about ringing Maxine, assuming she was home, and asking her to find out if Boucher was in residence. But that would involve an innocent party and possibly even get her killed – who could say?

No sooner had she thought this than the stair door opened – her heart quickened for a moment – and out stepped Maxine and Michael, both wearing overcoats and berets, off no doubt to some arthouse screening or gallery opening. Cat felt a wave of affection for them – such a sweet-natured, fun-loving couple, a million miles away from the sick-minded devils who populated her own private hell. Then she fixed her eyes back on the door.

Another two hours passed and most of Dean Village was in shadow. The top half of her building was aglow, almost amber. She could see through her bedroom window, for God's sake – even the blue smudge of the Monet print on the wall. And Boucher's skylight above that. But she could see nothing of the man himself. She wondered what he was thinking. Whether he had learned by now of her absence. Whether, if he could read her mind, he already knew where she was. And whether he would—

There was a sharp knock on the door behind her.

Cat's heart somersaulted. She couldn't answer.

Another knock, more insistent.

She had a vision of Boucher, having been led to her room by his acolytes, beaming at her from the corridor. 'Cat, my dear, I wish it hadn't come to this.'

Then she heard rustling. The sound of a card key *thunking* into the lock. An almost inaudible buzz. And the door was swinging open. Cat braced herself.

But it was only a maid. With a perplexed expression on her face.

Cat nodded impatiently. 'It's already done,' she said. 'It's already been cleaned.'

'You in right room?' the woman asked.

'Yes, yes, check downstairs. Ca' – she corrected herself mid-syllable – 'Stella. Stella Vidales. Check at the desk.'

The maid nodded and retreated.

Cat turned back to the window to find an abrupt change in scenery. An unmarked saloon had pulled up in front of her building. DI McReynolds was getting out. He was buttoning his jacket and going to the stair door. He was pressing on one of the buzzers – no need to guess which one. He was waiting for an answer. His body language, even from a distance, looked tense. He was pressing the buzzer again. Still no answer. He was dragging out his phone, tapping a number. Was he calling her? Or headquarters? Was he even supposed to be on the case?

Whatever. He was putting the phone away and trying one last time on the buzzer. And then, defeated, he was ambling back to his car and driving away.

But to do what? To check with ABC? To summon a locksmith? To round up a posse of constables with battering rams?

She stood for another hour and the sunlight faded completely. The sky was slate blue. The streetlamps flickered on. There were still acolytes milling around – a whole swarm now, more of them than ever. Cat's throat was parched, she was hungry and desperate for a pee. But she couldn't leave her post. To have stood this long without seeing Boucher surely meant he was bound to appear at any moment. Unless he had slipped out of the building at the precise moment she had turned to deal with the maid? Or unless he had already departed – because he was hunting for her?

Then another car pulled up – the third-hand Clio that Agnes had driven to Aileanach Castle. And there was the driver herself, throwing open the door.

Cat was no longer sure what she thought of Agnes. On one hand it was Agnes who had led her into this trap in the first place, who had shamelessly set her up, who to the last did not seem to comprehend why she was not delighted by the deadly turn of events. She was as manipulative as Boucher himself. But Cat still couldn't hate her.

Agnes shuffled to the stair door and hit the buzzer repeatedly. When there was no response she turned to the acolytes – a couple of them were milling around – and asked them a question. Gestures, raised hands; she seemed to be arguing with them. Then she shook her head and got back to pressing the buzzer. Again and again, as though convinced that Cat was ignoring her.

Belatedly it occurred to Cat that she must be trying Boucher's buzzer as well. Well, of course she would – as a last resort Agnes would naturally call upon her dear friend Cock Robin. But wait. There was no answer from him as well. Agnes kept trying – possibly both buzzers at once – but was getting no response from either flat. And now she was retreating. She was heaving herself into the Clio, doing a messy three-point turn and blurting off.

Cat was convinced of it now: Boucher was not home. He had not been home for hours. But that only meant he might be right around the corner. So there was no time to waste – she had to get in and out before he returned.

She took a deep breath and went for broke. She raced down the hotel stairs and rushed around to her VW and tore open the door and threw herself inside and span around the block to Bell's Brae and down the slope and across the stone bridge and deep into Dean Village, steering between a ludicrous number of acolytes to her parking space beside Boucher's MG, then flinging open the car again and dashing for the building and fumbling for her key and getting it into the lock and throwing the stair door open and slamming it in the faces of the acolytes and bounding around the swirls of the staircase with her other keys poised and finding the locks of her own door – too many goddamn locks! – and hurling the door back and launching into her flat and throwing on the lights and heading for her living room and finding the drawer with her passport and birth certificate and other valuables and fumbling around and finally getting the damn thing open and dragging everything out and oh yes she needed a suitcase and there was one in her bedroom and she was turning for the door and almost tripping over the black cat when she noticed that the light in the living room was strangely lurid and looking up she saw her paper globe lamp . . .

She froze, staring at a stain bleeding through the ceiling from above, just as it had done when Moyle had died . . . a great rusty bloom that could only mean that someone upstairs had been ripped apart, torn to shreds, eviscerated . . . that someone upstairs had been killed . . .

Oh no, oh no . . . oh no . . . not again . . .

She stared and gasped and stared and gasped . . . then ducked into the bathroom and had an insanely long pee . . . and then came back and stared and gasped some more.

CHAPTER
SEVEN

C AT'S FIRST THOUGHT WAS THAT IT must be some sort of Satanic message, because the blood was almost exactly where she had painted over the stain left by Moyle.

Her second thought was to wonder who it was that Boucher had killed.

Her third thought was to wonder if the blood was human.

Her fourth thought was to consider the possibility that the blood might belong to Boucher himself.

Her fifth thought was to speculate if that meant the Devil was dead.

Her sixth thought was to wonder if the Devil had killed himself.

Her seventh thought was to wonder why the Devil would do that.

Her eighth and final thought was a slowly dawning acceptance – that if Robin Boucher was truly dead then he could not have been the Devil after all.

She retained enough sense to switch off the lights but she could not bring herself to leave as planned. She collapsed into her armchair and sat in the dark and cold and stared at the ceiling as lozenges of light streaked and bloomed across the bloodstain. Part of her knew she was in danger staying where she was. Another part told her she was in even greater danger if she fled.

As to who had actually killed Boucher, if indeed anyone had killed him, was not a line of enquiry she chose at that moment to contemplate.

She wallowed for so long in her own sense of disconnection – of floating untethered in deep space – that she lost track of time. The flaring lights became less frequent and the room even chillier. Thomas Cat curled around her legs, looking for warmth.

After a while there was a buzz from her intercom – startlingly loud in the midnight silence – but she moved not an inch. Another buzz. She wondered who it was but couldn't bring herself to check from the bedroom window. One last buzz and whoever it was seemed to surrender.

The phone rang.

Not her mobile but her landline. She'd only had it connected as part of her Internet package and had shared the unlisted number with very few people. So who the hell could be calling?

It rang out.

She wondered if it was the police – though surely, if they really thought she was home, they would have forced the door by now? Then she wondered if it was Stella, concerned for her welfare. Possibly her sister had called back on the hotel line and somehow worked out that Cat had fled. Maybe she'd even tried calling Cat's cell phone, only to discover it was switched off. Maybe she was panicking right now, imagining the worst.

Cat took out her mobile phone, stared at it for a few minutes and then decided to risk it. She turned it on.

Immediately there was a flood of purrs and vibrations. Messages and missed calls from Agnes, from ABC, from a flurry of unregistered numbers. Cat experimented with what seemed the most harmless one of all, a text sent by Maxine the previous day

You OK, hun? Heard nothing from upstairs last night
except a ROAR. Any idea what's going on?

And then switched it off at once. And continued sitting in the darkness. Trying not to make a sound. Feeling as though she wanted to crawl up in a ball and squeeze into a tight space. Thomas Cat, licking his lips, was watching her expectantly.

The landline rang again. It was so late now that it seemed unlikely that it could be anyone local, and Cat – considerate to the last – thought she had better stop the din, if only to prevent any further disturbance to Maxine and Michael downstairs.

She got to her feet and raised the receiver. Heard not a peep from the other end, then issued a tentative, 'Hello?'

'Ha!' exclaimed Agnes. 'Knew you were home!'

Cat almost hung up immediately.

'Are you gonna let me in or what?'

Cat wasn't breathing.

'Are you gonna open this door or am I gonna have to fly through the window on a broomstick?'

Finally Cat exhaled. 'Where are you?'

'Downstairs. Come to the window if you don't believe me.'

Cat hesitated.

'Don't make me use that buzzer again! I'll keep banging it all night if you don't open up!'

Cat couldn't bear that possibility. 'OK, OK. Come up, then. Just . . . be quiet about it.'

'Aye right, I'll be quiet.' With a snigger.

Cat went to the intercom, pressed the stair door release, then opened her own door on the darkened stairwell. Agnes tramped up the steps – God, she was loud – and then appeared in front of her, panting from the exertion.

'Phew! It's like climbing the Scott Monument!'

Cat said nothing and Agnes chuckled.

'Not still angry with me, are you? Oh, what's that? A cat? When did you get that?'

'Just . . . step in,' Cat said, standing aside.

'We really gotta talk.' As Agnes crossed the threshold her face crinkled. 'Bloody hell, girl, it's dark as a crypt in here. What are you doing with yourself?'

Moving presumptuously inside, she fumbled for the light switch. 'There, much better. And where's the heating control? You got a goddamn thermostat in this place or is home-heating against your religion?'

In looking around the room – Cat remained blank-faced, awaiting the inevitable – Agnes finally noticed the red-stained light and the swelling bloodstain. And that stopped her in her tracks.

'Holy shit,' she said. *'Holy shit.'*

Staring at the stain. And eventually turning to Cat.

'Is that what I think it is?'

Cat didn't know how to answer.

'Cock Robin? Really?'

Cat only blinked.

And Agnes chortled. 'Jesus, Mary and the Cuckold,' she said. 'And to think . . . we were all hoping the two of you would, you know . . .' But she only shook her head and chortled again. 'Well, well . . . glory be.'

Cat couldn't decide if she should be angry. 'Glory be . . .'

'Yes, glory be.' Agnes frowned at her. 'What happened exactly? Did he get a bit fresh with you? Eat a rare steak in front of you? What?'

Cat frowned back. 'Are you trying to say that I'm responsible?'

Agnes spluttered a laugh. 'Who else, if not you? Poor guy. The grandmaster didn't see *that* coming, did he?'

279

Cat was still puzzled and it must have showed.

'Oh my. Oh my.' Agnes was still piecing things together. 'You still don't know, do you? You still don't know. Even though I told you last night, you . . .' Another possibility seemed to occur to her and she glanced at the ceiling. 'Oh, dearie dearie me. I see now, I see. You thought it was *him*. You really thought it was him. *Oh my.*'

Cat wanted to slap her for looking so amused.

'And I suppose when Dunn and the Wing Commander . . . after you'd complained of them, and they were taken out, I suppose you . . .'

Cat just looked at her.

'And then' – Agnes was still thinking things through – 'when I said it was all the fault of the one up top . . . oh my.'

Cat still stared at her.

'Now that's a wee shame, isn't it?' Agnes shrugged. 'Still, he's not the first man who's been mistaken for the Devil, I suppose. Not the first and won't be the last. And he was probably hiding something anyway – you suspected as much, didn't you? Well, well, well. That's the way it works, isn't it? That's always the way it works. When you project your evil onto others, the innocent always die.' She glanced up at the ceiling again. 'On the plus side, I suppose, it can always be a lesson to you. It's probably a good thing, in a way.'

'A good thing . . .'

'A good thing because . . .' Agnes seemed to change her mind. 'No, you just sit down, Cat – sit down and take it easy. This is gonna take some explaining. *Oh my.* Have you got anything in the kitchen other than nuts and leaves? I'll toss something into a pan.'

'I don't feel like eating.'

'Well, you're gonna get something whether you like it or not. You look terrible. And I could do with some scran myself. So set your glutes down, Catriona Thomas, and let the witch take care of everything.'

Cat slumped again into the armchair as Agnes strode into the kitchen, flicked on the lights and started browsing through the fridge, watched closely by Thomas Cat.

CHAPTER

EIGHT

'ASK NOT AND YE SHALL RECEIVE,' Agnes was saying from the next room. 'Ask not and ye shall receive.'

Cat assumed she was talking about something she'd found in the kitchen. But then she went on, 'That's a central tenet of Satanism. That people who are self-reliant and adaptable are the ones who should be rewarded, not those who always come looking for assistance. Call it Nietzschean, if you like. Call it fascistic. But it's not. It's much more complex than that. Bloody hell, have you got anything edible at all in here?'

Cat, despite everything, was still bothered by the noise. 'Keep it down. And what do you mean by edible?'

'I dunno – something with a bit of flavour.'

'Try making an omelette.'

'An omelette – with this soy milk shit?'

'Why not?'

'OK, OK, if you're happy with that. Anyway, what was I saying? Aye, ask not and ye shall receive. Well, in your case you *did* want something done for you, I suppose, and you got exactly what you wanted in the end. But make no mistake, we knew you were

282

sceptical, we knew it was a symbolic measure for you, we knew you didn't take the whole thing seriously. But that was fine, that was good, that was actually in your favour. The important thing was that you *acknowledged* your inner demons. You acknowledged them, you *owned* them, and then you went ahead and proved exactly how analytical and dispassionate you can be. Have you got anything I can use for filling in this so-called omelette?'

'Try the vegan sausages.'

'There are vegan sausages?'

'In the fridge. Chop them up with some tomato. Are you talking about those Scruples questions? At Aileanach Castle?'

'The "aptitude test", as you called it, aye,' said Agnes, clattering about with pots and pans. 'But it was already pretty clear – to me, anyway – that you fit the bill perfectly. Sharp as a knife, even-tempered, discerning, a single-minded predator . . . and just a wee bit fucked up. I knew you'd pass the test with honours.' There was a slight sizzling sound as the margarine melted. 'What am I going to use for eggs? There are no eggs.'

'Vegans don't eat eggs.'

'Then what am I gonna use? How can I make an omelette without eggs?'

'Use the black salt.'

'Black pepper?'

'Black salt. It's basically sodium chloride. Has a very eggy flavour.'

'Black salt, for fuck's sake. Where is it?'

Before she knew it, Cat was in the kitchen reaching into her spice cabinet. 'Here. You whisk it into the soya.'

'Let me do that,' said Agnes. 'And sit down, girl. I know how to make an omelette – when I've got the proper ingredients, anyway.'

Cat took a seat at the kitchen table. The cat was still wandering around, looking for food.

'Anyway,' Agnes went on, 'you got what you asked for, regardless of whether you really wanted it or not. The musician upstairs – *gone*. Vamoose. But you also got what you *didn't* ask for. And that was a thousand times more important.'

'And what exactly *didn't* I ask for?'

'Easy, tigress, I'm getting there. You reckon I'm using enough of this black pepper, by the way?'

'Black salt – yeah, I think you're doing fine.'

'Anyway, I guess we should've considered the possibility that there'd be a spanner in the works. Life never unfolds as expected, does it? Chaos theory and all that. I guess we should've expected that you'd think Mr Grandmaster was part of a stratagem or something. But in truth we just wanted you two to be happy – to, you know, procreate and be content and have a little responsibility.'

'Procreate . . .'

'Never hurts to have a stake in the future, you know. A little skin in the game, as they say.'

'I think that margarine is drying up.'

'Yup yup.' Agnes stopped swilling and added a dash of olive oil. 'Anyway, we tried easing you into it – full revelation, I mean. We did our best to grease the rails, get you comfortable with your new responsibilities. Madam Morganach, for instance – after your meeting in Corstorphine, she assured us you were well on your way.'

'Madam Morganach was one of yours?'

'Aye, of course.'

'An actor?'

'Well, acting a role. But that was the only way to get you to listen. And she said you looked comfortable with what she was suggesting – cool and calm, not particularly alarmed at all. If you were inwardly disturbed, she said, you'd get over it.'

Cat closed her eyes, remembering Morganach saying something

about Satanism bringing the powers of God to mortal human beings.

'So anyway, we hoped to get you settled into your new role before you did any harm. It's a shame about the grandmaster, it really is, but as for the others . . . well, the world isn't really gonna be any worse off without Alistair Dunn and the Wing Commander. And the musician upstairs, for that matter.'

'I don't understand,' said Cat. 'You seem to be . . .'

'You wanna help with the filling, by the way?' Agnes said. 'I've already got my hands full here.'

'You said you didn't need any help.'

'I've changed my mind. This is more complicated than it should be.'

Cat got to her feet and started chopping the sausages. 'You were saying,' she said.

'Aye, look, you shouldn't be angry. You *really* shouldn't be angry. This sort of thing needs to occur to you organically, so you can *own* it, you know. So you can deal with it your own way.'

'What sort of thing? What are you trying to tell me?'

'I'm trying to tell you that Satanism has always been a bit of yin to the yang. When the world was more puritanical it was all about indulgence and debauchery, there's no doubt about that, and that helped blacken Satan's name.'

'Blacken Satan's name . . .'

'Aye, it sounds ridiculous. But things have changed, you can't dispute that. Look at the world today. There's a lot more tolerance for lifestyle choices but the levers of power are still controlled by psychos. And these days those psychos have infinitely greater power for death and destruction. But the ground is shifting under their feet, they can't control the discontent, the anger, the growing rebellion, and they retreat into their little mental fortresses, becoming even more brazen and delusional. Am I sounding radical enough for you?'

'You need to add some mustard to that mixture.'

'Huh?'

'Dijon mustard. It's in the cabinet above you.'

'Oh . . . oh aye.' Agnes chortled and reached for the jar. 'At least you're not disagreeing with me.' She tipped some mustard into the mix. 'Anyway, it's critical-mass time. The end of the world is not just some batshit biblical prophecy but a distinct possibility. More than that, it's a damn good wager. Bet you never expected a Satanist to speak this way, huh?'

'Just . . . go on.' Cat was prodding the filling around the pan.

'But that's the point exactly. Satanism has always been about life. A love of life, a real zest for it – and a genuine hatred for those who won't allow us to enjoy it. But the way we're going, let's face it, there might not be anything to live *on*. The wise parasite never kills its host.'

'I think you're overheating that omelette, by the way.'

'Yup, OK. Anyway, that's where Lucifer comes in. That's where you come in.'

'That's where *I* come in.'

'Sure. Don't try to look surprised.'

Cat dived into the fridge and emerged with a packet of powdered vegan cheese and some basil leaves, which she started to tear apart. 'That's where I come in?' she prompted again.

'Aye, that's what the whole ritual was about. That was the gift that was given to you. The gift that was *unlocked* in you.'

'What gift?'

'What do you think?'

Cat tossed the basil into the mixture. 'I hope you're not seriously suggesting that I have some sort of . . . supernatural power?'

'I can't think of a better person to have a supernatural power, can you?'

'Stir it a bit faster, will you? Oh Jesus.' Cat stopped for a second, thinking about it. 'Oh Jesus – what are you saying? What am *I* saying?'

'Oh Jesus, indeed. Don't try to make it sound like we did something *evil*.'

'But you're being absurd. You can't be serious.'

'I've never been more serious. We unleashed a great power in you.'

'What power? What sort of power?'

'What do you think? Are you in denial? *You?* What power do you think?'

Cat turned the gas down. 'Are you seriously trying to tell me that I have the power to *kill*?'

'With a thought, girl. With a simple wish.'

Cat stared at her, not blinking for ten seconds. 'And all of those men who've been killed – you're telling me that *I* was responsible?'

'You must have felt it? You must have known?'

Cat thought of Scottie and Paulie Scicluna, and Robin Boucher, and Nick Bellamy, and Alistair Dunn, and Blair Griffon, and Dylan Moyle, and maybe even Angus Blinny the ogre. And it occurred to her that, if this was all true, her mind was even more homicidal than *she* had been prepared to admit.

'No . . . no,' she said. 'No . . . it's ridiculous.'

'It's difficult, I know,' said Agnes. 'But you more than anyone must be capable of seeing the logic. It's the very reason you were selected. Your intelligence, your reason. And your predatorial instincts.'

'Predatorial instincts.'

'Well, don't try to tell me you wouldn't find such a power a wee bit *useful*, huh? In a broader sense?'

287

'I don't know what—'

'Oh, come on, Cat,' said Agnes 'You can't seriously tell me you're not sick of the way things are in the world? The way the shit always floats to the top? And that you're not tired of just accepting it, being philosophical? As everyone clings to the life rafts?'

'Spoon out that omelette, will you?'

'Aye, I think it's well and truly cooked now. Looks OK, eh? Not bad for a first try with black pepper.'

'Black salt.'

'Whatever. What am I supposed to spoon it onto?'

'There are two plates in the drawer there. Can you spare some for the cat?'

'A vegan cat, is it?'

'Until he tells me otherwise.'

Agnes scooped out two servings of omelette and Cat scraped the rest onto the cat dish.

'So you're seriously trying to tell me I'm a witch?' she asked, rising.

'Oh, fuck no,' Agnes said. '*I'm* a witch. Maggie Balfour is a witch. And Lucifer would never unlock any power in someone as petty as us two. I mean, hell's bells, there'd hardly be anyone left.'

'So what am I?' Cat asked, as they took their plates to the kitchen table. 'What on earth am I – according to you?'

'You need some wine with that. You got some wine?'

'There's grape juice in the fridge.'

'Grape juice, for fuck's sake.' Nevertheless, Agnes bent over to fetch it.

'Then what am I?' Cat asked again. 'You still haven't answered.'

'What do you think, girl? What the hell do you think?'

'Some sort of devil?'

'Not *a* devil.'

'You're still speaking in tongues.'

'OK, let me say it then. Let me say it out loud. You're *the* Devil.'

Cat settled back into her kitchen chair. 'This is getting more absurd all the time.'

'I'm *not* being absurd. You're *the* Devil. You always have been.'

'Stop this. *Stop*. Now you're starting to annoy me.'

'Oh, hell no, we don't want that.' Agnes grinned. 'We certainly don't want that.' She set the glasses on the table and started pouring the juice. 'I'm just telling you what you already know. Everyone carries the Devil inside – in the heart, in the head, in the instincts – but the magic that goes with it, the full powers of Lucifer, they're almost never fully realised. They're never *unlocked*.'

Cat had a vision – a memory – of a huge leathery hand descending on her head as the Satanists chanted in Aileanach Castle.

'You know what?' Agnes said, surveying her. 'I can see it in your face. It's all falling into place, isn't it? You're reliving it right now – the coronation.'

'The *coronation*?'

'The moment the Laird of Howgate unshackled your powers. And relinquished his own. The moment he released the Devil upstairs . . .'

Cat continued to stare into middle space, feeling everything coalesce. Simultaneously she heard the acolytes outside starting to chant, as if purposely to remind her of the ritual.

'That's it, girl, that's it,' Agnes said. 'The reckoning. It's not so hard, is it? It's a moment of *triumph*. The baton has been passed, girl – to a woman for the very first time – and now it's your turn to sprint. I always said you were awesome. And' – with a chuckle – 'no one's gonna argue with me now.'

Cat lowered her eyes. 'The acolytes . . .' she breathed.

'The what?'

'The acolytes . . . the people outside . . .'

'Oh, the disciples, aye. Crackpots, most of them. They shouldn't even be here but it's hard to keep things completely secret. I blame Petra Varga – that bitch never shuts up.'

> '*Salute o Satana,*
> *O ribellione,*
> *O forza vindice,*
> *De la ragione!*'

Agnes repeated their litany. 'Hail Satan, o rebellion, o you avenging force of human reason.' That's the "Hymn to Satan", you know.'

Cat shook her head. 'They're making too much noise.'

'Come again?'

'I said they're making too much noise – they'll wake the neighbours.'

Agnes laughed. 'Still thinking about noise, are you? Cat, you're a classic. Anyway, don't worry your pretty head about it. The disciples will disappear as soon as you order them to. Nothing is going to be a problem. *Nothing.* The plods will never be able to pin a thing on you. And if anything does become a bit of a bother . . . well, you can always deal with it. You can deal with it the same way you dealt with the fud upstairs.'

Cat, with her fork poised over the plate, looked up at her sharply.

'I meant the musician,' Agnes clarified promptly, 'not the grandmaster.'

Cat sighed ruefully. 'Robin didn't deserve to die.'

'Of course not.'

'None of them did.'

'Just eat your omelette, girl,' Agnes said. 'Drink your grape juice. You'll need some strength. Sounds like this is still going to take some time to sink in. And then, when you're ready, you can start the revolution.'

The two women finished their meal in silence, the cat groomed its whiskers, and the clock ticked on into the wee hours of the morning.

CHAPTER
NINE

NOTHER WISTFUL LOOK UPWARDS at the ceiling, another lament for what might have been, another gut-wrenching wave of shame, another feeling of having been emotionally torn apart, and then Cat helped Agnes wash and tidy the dishes. They repaired to the living room, sat on the sofa amid the darkness and the warmth, and turned on the TV for the overnight news – yet more launching missiles and raging forest fires – and Agnes even fell asleep for a while, snoring again like a grizzly, before snapping awake when an early morning van rumbled past. She blinked and stretched and looked at Cat, who was stroking Thomas Cat expressionlessly.

'So, are cool with it yet?'

Cat was staring at the switched-off television.

'What's the matter?' Agnes said, frowning. 'Have you accepted it?'

'They were showing something . . .' Cat began.

'Huh? I can't hear you.'

'They were showing something on the news,' Cat said, louder. 'A live press conference . . . from a military base somewhere.'

'Go on.'

'And there was this guy, someone Robin Boucher called "the

Most Dangerous Man on the Planet" . . . he was announcing a new series of air strikes or something.'

'I think I know the fud you mean,' said Agnes. 'Go on . . .'

'And for a moment,' Cat admitted, 'I felt a flicker of anger – "fox devil rage" or whatever the Germans call it.'

'Oh?' This got Agnes's attention. 'Go on.'

'And I decided to test it out . . . the powers or whatever you've talked about . . . to concentrate my thoughts for a second.'

'And what?' Agnes leaned forward. '*And what?*'

Cat looked at her guiltily. 'And the guy . . . the Most Dangerous Man in the World . . .'

'He what?'

'He *exploded*,' Cat said. 'Right there on live TV.'

Agnes paused for a moment, as if to verify that Cat wasn't joking, then exploded as well – into laughter.

'Way to go, girl! Way to go! So you see? You see it now? The sort of thing you can do?'

Cat looked back to the blank television. 'It was *horrifying*.'

'It was *liberating*.'

'You didn't see it.'

'I don't need to see it. And neither do you, if you don't want to.'

Cat grasped for words. 'But you can't just . . . you can't just *do things* like that to people.'

'Of course you can do it. He deserved it, Cat. In one stroke you probably saved a hundred thousand people. A million people. You might even have saved the world.'

'You don't know that.'

'He's a fud, Cat – or at least he *was*. A genuine fud.'

'One person's fud is another person's messiah.'

'Pffft. Stop getting yourself tangled up with questions of morality. The sociopaths never do – it's a dead giveaway.'

'But the sort of power you're talking about,' Cat insisted, 'it's not for mortals. It's really, really not.'

'And it's because you really, really believe that,' Agnes returned, 'that you're exactly the right person to command it. It's supremely logical, Cat, and you know it. You *know* it. It's why you were chosen.'

Cat was silent for a few moments and finally she sighed. 'I don't want any more problems.'

'You won't *have* any problems.'

'I don't want to leave Edinburgh.'

'And you won't have to leave Edinburgh. Hell, you won't even have to leave this *building*. There's a property upstairs that'll soon be on the market, from what I hear. Why not buy the place and merge it with this flat? Make it a duplex? Why not turn this whole building into your castle? It's not beyond you now, I promise you.'

Cat shook her head. 'You're trying to make everything sound so simple.'

'That's because it is simple. Relax. You're already across the Rubicon – whether you know it or not.'

'Am I?' said Cat. 'Am I really? I still don't believe in the Devil, you know.'

'Then you don't believe in yourself.' Agnes frowned at her impatiently. 'Scot or not?'

'Sorry?'

'Are you a Scot or are you not? No true Scot would ever be frightened of being the Devil.'

'I'm not frightened.'

'Well, that's settled then. Hey' – Agnes cocked an ear – 'I don't hear your disciples.'

'They stopped chanting about an hour ago.'

'They're only human.'

'That's a relief.'

'Maybe it's time, you think?'

'Time?'

'Aye, you know . . . for the sparrow to take up her bow and arrow? And march forth into the great city?'

Cat nodded resignedly. A brisk pre-dawn walk might be just what she needed to get a grip on things. She got tentatively to her feet – Agnes was nodding in encouragement – and wrapped a scarf around her neck and very quietly opened her door – the stairwell was still pitch-dark – and went down the granite steps on hushed feet.

'I'm right behind you, Satan,' Agnes whispered.

When Cat opened the stair door she discovered that Dean Village was full of people – acolytes, disciples, whatever – all huddled in the darkness. They must have come from everywhere. They must have *known*.

Cat looked back at Agnes. 'You coming with me?'

'This isn't my moment, lassie.'

'Uh-huh.' Cat was about to turn but then paused. 'You never did tell me what a fud is, by the way.'

'A cunt, basically.'

'OK.'

The acolytes were muttering and pointing – word was spreading fast – and the frenzied chant was building again.

> *'S'innova il secolo,*
> *Piena e' l'etate.'*

Agnes translated: 'The new age is dawning; the time has come . . .'

Then Cat Thomas – with Thomas Cat hugging her heels – made her way out from the building and through the disciples, who were bowing and peeling away from her while renewing their acclaim.

'Rege Satanas!'

'Ave, Satanas!'

'*Die Frau ist Gott!*'

'*Gott ist die Frau!*'

'Hail Satan!'

Cat went all the way to the wrought-iron footbridge with the stars gleaming above and the river burbling below and she paused there in the middle, surrounded by magisterial Victorian tenements, watched by hundreds of adoring eyes, feeling an immense sadness mixed with an immense joy, and an extraordinary sense of power. And though she normally derided such whimsies, she felt that this was somehow right – it was destiny, it was the moment she had been born for.

EVERYTHING IS GOING TO BE ALRIGHT.

Because when you thought about it . . . really thought about it . . . and took all the variables on board . . . and came to terms with all the pros and cons . . . well, it was right, wasn't it? . . . right and proper, after all these centuries, that the Devil should be a woman . . . a level-headed and self-analytical woman at that . . . a discriminating and compassionate one . . . and a vegan . . . and for that matter a Scot.

I mean, who better to shake up the world? To challenge the indifference of the heavens? And *do* something?

So Cat Thomas and Thomas Cat continued across the Rubicon – or at least the Water of Leith – and headed up the steep stone stairway, climbing out of Dean Village into Belford Road, into Edinburgh, into the world, and into the brightening dawn.

She couldn't decide which fud she would kill next. But she would think of someone.

'But at the Dean Bridge, you may behold a spectacle of a more novel order. The river runs at the bottom of a deep valley, among rocks and between gardens; the crest of either bank is occupied by some of the most commodious streets and crescents in the modern city; and a handsome bridge unites the two summits. [...] And yet down below, you may still see, with its mills and foaming weir, the little rural village of Dean. Modern improvement has gone overhead on its high-level viaduct; and the extended city has cleanly overleapt, and left unaltered, what was once the summer retreat of its comfortable citizens. Every town embraces hamlets in its growth; Edinburgh herself has embraced a good few; but it is strange to see one still surviving—and to see it some hundreds of feet below your path. [...] The smoke still rises thriftily from its chimneys; the dusty miller comes to his door, looks at the gurgling water, hearkens to the turning wheel and the birds about the shed, and perhaps whistles an air of his own to enrich the symphony— for all the world as if Edinburgh were still the old Edinburgh on the Castle Hill, and Dean were still the quietest of hamlets buried a mile or so in the green country.'

ROBERT LOUIS STEVENSON,
Edinburgh: Picturesque Notes

ACKNOWLEDGMENTS

With humble thanks to my editors, publishers, agents and inspirations: Emma Hargrave, Campbell Brown, Rod Morrison, Ali McBride, Dr Ariel Moy, Debs Warner, Janne Moller, Thomas Ross, Alice Latchford, Guy Carvalho, James Graham (Jim's Barbers) and David Forrer at InkWell.

Also by Anthony O'Neill

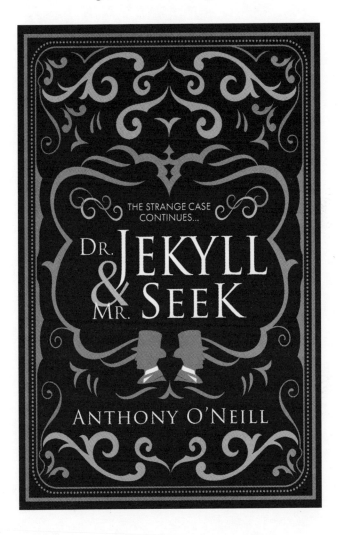

The strange case continues . . . in this 'fiendishly ingenious'
and brilliantly imagined sequel to *Dr Jekyll and Mr Hyde*.

blackandwhitepublishing.com